CRYING MEADOWS

A TALE BY
AVERY GOODE

A Blessingale Family Tale

Crying Meadows

© 2018 by Avery Goode

Leverage Media Group, LLC

P.O. Box 311822 Atlanta, GA 31131

ISBN 10: 0-9975164-2-9

ISBN 13: 978-0-9975164-2-5

DEDICATION

*This book is dedicated to Blayke "SingToMe" Ladd
who was the real hero is so many people's lives. We love you
Blayke and can still hear your melodious voice in the wind.
Keep watching over us!*

ACKNOWLEDGEMENTS

I would like to say Thank You, Jesus for blessing me with another witty and creative idea. Thank you for blessing me to grow in faith and love. Thank you for blessing my hands and my thoughts and helping me to construct better stories each time I sit to write. You are the G.O.A.T. Jesus, and I am nothing without You.

Much love to my children who challenge me and change me for the better. You all are my Earth, Wind and Fire. The three of you and the little kiddles are my reasons WHY.

To my entire family who has shown tremendous support of me throughout my career, thank you.

I am not going to name each individual name this go-around but please know that I am grateful for every frister, friend, broski, editor, typesetter, and graphic designer who supports me and prays for me.

Special thanks to Leonard Kinsey of LKP Photography for doing such a fabulous photo shoot in a graveyard. You are an amazing photographer, and I am honored to work with you time after time.

Last, but certainly never least, I want to send a huge hug of love to all my readers who stick with me book after book. You all make writing purposeful and your feedback helps me grow. I love you all and I appreciate you. -Avery

Let's connect:

FB: Author Avery Goode

Instagram: thegoodescribe

Twitter: thegoodescribe

Periscope: thegoodescribe

Snap Chat: SheGoode

Website: averygoodesworld.com

Email: averygoodesworld@gmail.com

Email: averyonthemove@gmail.com (For bookings
and tour date inquiries)

Other Goode Books:

Dishonest

Pillow Princess Part 1

Pillow Princess Part 2

Head Doctor

Private Practice: Head Doctor 2; A Freakquel

Pen Pals (Available in E-book Only)

CHAPTER 1
NO MONEY, MORE PROBLEMS...

THE COUPLE IN THE PICTURE was happy. He, a successful businessman who was once the captain of his college football team. She, a former beauty queen, who was the belle of the ball in Georgia's high society. Their smiles gleamed as brightly as the polish on the mahogany desk that the framed photo sat on. Anyone looking at them would think that they were the perfect couple. They were everything but. The picture was only a reflection of the people they longed to be once more. Preston Meadows was perfectly tanned all year around. His nose was straight and his lips just full enough to make kissing a pleasure. He had deep blue eyes that were daring and telling at the same time and soft, dark brown hair that had waves that made a woman want to run her fingers through it. His finely chiseled physique complimented each suit and was the envy of all women and even some men. He was gorgeous.

His beautiful wife was just as easy on the eyes as he was. With long auburn hair that cascaded over her shoulders to the emerald green eyes that held people captive, Amy Meadows was every bit a trophy wife a man could desire. Her thin, yet curvaceous frame was kept well-toned, by daily workouts in the couple's home gym. It was her full pouty lips that turned up at the corners and deep dimples that had made her the most sought-after debutante in Buford County, Georgia. It was no secret that Preston and Amy would be married one day. Their fathers were best friends. Each man headed up his own Fortune 500 Company and it was rumored that the two had

1

been contemplating a merger for years. While Preston and Amy married for love, their marriage was also the ultimate business merger. A union that was inevitable. It was supposed to be a lucrative match for both families. And it was, for a while. Before the debt. But now, next to the beautiful photo sat a stack of daunting bills. Many of them went unopened because they pretty much said the same things.

Past Due.

Delinquent account.

Final Notice.

It was easy to ignore the mail, but the incessant collection calls were harder to dodge. Even with call filtering, a few savvy bill collectors managed to get through the line.

"Hello, this is Pat from First Bank regarding your past due credit card account. Before we proceed, I need to inform you that this is an attempt to collect a debt and any information obtained will be used for that purpose."

Preston had heard it all before. Calls like this were expected for a regular Joe Schmo with money problems, but not for him. Not someone of his standing. Hell, he was a Meadow's for God's sake! His family had Mayflower descendants in its lineage. Blue blood. Abbott Meadows Sr., Preston's father, owned more real estate in the state of Georgia than the state did. The Meadows were Southern aristocracy. It was unheard of that someone of his caliber would have money woes. The wealthy did not let their skeletons out of the closet. It was taboo that they even admitted to having any. Most of the secrets in the Meadow's family were long buried and never spoken of. Having financial issues in a wealthy family was about as hush-hush as incest was in a poverty stricken one. No one in Preston's family knew that he and Amy were having money troubles. No one would either. Soon, things would change, and he would be able to set things right again. Preston was expecting a huge financial windfall. It was not clear exactly what day it would come, but he knew it was on its way. He was banking on it. Until then, the collection calls would continue.

He looked down at the smart phone in his hand where he had pulled up one of his bank accounts. It was in the red almost fifteen hundred dollars and that was just the beginning. Once all the other checks and transactions hit the account, he'd owe closer to twenty-grand if not more. Disgusted, he looked out of his second story master bedroom window that overlooked his wife's newest hobby, her garden.

It was ugly. Flowers were wilted and bent over as if they were tired of struggling to grow. The grass was brown and yellow in some spots and weeds were overtaking the small plot of land at a rapid pace. Preston's gaze shifted to the right as he spotted his wife making her way to the pitiful patch.

Basket in hand, she strutted across the yard as if she had not a care in the world. She wore a straw hat, an oversized gardener's smock and a pair of gardening Crocs that turned up slightly at the toes. He could not see her face, but he imagined she was frowning as she looked down at the garden. Day in and day out she toiled, digging, planting, and watering but none of her efforts yielded good results.

Preston had seen this happen many times before. She would take on a new pastime that the women's league offered and when things did not work out to her satisfaction or she got bored she found something else that tickled her fancy and moved on. It was only a matter of time that she would give up on this as well. In a way, her husband pitied her. She did try her best at the activities she participated in, but nothing panned out. Archery was a shot in the dark. Baking was a flop. Sewing caused her to need stitches.

Now gardening. This was her last opportunity to redeem herself. The women in the league felt that Amy Meadows was nothing more than a pretty face with a nice body. Preston knew that because his wife told him that repeatedly. Many a night she had cried to her husband about the ladies.

"None of them take me seriously, honey. It's as if they laugh at me behind my back," she whined to him one day.

The truth was they laughed at her in her face, but she was too daft to realize it. She was met with condescending tones and the "how nice dear's". The chairlady even went so far as to pat Amy on the head like a pet. No, they did not respect her at all. They barely even liked her.

Preston knew that Amy was the most beautiful woman in the Distinct Ladies of Leisure Women's League. She was also the youngest. Many of the husbands openly appreciated his wife's attributes. The women overheard their husbands on several occasions commenting on Amy's assets and that sparked a bit of jealousy within them. The men may have been checking her out, but she only had eyes for her husband. That much Preston knew.

However, his knowing how much she loved him did little to improve his sour disposition now. He needed money and she was in part to blame for their financial demise. Amy was so hell bent on keeping up with the latest fashion trends and outdoing the next socialite that she spent frivolously. Preston wasn't like the other husbands. He didn't keep things from his wife that concerned them both. As soon as he realized that they're money was dwindling he told his wife about it.

That conversation, like so many others they had was futile. She showed a blatant disregard to everything that they spoke about and continued to spend as if they had all the money in the world. Because she came from a privileged background, Amy didn't understand moderation. Preston didn't either, but he knew that if they continued in the manner that they were that the two of them would be on skid row.

The communication in their relationship, among other things began to wane. There used to be a time when the two of them could talk about anything to one another. Now he could barely stand to speak to her. The sound of her voice grated on his ears. They weren't making love much these days either. He used to love coming home midday to ravish his wife and then return to work. Thoughts of their rendezvous helped get him through many a boring meeting. Not anymore. Amy was so obsessed with having a baby that sex became mechanical. In, out. Up down. She bought a fertility calendar and ovulation schedule into their bedroom, so the couple no longer enjoyed random acts of unbridled passion. Their lovemaking was reduced to timing and temperatures.

Frustrated, Preston walked over to the mini bar and fixed himself a drink. He walked back over to the window and stared down at his wife. Shaking his head, he lifted the snifter of brandy to his lips and took a long swig. He needed relief. As if on cue, the Meadow's housekeeper appeared in the doorway with a dusting cloth and aerosol can in hand.

"Excuse me, Sir. May I come in and polish your…wood?" She inquired seductively.

He nodded. "You always seem to know what I need exactly when I need it, Marisol. Come here."

Marisol obeyed her boss and went to him. Kneeling in front of him, she slowly unzipped his pants and released his hard member.

"Seems you have been having a, hard time. Let me handle this for you."

Skillfully, she began pleasing her boss with her mouth as he looked out the window. When the pleasure began to overtake him, Preston threw his head back and relaxed into the moment. This was exactly what he needed. For a little while, he could forget about his financial woes and his failing marriage. All that mattered was this moment.

CRYING MEADOWS

Soon, Preston found the release that he sought and was satisfied temporarily. Helping the beautiful housekeeper to her feet, Preston looked on as she righted her uniform.

"Will I see you later in my room?"

"Of course, Mari. Why wouldn't you? Now run along like a good little girl and ask Miss Ruthie to please fix my dinner. I am hungry."

"Yes, Sir."

The phone vibrated in Preston's pocket. "Meadows."

"Hey Pres, dad has taken a turn for the worse and is in the hospital. Mom is asking all of us to meet her there," his oldest brother Albert, Jr. or A.J., as they called him, said.

"Damn. Is the old man going to pull through?" Preston could care less. The financial windfall he was expecting would only come when Abbott, Sr., died.

"I'm sure. He's a tough old fart. Anyway, put some fire under your feet and head this way. I'm about five minutes away myself. See ya'".

Preston hated how his brother ended phone conversations. He just hung up. He never said 'good-bye' or anything. And he was so damned bossy. Growing up all he did was tell Preston what to do, how to do it and when to do it. It was torture. Especially since he was the youngest of three boys. He got punished by both his brothers.

Jealousy, competition, and fighting were a constant companion in the Meadow's mansion. Robert, the next to the oldest wasn't as much a bully as A.J. He was more verbally antagonistic than he was physically. Being the younger brother, Preston knew just what to do to push both of their buttons. One thing that used to drive A.J. crazy was when Preston deliberately did the opposite of what he told him to do. The thought crossed his mind to do that now, but this wasn't an order from his big brother. It came from the top. His mother.

6

Reluctantly, Preston made his way out to his car. He didn't bother telling his wife where he was going. He pulled the key fob out of his pocket to unlock the car door and he dropped his cell phone on the concrete. Preston picked it up, got into the car and looked at the phone. It was exactly what he was praying he wouldn't end up being. Broke.

CHAPTER 2
NO FLOWERS IN THE GARDEN...

AMY MEADOW'S CHEEKS BURNED FROM the hot tears she cried. Angrily she dug her trowel into the ground not caring that dirt flew everywhere.

"What have I done wrong? I've planted, watered, trimmed, and fertilized and this stupid garden still won't grow. How could it be dying after all I've done?"

She wasn't just talking about the garden. She was referencing the state of her marriage also. She loved her husband and had tried just about all she could do to make their life perfect. Preston wasn't satisfied. Despite all she did to please him, he still felt compelled to step outside of their marriage. A blind man could have seen that he was cheating because he didn't bother to hide it. Amy had chosen the wrong moment to look up from her garden. When she did, she saw her husband with his head thrown back and knew instantly what it was. She had seen the stance before. In times past, it was she who caused it by performing oral sex on him. He was having an orgasm. He was with her. Marisol. It was bad enough that he was cheating with their housekeeper but to allow her into their bedroom was disrespectful. Amy had told her before to stay away from her husband, but Preston instructed the buxom housekeeper not to pay any attention to his wife.

"Don't listen to her. We're married in name only at this point. You're the only woman I want in my bed," he said.

Now, no matter what Amy did or said, the insolent housekeeper disregarded everything that she told her to do. Marisol walked around haughtily as if she was the woman of the house. From the outside looking in, one would think that the roles were reversed. Amy did more cleaning than the actual housekeeper.

Because of the hostile relationship between the two women and to save face, Amy always gave Marisol the day off whenever she would have guests over. The last thing she needed was for the women in the league to see how she was disrespected by the help. Surely, they would question why Amy hadn't fired the wench and she couldn't tell them the truth. How could she? What would she say?

"Oh, I can't fire her because she's not just any maid, she's my husband's paramour and he prefer her more than he does me?"

No, she couldn't do that, and she most definitely couldn't tell any of the women that her husband was humping the maid. It wasn't uncommon for the men in their society to keep mistresses. Amy had overheard many of the women in the league talking about the random affairs before. What was unheard of was the man cheating with someone so far below his social station. Preston was scraping the bottom of the barrel with Marisol.

Shaking her head, Amy went back to shoveling dirt and tried her best to clear her mind, albeit unsuccessfully. The more she pounded the dirt the more she thought about her past failures with the other activities the women in the group did. The Distinct Ladies of Leisure Women's League was involved in various charitable and philanthropic activities. Just recently the group voted to include more 'hands-on' duties.

"D.L.L is more than a wealthy group of beautiful women. We are a hands-on league who doesn't mind working with our hands like common folk." Louise Belfair, the leagues chairwoman stated a few months ago. "What greater way to motivate the lower class than to show them that their 'betters' understand their plight."

Amy hated Louise's thick, Southern accent. It reminded her of the way Blanche Devereaux from The Golden Girls television show used to speak. It was an exaggerated drawl that dripped with saccharine. But there wasn't too much that was sweet about Louise. Of all the women in the league, she was the one who made it apparent that she held some level of disdain for Amy. When Amy hurt herself trying to sew a blanket, Louise was right there.

"Why bless yo' 'lil' heart," she uttered.

Everyone knew that when a Southerner said that, the phrase had little to do with religion and more to do with a passive-aggressive way to call you an idiot. The way Louise said "bless your heart" to Amy stung worse than any insult. That's why making a go of this garden was so important to her. Not only was she trying to prove something to Louise and the other ladies, but she also needed to show Preston as well. They all needed to see that she could do something right. If she could convince her husband that she was not a total failure in everything, maybe he would start seeing her as an asset instead of a liability.

When they first got married, the two of them had big plans. Preston was going to head up a division of one of Abbott's company's and she was going to raise their children and take care of their home. They had accomplished neither of those goals. At twenty-five years, old, Preston was flying high.

"We've got plenty of time to do all that, babe," he stated.

"Let's live a little. Travel and see the world. We won't be able to do that as much after we start having kids."

A twenty-three-year-old naïve Amy believed everything he said. Her father had given a sizeable dowry to Preston after their marriage and even though some of it was supposed to be held in trust for Amy's personal use, the couple pretty much blew through ten million dollars in two years. They went to the finest restaurants and stayed at the best hotels when they traveled abroad. Both dressed to the nines always. In Paris, they had commissioned original designer pieces from Jean-Paul Gaultier that had cost well over two-hundred fifty thousand dollars just for one suit and one gown.

"My, my. Aren't we living in high cotton?" Cora Lee Meadows, Preston's mom, expressed when they came to the Meadow's annual Christmas Cotillion after they had the garments made.

"We do alright for ourselves, Mother Cora," Amy replied. "Surely not as well as you and Abbott, Sr., but we manage."

Both Amy and Cora Lee were the descendants of cotton growers. If you're living "in high cotton," it meant you're feeling particularly successful or wealthy. And they were. That night at the ball, Amy simply smiled at her mother-in-law's comment but inside she fumed. She wanted to chastise the older lady for bringing up money in a public, social setting. That was impolite.

Right after the cotillion, Preston was slated to begin work as the vice-president of marketing for Meadows Textiles. He had plans to launch major campaigns and foster relationships with local designers who would use Meadow's fabrics exclusively for their designs. This was going to increase the company's bottom line by forty-two percent in the first year with consistent growth annually. However, on Preston's first day of work, his father had another plan for him. Instead of a vice-presidency, he was given an entry-level marketing position.

"You need to start from the bottom and learn the business," Abbott, Sr. told him. "No one starts from the top."

CRYING MEADOWS

An angry Preston wanted to curse his father and remind him that he had started both Abbott Jr. and Robert in VP positions, but he kept his mouth shut. Amy witnessed the pain in her husband's eyes and tried to comfort him.

"Honey, don't you worry about anything. You show your dad that you are handier than a hip pocket and watch how he promotes you in no time."

That was four years ago.

Today, Preston was just now becoming the manager of the junior southeastern region which consisted of Georgia, Florida, and Tennessee states. Abbott cited Preston's lack of work ethic and creativity as the reasons for the slow ascent within the corporation. Amy thought that her father-in-law was full of malarkey. Her husband was hard working and had brilliant ideas. But those were his reasons, and she had no choice but to respect them.

As for her, Amy didn't have any reasons to explain why she hadn't given her husband any offspring. They had been trying over three years to have a baby. She had seen multiple gynecologists and fertility specialists and they all said the same thing. There was no known medical reason for her not to reproduce. She had taken every test imaginable, followed each instruction they gave her and had given up caffeine. Her doctor told her to give it time.

"You and Preston are still young, Amy. Don't be in such a rush. I'm sure the moment you forget that you're trying to have a baby and just enjoy the process, is the moment that you and your husband will conceive."

But Amy couldn't stop thinking about it because every other month her husband reminded her that she still wasn't pregnant.

"What kind of half-witted woman did I marry? You can't cook. You give the worst head imaginable and your pussy is drier than the Mojave Desert! I was hoping to have gotten you pregnant at least twice by now, so I could stop climbing on top of your stiff ass. It's like I'm having sex with a log that has tits. I hate that my dad made me marry a fuckin' virgin. If I would have sampled your goods beforehand and saw that it wasn't worth it, I would have married Harper Rankins. She's not as pretty as you but at least she's given her husband three kids in three years."

The scathing remarks that Preston made about Amy's infertility wounded her deeply. Upon the advice of her nurse, she began tracking her menstrual cycles, temperature, and ovulation days. She hoped that it would help but her constant requests to have sex only seemed to anger Preston more. He lied to his buddies about the hot sex he had with her to save face. People thought that the reason they didn't have children yet was because they were still reveling in one another. No such thing.

Preston and Amy's perception about their relationship was vastly different. While in his mind, he was a good husband who loved and cherished his wife, the reality to Amy was that he hated her. Outwardly, it seemed as if he enjoyed coming home during the day to make love, but his actions said something different altogether. He wouldn't allow Amy to get on top or try any other position to help spice up their lovemaking. It was always the Doggy-style position. The one with the least amount of contact.

If he were assured that Abbott, Sr., would not cut him completely out of his will for divorcing Amy, he would have. This was the only thing keeping the two of them together now. To her, any reason was better than none. Amy was determined to win her husband over again and save their marriage at any cost. So, if that meant that she allowed him to hump the maid for now, then so be it.

Amy foresaw a day that she and her husband would be happily married, and Marisol would no longer be in the picture.

CRYING MEADOWS

Until then she would bite her tongue and keep her unhappiness a secret.

She stood and dusted the dirt off her knees. She had been in the sun too long and was beginning to feel faint. Slowly she walked over to the garden shed and replaced all the tools she'd been using then made her way towards her home. As soon as she opened the door to the main house, the gust of cold air enveloped her. She made her way upstairs to her bedroom and removed the dirty clothes. After a hot shower, Amy donned a silk robe and walked over to her five-hundred square foot custom closet. Today she was having lunch with the women's league. They had to wear something peach.

She chose a simple, yet stunning soft peach colored, knee length silk Chanel day dress. It had subtle pleats beginning at the waist and stopped at the bottom hemline. Trimmed in lace at the neckline, the shoulder strap and the bottom had three embellished pearls down the left torso of the dress. She picked a soft peach pair of sling-back, two-inch heeled sandals and white silk panty hose. The women may have many negative things to say about her, but lacking style and class wasn't one.

It didn't take her long to dress. Once she got downstairs, she took one last look at the dusty foyer and shook her head. She couldn't wait to get rid of the lazy, insubordinate, poor excuse of a housekeeper. It was high time. Amy walked to her car and got in, turning on the air conditioning as soon as the ignition turned over. She adjusted her mirrors and drove slowly down the driveway. She knew that Preston left already because she heard his engine roaring as he sped off. He didn't even have the decency to tell her where he was headed.

Exhaling loudly, Amy drove on. One day things would change. That's what she kept telling herself. As she drove past her neighbor's homes, she admired the beautiful flowers that colored their lawns.

"One day, the seeds will grow in my garden, too," she mumbled quietly rubbing her tummy. "One day."

CHAPTER 3
FAMILY AND FINANCES...

A CHILL RAN DOWN HIS spine as he walked through the sliding glass doors. The lobby of the hospital was beautifully decorated with warm browns and spa greens. Modern sofas and armchairs were set up next to expensive, hand carved cherry wood end tables that held an assorted selection of magazines for the guests' reading pleasure. The atrium had a gorgeous skylight that allowed natural light to bathe the host of plants that grew there. A quiet spring of water flowed from the rocks down to the Koi pond that sat in the center of the lobby. The streaming water was calming and peaceful.

The new lobby was a gift courtesy of the Meadows Foundation. Cora Lee sat on the hospital board and when it came time to upgrade the dingy hospital, she was more than happy to get her husband to cut the check to make it happen. Not knowing that one day, the very hospital he helped save would soon help save him in return.

There was a small crowd of people waiting for the elevator when Preston got nearby. Smiling politely, he waited impatiently, tapping his foot as he watched the numbers slowly light up, marking the elevators descent. When it arrived, the red arrow flashed downward, and the doors opened. All the waiting people stepped inside, and the doors closed. Frustrated, Preston stabbed the up arrow to get an elevator to take him to the floor his father was on.

In a daze, Preston looked out of the window not seeing anything, but staring at everything. The ding of the elevator broke the trance and he stepped on alone. Just as the door was about to shut, a small, dainty hand stopped it and the door opened. Preston gave the pretty woman his most flattering smile.

"Hello," he said smoothly.

"Hi," she replied, winded. "Hurry up you guys, we're running behind as it is," she yelled to people that Preston couldn't see. Oh, but he could hear them.

The pitter patter of anxious feet hurried towards the elevator and six children, ranging in ages from five to fifteen, ran inside.

"Thanks for the holding the elevator for us, Mom. Retard Pete here had the brilliant idea to stop and tie his shoe," the oldest said.

"Don't make fun of your brother, Tyson. You were his age once and tying shoes weren't easy for you either," the mother reprimanded.

Are all these children hers? Preston wondered. If so, she looked amazing. The woman was almost in better shape than his wife and Amy was fit. Preston admired the way the mother lovingly held the child named Pete, her youngest son in her arms. So many times, he wished he could see Amy doing the same thing, but it wasn't to be yet. Looking away from her and her brood, Preston pressed the number ten and rode the elevator in silence until he got off.

The combination of lemon-scented ammonia and depression hit him in the face when he exited the elevator. The stench made him sick to his stomach. He looked at the numbers on the wall and followed the arrow to room ten-fifty. It was at the end of the corridor. Patients and their families visited with the doors open. Preston kept his eyes averted to avoid seeing any more patients. Sick people disgusted him. He walked in a straight line refusing to turn his head.

At the end of the hall there was the creak of a door opening and Bill Corley, Abbott's attorney, walked out, with his briefcase in hand and his paralegal in tow.

"Hey Preston," the lawyer acknowledged.

"Bill. What are you doing here?"

Before the lawyer could respond, Cora Lee Meadows stepped into the hallway.

"About time you arrived. Your father has been asking about you. Why are you out here, jabbing your jaws with Bill? Get in there. Bill, thank you for everything. I'll talk to you soon," she said, dismissing the attorney.

The hospital room that Abbott Meadows, Sr., occupied was large. As far as hospital rooms were concerned, this one appeared to be somewhat luxurious. It was a private room with the standard bed. Instead of the silver metal rails on the side, this one had hard plastic railings that had the controls on a touch pad attached to the sides. There was an antique looking armoire that held a forty-inch plasma television with over a hundred cable channels. Two matching, one drawer nightstands flanked the bed. A Naugahyde sofa bed and matching recliner sat across the room with an end table between the two.

"Nice digs you have here, A.B.," Preston said to his father.
        "Considering how much you gave this place; I would expect no less."

"Always preoccupied with money, aren't you Pres?" His sister Bella Rose observed snottily. "You didn't even say hello to Father or hug him."

"Mind your fucking business, Bella. I swear-."

"Preston Scott Meadows, that is no way to talk to your sister or speak in front of your father. Sometimes you act like you were raised in the inner city. Apologize this instance!"

Preston mumbled a meager apology to his sister but only because his mother commanded him to. He didn't bother speaking to his other sister, Jennifer or her husband, Dustin. He couldn't stand either of them and they knew it. They were both snooty and condescending and looked down on Preston like he was a second-class citizen. His perception anyway.

Truthfully, Preston didn't care for anyone who was doing better than he was. And in his current state, the guy who pumped his gas an hour ago was among that number. But Dustin Reynolds was the solitary heir to one of the world's largest fortunes and his baby sister had managed to snag him. The two of them were married six months after he and Amy and his sister had already had two beautiful daughters and was pregnant with their third child. A son, to be named after his father. Something Preston always wanted.

He sat in a chair on the other side of the room while the women in his family fussed over his father. Bored, he looked up and counted the holey, square tiles on the ceiling until he fell asleep. A hard punch on the side of his leg jarred him awake.

"Wake up old man," his brother Robert barked. "The doc has something he wants to tell us."

Preston opened his eyes in time to see a foreign doctor enter the room. Abbott, Jr., cut his eyes at Preston and shook his head, looking away from him and towards the physician.

"What's up Doc?" Preston joked, receiving dirty looks from his parent's and four siblings.

The doctor quickly gave Abbott and his family a quick break-down of his health and what it was going to take to get him up and running again.

"I've scheduled you for surgery in the morning. We're looking at about three to four hours in the O.R. In about an hour the nurse will come in and take you for your EGD. I want to look around and see what else's going on inside. Any questions?"

There were many.

"How risky is the surgery?"

"Will he be okay?"

"Is his heart strong enough for the procedure?"

Core Lee and her children were concerned and had so many more questions.

"Listen, I've been Abbott's doctor for years. He's my favorite patient. I promise, I'll be back to answer all your additional questions. Let me make my rounds and I will return."

The only question Preston had was why his father's attorney and paralegal were at the hospital. Had he changed his will in any way? As much as he wanted to call Bill, he knew that it was too soon. He'd wait until morning to follow-up with the lawyer and find out what was going on. Maybe he'd pay the paralegal a visit also. She was nice-looking and stacked in all the right places. It would do him well to have someone on his side with an inside track to what was going on concerning his father's will.

"Earth to Preston," Abbott, Sr. said. "Are you listening to me, Son?"

"Sorry, Father. I was thinking about Amy," he lied.

"How is she? Why didn't she come with you?"

"She really wanted to, but she had a meeting with the ladies' league today."

"That was today?" His mother chimed in. "I completely forgot. Excuse me dear. I'm going to step out into the hallway and phone Louise. I'm sure she's concerned about my absence."

"Sure, take your time, Dear. But don't go telling all my business to that old biddy. Before long, the whole state will know what's going on."

"Yes, Dear."

After his wife left the room, Abbott excused his daughters and son-in-law. He looked out the window for a moment before speaking.

"It's time to get down to business. Now I didn't want to tell your mother or sisters this, but things aren't looking too good for me health wise. It is a high probability that I may not make it out of surgery alive," he stated gravely.

"Father don't say that. We must keep our heads about this. Dr. Halal is a great physician. I know that he is capable of finding out what's wrong with you."

"That's what I've always loved about you, Robert. Always the optimist. But let's face it, Son; your old man is not as strong as he once was. Hell, I'm old. Pushing ninety in the fall. I've lived a good life. No complaints."

"I know. But why do I feel like there's something you're not telling us?"

"I'm telling you all I feel is necessary, Rob. Just know this; Death is as much a part of life as birth is."

"Is there anything you need us to do, Dad?"

"Just take care of Cora Lee. She's as stubborn as a mule that one, but she needs her boys. Just be there for her, A.J."

"Will do, Sir."

"Why don't you fella's step out and gimme a minute with Pres, here."

Obediently, Abbott, Jr. and Robert walked out of the room, leaving their father and younger brother alone.

21

CRYING MEADOWS

"I know you were probably madder than a deaf-mute playing bingo, when I didn't give you a VP position at the textiles plant all those years ago."

"It was fine, Sir. I learned a lot." Lie.

"Stop bull-shitting me. I know you were pissed. Hell, I would have been too, if my old man did that to me. But I was trying to build character within you, Son. You've always acted like a pansy and I was hoping that starting at the bottom and working hard would toughen you up. Seems like my plan backfired."

Preston couldn't believe what he was hearing. Not only was his father insulting him, but he was admitting that he had purposely given him the shitty job. And for what? A lesson to toughen him up?

"How was that pray tell, supposed to toughen me up?" He asked incredulously.

"Hell, I thought if you saw how shitty it was working at the bottom that you would strive to be the best and move up. Your lazy ass didn't see the value in the position though. You were late almost every day. Played golf at the club when you should have been in meetings. Taking advantage of your name all around. It's my fault you act like this. I let your mother keep you on her titty too long. Made you rotten it did. You sucked on that damned thing 'til you were damned near two. It wasn't right I tell ya."

A thick vein appeared on the side of Preston's neck and he balled his fists at his side. He walked slowly over to his father's bed and looked down at him.

"Old man, I swear if you weren't dying, I'd kill you."

Abbott let out a hefty laugh. "Now that's the fire that I've been waiting to see. Finally got some gumption in your belly. Good for you. Won't do you much good with me, but maybe if you use some of that fire on your wife you can manage to give her a baby. She's a comely wench. I wouldn't have minded taking a poke at that prime ass."

"How dare you speak about my wife that way? What is wrong with you, old man?"

"Old that's what. I can say whatever the hell I please. It's the truth, though. I can't tell you how many nights I laid awake, stroking a hard one, thinking about those lips of Amy's. She gets it from her mother you know. When I tell you that LaRue Blessingale knew what do with those juicy lips. Well doggy! She kept me harder than a diamond in an ice storm."

Abbott watched as his son turned a light shade of red. It was laughable. The older Abbott knew more about his young son than he was going to let on. He knew about his and Amy's fertility complications. Their money issues. And even the affairs that his son was having. Especially the one with the housekeeper, Marisol. He wanted to intervene on that one, but...now was not the time. He'd always prided himself on letting his children make their own decisions and he wasn't about to change. Preston would find out soon enough.

"Why are you squirming, Son? Don't tell me that you actually love your wife?"

"Of course, I do, Father. This, conversation... it's all ridiculous."

Laughing, Abbott said, "Oh well ain't that sweet. You married George's daughter for love. And all this time I thought it was because she had a nice ass and a shit load of money."

"I will not stand here and continue to be disrespected by you. Father or not."

"You'll stand your lily-livered ass right there until I tell you to move. I own you. You have no power here, Son. Hell, I know that the only reason that you even came to the hospital is to find out when I'm doing to kick the bucket. You're transparent, Preston. That's why you never made a good poker player. You wear your heart on your sleeve and your emotions are written all over your face. You sicken me."

"That goes both ways, old man."

"You do have some redeeming qualities though. You're creative. I'll give you that much. Too bad I won't be around to see how creative you're going to be when...," Abbott's voice trailed off.

"When what?"

"It's nothing. You'll find out soon enough. Now go home. I'm getting tired. Send my Cora Lee back in here. I wanna spend time with her."

An angry Preston stormed out of the hospital room and told his mother that she was needed. Without bothering to say goodbye to his siblings, Preston left the hospital and drove around the city aimlessly, trying to clear his head. His father had always been an asshole and the illness only made it worse.

Usually, when a person found out they were terminal, they changed for the better. Became humbler and tried to make amends to the people they have wronged and hurt. But not Abbott, he seemed to get worse. His illness made him bluntly honest. He had always lacked tact and now he spoke with no filter or regard to anyone's feelings.

Before long, Preston found himself at a seedy hole-in-the-wall bar on the southeast side of Atlanta. There, he drowned himself in cheap booze and self-pity. He managed to pick up a prostitute who gave him some mind-blowing sex for fifteen minutes and robbed him of what cash he had on him. Once he finally made it home, he climbed the steps to his bedroom where Amy lay awake waiting for him. He passed out on the chaise lounge and never made it to the bed.

The next morning, a hung-over Preston decided to forego the trip to the hospital and opted to go play a round of golf with some friends instead. His mother called and berated him.

"What is wrong with you Preston? Your father just came out of a three-and-a-half-hour surgery and you are nowhere to be found. The entire family is here, even Amy. Yet you're missing in action."

Damn, Preston didn't even pay attention to the fact that he was alone. He could care less.

"Mother, I had a prior engagement. Father of all people will understand. After all, he missed several family functions because of business. I'll come tomorrow and visit. I've got plenty of time."

Two days later, Preston still hadn't visited his father. And time ran out.

CHAPTER 4
DEATH AND DISHONOR...

ABBOTT MEADOWS, SR., WAS DEAD. Sometime during the night his heart gave out. He went peacefully in his sleep. Preston couldn't have been happier. While the others mourned the patriarch of the clan, the youngest son silently rejoiced. Cruel he knew, but he didn't care. All his life, his father had made him miserable. He treated him differently from his older brothers and showed favoritism among them all. He was ready to finally get what he had coming to him.

Bill Corley, Abbott's attorney had already told Preston years ago that he was in line to receive a hefty inheritance. That's why Preston spent without reserve. His father was worth billions and if Bill was right, Preston was in line to receive a nice percentage of it. Of course, there was his mother and four siblings to consider but he could care less about them. All he wanted was his piece of the old man's pie.

Cora Lee asked all her children to come to the family home to help plan the funeral. Meadow's Estates was a sprawling thirty-thousand square feet mansion that had nine bedrooms and thirteen bathrooms. There was a twenty-seat media room, indoor basketball court, state-of-the-art gym, and a Tuscan inspired chef's kitchen. The home was nestled on fifty-acres.

Driving up to the vast estate brought back lots of memories for Preston. Some good. Some bad. He and Amy

26

were married here. That was a good memory for him regardless of how rocky things were for them now. But he also remembered being chastised harshly by his father and those memories he wished he could forget. He parked his car in the circular driveway, killed the ignition and got out of the car. He was halfway up the stairs when he turned around towards the car.

"Are you coming or what?" He questioned Amy.

"Yes. I was hoping you'd open my door for me. After all, that is the gentlemanly thing to do."

"What's wrong with your arms? Come on, Amy. Cut the crap. You've already made us late."

Preston turned on his heels and trotted up the steps. Before he could even knock the door swung open.

"Welcome, Master Preston," the butler said.

Preston gave the man a bear hug. "Sloan, my good man. How have you been? I sure have missed you," he ended sincerely.

"All is well, Sir. You're looking mighty dapper. I am deeply sorry for your loss. Master Abbott was a fine man."

"Thanks. But you and I both know that you were more of a father to me than he ever was. Where's everyone?"

"The parlor, Sir. Shall I announce you?"

"Don't bother. I'm going to the bathroom."

Preston wanted to end the conversation quickly before he got emotional. He did have a special attachment to the butler. The man was always there for him when he was younger. Nurturing him and teaching him, much like a father should. It was Sloan who fostered the love of football in Preston and when he was recruited out of high school to play college ball, it was Sloan he sought out first to share the great news. On a dark, lonely night, when Preston contemplated suicide, it was the butler who talked him off the ledge. Literally.

By the time Preston made it to the parlor, Amy had joined the rest of the family. She was standing next to Preston's sister, Jennifer, rubbing her stomach.

"Rubbing it like it's a magic coin isn't going to make you pregnant," he whispered softly in her ear as he walked behind her.

"I swear you're the demons spawn," his sister retorted, overhearing her brother's hurtful comment.

"So, it would seem," he laughed.

Cora Lee cleared her throat to get her family's attention.

"I've called you guys here to talk about the funeral arrangements. Abbott was a special man and I want to send him off the way he lived...in grand style. Murray's Funeral Home will prepare his body and host a viewing there Wednesday. The funeral will be Thursday at 11a.m."

"So soon?" Bella Rose, the oldest daughter asked. "But we haven't even had a chance to look at caskets."

"That's already taken care of, dear," her mother replied. "Your father obviously knew more about his condition than he cared to let on. These arrangements have been made for many months. Now, where was I? Oh, yes, after the service we will release doves in your father's memory. That was his favorite bird. The repast will be at Abbott's. I don't want stranger's milling around my house. Funerals attract vagabonds."

Abbott's was the upscale restaurant that Cora Lee had formed with her husband over ten years ago. It was a white tablecloth establishment that was so elite, one had to make reservations months in advance just to drink at the bar. Since the flagship restaurant performed so well in its first year, the couple opened a location in Los Angeles, Manhattan, Washington, D.C., and Paris, France.

"Are you planning on hosting the repast there and still operate normal business?" Abbott, Jr. asked.

"No, Son. We will close for the day and only have a skeleton crew work for a few hours. Your father would have wanted it that way."

"Can we afford to halt operations for an entire day?" Preston spoke up.

"Here we go," Robert said rolling his eyes in the top of his head. "I was waiting for you to bring up money."

"Lay off, Rob! I'm just thinking about the family here."

"More like thinking of you, right Preston?" Jennifer added.

"Look here, you bi- "

"Silence! All of you!"

It got so quiet one could hear a pin drop.

"Now I've had just about enough of all this bickering!" Cora Lee lamented. "Your father has been gone less than twenty-four hours and look at all of you, falling apart. Get it together!"

Sloan walked into the room and cleared his throat.

"Dinner is served Madam, or should I have Cook hold service?"

"No, thank you, Sloan. We'll come now."

The Meadows family adjourned to the formal dining room where they ate in silence. Cora Lee looked down the length of the table and was immediately saddened. This was the first meal that they'd had in Abbott's absence. Tears flooded her eyes but didn't spill over. Now was not the time to show signs of weakness. Abbott hated that. She was stronger than that and was determined to show everyone. She was the head of this family now and she was going to make her husband proud. Lifting her fork, she tapped her water goblet three times.

"Now that we've had sufficient time to cool off, I can continue. After the repast, we will attend Catholic Mass that evening. It's Holy Thursday."

"With everything that has gone on, I forgot that this was Easter weekend," Amy observed.

"Yes, dear. And in observance of Good Friday, we will postpone the reading of the will until the following Monday."

"Reading of the will? I thought that was only done in movies?" Jennifer said.

"Yeah, Ma. Me too," Abbott, Jr. agreed.

"Well children, you know how your father was. He had to have his own way of doing things."

Peachy. Preston was going to have to wait a week to find out exactly how much money his father left him. If one more bill collector called him, he was going to hunt them down and shoot them in the foot. It was frustrating, but hell, he had waited this long. What were a few more days?

"Did Father leave all of his affairs in order, Mother?" Bella Rose questioned.

"Did he? You know how meticulous your father was. He didn't leave a stone unturned. Everything that your father ever purchased has been paid off. We've lived debt free for years."

"Even this estate?" Dustin, Jennifer's husband challenged.

"Especially this estate, dear boy. My husband wanted to ensure that I didn't have a care in the world. He will be sorely missed."

"Yes, he will."

"Indeed."

The family agreed.

"Your father has put a contingency clause in his will," Cora Lee continued. "To receive your inheritance, you must attend the funeral, the repast, and Thursday Mass and Easter Service. *With* the family."

Everyone turned their heads to look at Preston.

"What are you all gawking at me for? I'm not going to miss my father's funeral."

"It's not just attending the funeral Pres. You must do all the things with the family. Don't forget that part."

"How could I Abbott, Jr., with you right here to remind me?"

"Always here to help, little bro. Always here to help." Abbott said, patting Preston on his back.

"Mother Cora is there anything that I can do to help you?"

"As a matter of fact, Amy, there is. Since you're the only one here who doesn't have any children to tend to, can you please double check with Chef Crane at Abbott's and make sure he has the menu I faxed over? Also, get with the florist to ensure the flowers are fresh and delivered on time. I will supply you with the information after dinner, dear."

Amy noticed how Cora Lee tried to skirt by the snide remark she made about Amy not having any children. It was hurtful that even her own mother-in-law would draw negative attention to her infertility.

"Thank you, Mother Cora. I'd be honored to help you."

Dinner continued without incident and the conversation flowed lightly. After dinner, the men went into the cigar parlor and the ladies had tea set up on the veranda. It was a cool Georgia night and Cora Lee wanted to enjoy the fresh air.

"Mother, it's getting late. Come, let's get you settled in for the night," Bella Rose offered.

CRYING MEADOWS

"Of course, you're right dear. But don't fuss over me; I'll have Guadalupe help me. You all head home. I'll see you tomorrow."

Cora Lee hit a buzzer and soon her beautiful housekeeper appeared. When Amy saw her, she couldn't help but notice how the woman seemed to get prettier and prettier as the years progressed. For an older woman, she was stunning.

Hmmm, she thought. *I guess that's what Marisol will look like when she gets that age, since most Hispanics look alike.*

On the ride home, Amy placed her hand over Preston's and caressed it gently. She was pleased when he didn't throw it off like he usually did. He looked over at his wife and for the first time in years, he was happy that she was there by his side.

"I know that things have been crazy, Ames. But I promise, we're going to get through this."

"Wow. You haven't called me that in years. It really felt good."

"I know I've been a bastard. It's just that with all this shit Dad threw at me and the mounting bills…well, I've not been myself. Just give me some time. I'm going to do right by you Amy. I give you my word."

"You mean it, honey?"

"Yes. I do. I'm going to stop fucking around with Marisol, too. I see how she disrespects you and that's my fault. I'm going to do better. Once we get this inheritance, things are going to change for us. You'll see."

That night when they got home, Preston didn't visit the housekeepers' room like usual. Instead, he made slow passionate love to his wife. It was the dawn of a new day.

CHAPTER 5
WHERE THERE'S A WILL...

DOLLAR SIGNS FLASHED BEFORE Preston's eyes. He was salivating. It was time. The will was about to be read.

"What's taking Bill so long?" Preston asked, fidgeting in his seat.

"We just sat down, Preston. Why are you so antsy? Are you high or something?"

"No A.J. don't be ridiculous. It's just that some of us have better things to do than to sit cooped up inside all day."

"Yeah, I know how busy you are. The back nine will be waiting for you. I assure you; it's not going anywhere."

"I do more with my time than play golf you imbecile."

"Ooh, name calling. How adult."

"Will both of you please shut up!" Bill Corley barked, walking into his massive conference room. "You all bicker like five-year olds. Now before we begin, I have a video that your father wanted me to share with you all. Perry, you can begin," he instructed his assistant.

The overhead lights were dimmed, and the screen lit up. Abbott Meadows, Sr., sat in his hospital bed. When Cora Lee saw her husband, she let out a soft cry. The assistant paused the video.

CRYING MEADOWS

"It's going to be alright, Mother. We will get through this together.

"Yes, we will my dear, Bella. I'm sorry Bill," Cora Lee apologized softly.

"You're grieving Cora Lee. We know how much you loved Abbott. It's perfectly understandable to feel the way you do."

Cora Lee simply nodded in agreement and the DVD was restarted.

"I, Abbott Charles Meadows, Sr., a resident of Georgia and Fulton County; and being of sound mind and memory, do hereby make, publish, and declare this to be my last will and testament, thereby revoking and making null and void all other last will and testaments and/codicils to last will and testaments heretofore made by me."

For the next few minutes, Preston tuned out his father's voice. He wasn't saying anything of importance, just spouting some legal jargon that was necessary to validate the will. Like radars, Preston's ears perked up when he heard the bequests being read. He began with some staff members and good friends who helped him along the way and then he got down to the nitty gritty.

"To My loving wife, Cora Lee of 58 years, I leave Meadows Estates in its entirety, which consists of the main home and the three adjacent properties that border our property. Also, I want you to have my art collection that is valued to date at forty-eight million dollars, and all cash, stocks, bonds, CD's, and money market accounts totaling four and a half-billion dollars. I love you Cora Lee to the moon and back. Don't spend it all in one place."

"I won't dear," she said to the screen.

"Now, to my children, who have made me so proud over the years, I leave the following:

Abbott, Jr. I leave Meadow's Textiles, Southern Belle Publishing Company and Media Group, my classic car collection and one hundred-

twenty million dollars' cash. To each of his children, I leave twenty million dollars to be held in an interest-bearing account until they reach the age of majority.

Robert, I leave Meadows Holdings of Georgia which includes Meadows Financial and Asset Management, Meadows Mercedes of Atlanta, the chateau in Paris, France and one hundred-twenty million dollars' cash. To each of his children, I leave twenty million dollars to be held in an interest-bearing account until they reach the age of majority.

To my lovely oldest daughter, Bella Rose who loved to cook, I leave the entire chain of Abbott's restaurants, the penthouse in New York on Fifth Avenue, the estate at Martha's Vineyard and one hundred-twenty million dollars' cash. To each of her children, I leave twenty million dollars to be held in an interest-bearing account until they reach the age of majority."

Damn, the old man is being mighty generous, Preston mused. I wonder what he left me. His loud thoughts caused him to miss the first few words of his father's bequest.

"...sweet young daughter, Jennifer, I leave Meadows Property Management which currently owns a two hundred-fifty-unit apartment complex, fifty-four homes, twelve condos, the Meadows Midtown Parking Garage and four commercial properties, the Georgia Meadows Private Airstrip and the 2015 Gulfstream GV private jet, and one hundred-twenty million dollars' cash. To each of her children, I leave twenty million dollars to be held in an interest-bearing account until they reach the age of majority.

And finally, to my youngest son Preston, I leave Lush Meadows Golf and Country Club and one hundred-twenty million dollars. The cash which is to be held in trust and overseen by Bill Corley until Preston and Amy Meadows produce an heir of their own loins. For each child, they conceive a twenty-million-dollar trust will be established and held in an interest-bearing account until they reach the age of majority. Should Preston and Amy fail to conceive within eight years of this date, the one hundred-twenty million will be forfeited and divided evenly among my four other children. In addition, the trusts that would have been created for the children will then revert to the Meadows Estate to my wife, Cora Lee Meadows.

Furthermore, it is prohibited that any person in this room, make available any funds to Preston Scott Meadows or Amy Jo Blessingale Meadows with the intent and purpose to loan, invest, donate, or endow in anyway. Such violation will result in the revocation of that person's inheritance in its entirety.

In Witness, Whereof, I, the undersigned testator, declare that I sign and execute this instrument on the date written below as my last will and testament and further declare that I sign it willingly, that I execute it as my free and voluntary act for the purposes expressed in this document, and that I am eighteen years of age or older, of sound mind and memory, and under no constraint or undue influence."

The television screen went black.

"What the fuck was that!" Preston screeched. "This is some bullshit! What in the hell just happened here?"

"Your Father made you all's inheritance based upon how many heirs you all produced. He wants the Meadows bloodline to continue," Bill disclosed.

"That's some first-class malarkey! And why in the hell would he leave me Lush Meadows? That place is run down and irreparable."

"Well baby bro, Dad clearly understood your love for golf. What better gift than your own golf and country club?" Abbott ribbed, slapping Preston on the back.

Angry, Preston charged his older brother and the two of them tussled in the conference room. The attorney, who witnessed the filming of the will, had the foresight to have security on stand-by just in case something like this happened. Two brawny guards pulled the brother's apart. They gave each of them a warning glance which settled them both down.

"And what the hell did he mean saying it's prohibited to make funds available to me or Amy?"

"That, my daft brother means that none of us can give you or your wife a dime at any time or we will lose our inheritance," Robert explained.

Preston gave Bill a questioning look.

"I'm afraid he's right, Son. Your father was very clear about that."

"I'm not your Son. Fuck you! Fuck them! And Fuck him!" Preston got ready to storm out.

"One more thing, Preston. This is from your father." Bill handed him a small envelope.

Preston snatched it and slammed the door behind him when he exited the room. On the elevator, he tore the envelope open and read the short note.

"You're damned right!" he said wadding the paper up and tossing it to the ground.

The woman who stood silently in the back of the elevator picked up the note and read it.

WISH YOU WOULD HAVE KILLED ME NOW, DON'T YOU?

CHAPTER 6
THE AFTERMATH...

FAMILY WEALTH CAN BE A CURSE. It potentially makes the kids lazy and dependent on the main money source. While most wealthy parents had lower expectations of their children, Abbott Meadows, Sr., was the opposite. He gave his children little to work with to see what they could make of it. All of them always surpassed his expectations. Except Preston. He was the typical rich kid. He spent recklessly, experimented with drugs, trashed hotel rooms, and got into boat loads of trouble, relying on the family name to absolve him from his guilt.

Therefore, Abbott put conditions on Preston's inheritance. At some point in his son's life, he wanted him to learn responsibility and grow up. Preston never saw his father's life lessons that way. He always viewed them as punishment. Preston was the black sheep of the Meadow's family and had no problem living up to the label.

He sped southbound on Interstate eighty-five. He needed to clear his head and see someone who could help him make sense of all that had happened in the past two weeks. His good friend was a master problem-solver. What Preston was dealing with right now, was a master problem. His destination was Newnan, Georgia, but first he had a stop to make.

༒ ༒

In the office, the siblings congratulated one another on their inheritance. They weren't at all surprised at the amounts of money that their father had left them. They were however surprised at how he handled Preston's share. Less than half an hour after the reading of Abbott's will, everyone in Georgia high society knew how much each of the Meadow's children was bequeathed. Thankfully, no one knew about the stipulations, regarding Preston's inheritance.

Fortunately, Abbott, Sr., made it clear that no one was to disclose the details or else they would run the risk of forfeiting their inheritance, as well. Bill Corley announced that just as Robert was about to call his personal attorney.

"Wait until I call, Mackey," Robert told Abbott, Jr., as he pulled out his cell phone.

"I wouldn't do that if I were you, Robert," Bill began. "If you all will look at the last page of the document you just signed, down at the bottom, you will see something very interesting."

The Meadow's children scanned the document. It was Bella Rose who saw it first.

"Dad definitely knew his kids, didn't he?" She surmised.

"Look here, it says, "If any of my children or their spouses find it so inclined to share the particulars of this will, expressly the details concerning Preston and Amy Meadows, they willfully forfeit all inheritance immediately."

"Phew, I almost lost it all," Robert said wiping his forehead. "That was close. Thanks for the heads up, Bill."

"You're welcome."

"Should one of us warn Preston? He stormed out so fast he missed this morsel of information."

CRYING MEADOWS

"Honestly, Jen, I think Preston is too prideful to tell anyone what happened here today. I don't think we have to worry about him."

"So, we can talk about our own inheritance, just not Preston's? Is that right?" Jennifer asked.

"That's correct," Bill answered. "Your father isn't trying to ostracize your brother in the community, and we all know how small Georgia is when it comes to money."

"But why did dad forbid any of us from helping him?" Bella Rose questioned.

"He wanted him to finally do something for himself, without the help of his family or the Meadows' name," Cora Lee told her children. "He felt as if Preston has been floating by on the name and not doing enough to establish himself. If he proves that he can make a go of the country club, he has an equal inheritance coming, like the rest of you."

"Really, but that's not what dad said on the video," Abbott Jr., queried with a twinge of jealousy.

"That's true, A.J., but your father left your mother a specific set of instructions concerning Preston. And this isn't to be discussed either. Especially not with Preston. Is that clear?"

"Crystal," they said.

The remaining Meadow's family signed the final documents, received last minute instructions, and was sent on their way. Bill Corley was happy to be rid of the lot of them. All except Cora Lee. She was going to be an on-going client. The Meadow's children weren't as bad as many children of means. Their main issue was that they argued too much and was always trying to outdo one another. Their father was responsible for their competitive nature.

"Rest in peace, Abbott, you ornery bastard. I'm sure going to miss you."

AVERY GOODE

A few people milled around the golf and country club. Some Preston recognized from school. Others from social gatherings he'd attended before. None of them mattered to him. Unless one of them was prepared to give him the money he needed to turn this place around, he could care less about their existence. Exhaling, Preston continued to tour the club.

Lush Meadows was once the most prestigious club in the Southeast. People would pay big bucks just to get on the coveted waiting list. The crème de la crème of Georgia society were all members there. They hosted the best galas, and it was the chosen venue for many government functions. Abbott, Sr., used to hobnob with only the best.

There was once a time that Preston would walk around the club with pride. Presidents and governors had dined there. Many had played a few rounds of golf on the greens as well, and many legends had performed in the ball room. Out of all of Abbott's children, he was the one who showed the most interest in the club. Growing up, Preston knew that one day, the club would be his. He used to imagine sitting in the large oval office that overlooked the back nine, giving orders to staff, while smoking on the finest Cubans. That's when the club boasted grandeur.

He never imagined this though. The ceiling tiles in the kitchen looked to be stained with urine because of water leaks from roof damage. Although the roof had been repaired, the tiles never got replaced. The freezer had a hairline crack in the glass and Preston knew that was a health code violation. There were mouse droppings behind a cabinet in the pantry that he spotted on his way to the dining room.

There he found some carpets that were unraveling and some small holes in the floor that the staff had used furniture to cover. The white linens on the tables were dingy but one couldn't tell so much because the bulbs were cheap, and the lighting was dim. Some of the plates had small cracks on the bottom, making it alright to still eat off, but not up to par for a club of that caliber. So many things that Preston witnessed in the club were off brand for the Meadow's name.

But nothing was more deplorable than the putting greens themselves. And this is the sole reason that membership was down. Dry, brown patches of grass were scattered over the one hundred seventy-five-acre course. Gone was the bold green grass that was so thick, it felt like carpet under foot. Some of the smaller bodies of water were drying up. The out-of-play areas resembled barren land and some of the outbuildings and hard structures were in desperate need of repair. Although elite couples joined the club, it was men who were the driving force of enrollment. Without them, their wives had no reason to join.

Shaking his head, Preston couldn't believe that this was his inheritance. It was going to take some serious capital to restore Lush Meadows to its former glory. It would take some doing but deep inside, Preston knew that he could do it. He had no other choice.

"This place is depressing," he voiced, walking out of the front doors towards his car. He had seen enough.

❧ ❧ ❧

"Are you inside? I don't see your car." Preston spoke into the phone's receiver.

"I am and it's in the garage. Come in. The door is unlocked. Come to the office."

Preston twisted the doorknob and walked inside the house. It was a beautiful four-bedroom craftsman bungalow that sat on a half-acre of land. There was a massive stone fireplace that sat on the far wall. It was the focal point of the room. The polished hardwood floors creaked under the weight of Preston's dress shoes.

"Have a seat while I make you a drink. You look stressed."

"You have no idea. I thought that my problems would end after my father died. It seems like they are just beginning."

"What did I tell you?"

"Never count my chickens before they hatch."

"You didn't listen. I try to give you advice but because I'm not rich like you, you never take it. Now look at you."

"I know. Don't rub it in. The last thing I need is to hear I told you so."

"I wouldn't do you like that. I love you. But one day, you will listen to me. This is what your father wanted. For you to learn."

"You're right, Marisol. But I did not come here to talk," he admitted, setting his drink down on the table and standing up. "That's a nice tie you have on. It looks familiar."

"It should. It's yours. I took it from the house the other day before I left. I figured you would love to see it on me."

"Indeed. It looks much better on you than it does me."

"You only say that because it's all I'm wearing."

The sexy housekeeper sat on the edge of the cherry wood desk in her home office. When Preston got closer, Marisol slid back just a bit and spread her legs wide open. Her knees were bent, and her feet were positioned at opposite corners of the desk. Preston got a full view of what she offered him.

"You look delicious," he told her.

"I am," she said as she helped him to his knees.

Kneeling before her, Preston sniffed her warm center.

"Hmmm. Peaches."

CRYING MEADOWS

He leaned in and nuzzled her womanhood with his nose then backed up slightly to lick her. Marisol rested her head on her shoulder as she watched him eat her out. Skillfully, Preston's tongue stroked her most sensitive spot. He played with the hard nub, flicking his tongue over it a few times before taking it into his mouth and gently suckling it.

Marisol moaned in pleasure as she gripped the back of his head and brought him deeper into her. She grinded her hips on the hard wood in ecstasy. The louder she moaned the harder he suckled.

"Aye, Papi. You love me so good," Marisol said, her thick accent coming through.

Preston added two fingers to the pleasure party and little sparks of electricity began to travel from Marisol's toes up her long legs. His stiff tongue moved in and out, making her center drip with hot nectar.

"Ooh, Papi, please. I need you," she exclaimed, pulling him up by the shoulders.

Quickly Preston unfastened the belt of his trousers and let them drop to the floor. Not wasting any more time, he pulled his hard member through the hole of his boxer shorts and jabbed it to the hilt of her womanhood. Marisol cried out in pleasure.

Preston grabbed the back of her head and kissed her passionately on the mouth, allowing her to taste herself. His mouth was hard on hers as the two of them fought hard to breathe. Their tongue's wrestled and danced as their bodies became one. Without removing himself from her center, Preston picked Marisol up and took her to the massive bed in the room adjacent to the office.

He slammed her down on the bed and began assaulting her hot cave. Their skin slapped each other loudly, and wet, suction noises could be heard throughout the bedroom. Marisol, who was on the verge of a powerful climax, flipped

Preston over and straddled his hard penis. Like a cowgirl, she rode her stallion into the sunset until her hot juices flowed out of her body and onto his stiffness. Shortly after her release, Preston found his own, spilling his steaming hot seed within her.

Marisol collapsed on his chest, breathing heavily. Her small fingers rubbed the beads of sweat that had formed on his forehead. Tenderly, she kissed his chest and made small circles around his nipples with her tongue.

"You're trying to re-ignite the fire, Mi Amor?"

"Mmm, while that sounds delicious, I know that we don't have time for another round."

"Baby, we always have time for round two."

"So, what are you going to do, babe?"

"About what?"

"Don't play that with me. You know what I'm talking about. Your wife and the stipulations of your inheritance."

Preston exhaled heavily. "You already know what I'm going to do," he answered with a little edge in his voice. "I'll do whatever I have to do to get my money."

"Even if that means, hurting me?"

Preston pushed the woman off his chest and sat up quickly.

"Amy is my wife, Mari. She's wanted a child for a long time now. My father wanted all his children to have an heir and create our own individual legacies. It's a win-win situation. She gets her baby. I get my money. You get my money."

"You make it sound so simple."

"Because it is."

"Nothing is that simple."

"It is if we want it to be. Now give me a kiss. I must go. I've scheduled some meetings with a few of my fraternity brother's in Chicago and Los Angeles and I have to get home to pack."

"How long will you be gone?"

"Since when did you start questioning me? I don't like it. Remember your place."

"I'm sorry. But I have some important things to discuss with you. I think- "

"That's the problem with women, they're always thinking. Whatever you want to talk about can wait till' I return. I'm sure it's not that important."

Preston smacked Marisol on her backside as he jumped out of bed. In less than ten minutes he was dressed and ready to leave.

"While I'm gone, I need you to do what you're told at the house. I told Amy that I was going to be more respectful to her."

"And how is making love to me respecting her? Or the trick you were with the other night?"

He gave her a scathing look. "You're pushing it, Mari. Like I said, know your place. Don't give Amy any problems while I'm gone. Or else…"

"Or else what?"

"You don't want to find out. Come on now, this isn't us. We don't get into petty arguments. I love you. Let's not argue."

Marisol didn't respond, and Preston paid no attention to the fact when he kissed her, she didn't kiss him back. He had a plan and that was all he cared about.

It didn't take him long to get home but by the time he left Marisol, darkness had fallen. He walked into a dark house and called out to Amy as soon as he stepped into the foyer.

"I'm in here," she called out.

"Why are you sitting in the dark?" He asked flipping the switch. "What's wrong?"

There were tears in her eyes and her face was tear streaked. Amy opened the palm of her hand. Inside was a pregnancy test.

"I was so sure this time. I had all the symptoms. I just knew…I thought…" The dam burst, and Amy broke down.

"Shhh, stop that now. It's going to be okay. We're going to have kids. Soon, this house is going to be noisy with the pitter patter of little feet and when they get older; it will be filled with friends we don't understand and music we hate or vice versa." Preston leaned in and hugged Amy.

"Your face smells like pussy." Amy removed herself from his grasp. "You've been with her again?"

"I never heard you talk that vulgar before. Yes, I've been with her."

"Dammit Preston! I thought that you said we were going to try to work on our marriage. How can we do that when you're still screwing the help?"

"Shit, Amy! I was stressed and needed something that she had to offer."

"What is it? I need to know. What is it that an undocumented maid from Mexico can do for my husband that I can't?"

"You don't understand, Amy. Drop it."

"I know I don't. That's why I'm asking. I'm trying to get an understanding. It's not like I'm ugly or out of shape. I do whatever you ask. I suck your dick, swallow your cum, let you fuck me in my ass. I do it all. So, tell me, what is it that she does for you that I don't?"

"I don't have time for this," he said leaving the room.

CRYING MEADOWS

"Of course, you don't. It's just like you to leave when things get uncomfortable. You are a runner, Preston. And a coward!"

Amy collapsed on the sofa in tears. This is not the way she had planned on their conversation going. She was so distraught about another negative pregnancy test and needed her husband's support. But she wasn't counting on smelling sex all over his face either. He didn't even have the decency to shower after lying with the other woman. It was getting to be a bit too much for her. For her and her husband to have a happy life, she was going to have to put an end to the torrid affair once and for all.

CHAPTER 7
QUEENS AND PEASANTS...

PRESTON DESCENDED THE STAIRS WITH a suitcase and carry-on in hand.

"You're leaving me?" Amy screamed.

"Don't be so dramatic," he rolled his eyes. "I'm going out of town. I've got to find some money somewhere, so I can get that dump of a club off the ground before we find ourselves out on the street."

Relieved, Amy said, "How long will you be gone?"

"I don't know. A week. Maybe two. Depends on how successful I am."

"Okay. I'll see if I can get some help here from my father."

"Don't!" He yelled. "I don't want your father thinking I can't take care of you. Let me handle this, please."

"Whatever you say. Have a safe trip," Amy said, walking him to the door. "Don't. Even. Think. About. It."

Preston had leaned in to kiss her and she rebuffed his attempt.

"Guess you're right. But she did taste like peaches. You may have liked it." Snickering, he walked out and slammed the door behind him.

Amy was livid. One day Preston was texting her I love you and *I miss you* and then he wasn't texting or calling her at all. She wanted to make her marriage work. But her husband was making it very hard. A woman could only take so much. Preston was the only man she had ever loved and felt that she could ever love. Since she was five years old, she's had the hots for him. She used to love watching him play catch in the yard with her brothers.

As she grew older, he didn't pay much attention to her because she had braces and wore corrective shoes. During those years, she stayed away from him. It wasn't until her mother sent her away to boarding school that Amy began to blossom. Surrounded by so many beautiful girls motivated her to step her game up. When the day came for her to remove her braces, she was so excited that she was half an hour early for her appointment. Next, were the ugly glasses that she traded out for contact lenses.

By the time Amy returned to Atlanta for her coming out party, she was a statuesque young woman whose dark red hair cascaded down her back. Her green eyes sparkled complimenting the emerald necklace her great-great-grandmother passed down to her. Her soft, sun-kissed skin was creamy against the gorgeous white dress she wore.

Preston was to be her escort. He hadn't seen her in two years. LaRue Blessingale, Amy's mother, knew that her daughter had a life-size crush on Preston, and she took great pains in ensuring her daughter was perfect that evening. Every detail was spot on from her hair to her make-up and nails. Amy glowed inside out.

When she reached the top of the staircase, Preston was flabbergasted. He knew that he would be escorting Amy, but no one bothered to tell him how much she had matured. And in all the right places. His mouth was dry by the time she descended the stairs and locked arms with his. He was smitten.

From that point on, the two of them were hooked on one another. They wrote letters three or four times a week and they talked as much as possible. When Amy was home for school breaks, he took her on chaperoned dates and spent as much time with her as possible. The day of her high school graduation, he was right there, cheering louder than anyone. He was her biggest fan. But that was then. This was now. Things were different.

Two days after Preston left for his business trip, Marisol returned to work. Obeying Preston's orders, the maid stayed home on her days off, so that she and Amy would spend the least amount of time together as possible. Amy was happy for the variation in their schedule. She would not have been happy if she knew that her husband purchased the home for his lover using some of the money Amy's father gave him in dowry for his daughter. No, she wouldn't be too happy at all.

Louise Belfair and the entire Distinct Ladies of Leisure Women's League were coming to her home tomorrow. She did not have time to sit and reminisce. Amy was nervous. Not because her house was not up to Louise's standards, but Cora Lee and the senior members were coming as well.

These ladies were the preeminent forces to be reckoned with in the entire state of Georgia. What made Amy so nervous was that Marisol would be on staff during the meeting and she wasn't sure how the housekeeper was going to perform in front of the ladies. This would-be Cora Lee's first social function since the death of her husband and Amy wanted to make it as nice as possible for her intimidating mother-in-law.

Amy pressed the intercom button and asked the staff to meet her in the library. She was almost speechless when Marisol showed up. For a moment, she stood quiet, staring at the maid.

"Um, Ma'am, you wanted to see us?" Ruthie, the cook asked.

"Oh, yes. Sorry. As you all know it's my turn to host the quarterly women's luncheon and we need to get a few things ironed out. Ruthie, I placed the menu on your desk in the kitchen. Did you see it?"

"Yes, Ma'am I did."

"Great. Do we have everything we need in house or do you need to send John to the store?"

"I have everything I need."

"Ok, then. Marisol, I need you and Tabby to make sure that the house is spotless. Cora Lee will come wearing a pair of white gloves and do a test. I need to pass." She paused to see if Marisol, who usually balked at that point, had anything to say. The housekeeper remained silent much to everyone's surprise.

Amy continued. "Leland, I know you've seen me working in the garden the past few days. Will you please make sure that all the tools are put away and the grounds look presentable? I don't know if the ladies will want to tour the grounds but let's be prepared should they desire that, okay?"

"Sure thing, madam."

Amy rattled off a few more orders to the staff members and sent them on their way to get busy. Marisol worked surprisingly well with no back talk. Preston said he would talk with the surly housekeeper. Maybe the talk they had did some good. Not one to look a gift horse in the mouth, Amy continued about her day making sure that everything was on schedule for her garden party. A soft vibration in Amy's pocket alerted her that her cell phone was ringing. It was Preston.

"Hey, Ames. Just checking in. I made it to Chicago and I'm at the hotel."

"That's great, dear," Amy said, trying to mask the hurt in her voice. He always did this. Hurt her, wait a little while and then call her or come talk with her as if nothing ever happened. All without ever saying sorry.

"Is everything okay on the home front?"

"So far so good. I'm glad that you made it safely. When is your meeting with Tim?" She said, asking about a friend of his who he hoped to get a loan from.

"In the morning at ten. I'm hoping he's willing to come on board with me. I could really use his help."

"Wonderful. Well, call me tomorrow after the meeting is over and let me know how things turned out." Click.

Amy didn't give Preston a chance to respond before hanging up. She had too much to do around the house and couldn't afford to stay on the phone with him. Shaking her head, Amy resumed working around the house. She and the staff worked well into the night before calling it quits.

The next day with butterflies in her stomach, Amy prepared to receive her guests. In true Meadows fashion, Cora Lee was the first to arrive, immediately followed by Louise Belfair. Twenty minutes later, all the Distinguished Ladies of Leisure were seated in the garden at Amy's home. Ruthie and the serving staff came out with large trays of appetizers and fresh squeezed, ice cold lemonade and cold, sweet tea.

"Lunch is served," Ruthie announced. "Miss Amy has selected a delectable menu for your dining pleasure this afternoon. For starters, we will be serving a savory spring vegetable and goat cheese tart and smoked salmon with lemon crème fraiche. Our main selection will be skillet fried chicken, sugar snap salad, roasted fingerling potatoes and roasted carrots, both with chive pesto. You will end your meal with the Apricot-Anise tarts. Enjoy your meal, ladies."

The ladies talked softly amongst one another, complimenting Amy on a job well done. This was the first time that Amy had won over the ladies. Hopefully, it wouldn't be the last. The staff made it through service without a hitch and cleared all the dishes away in record time.

CRYING MEADOWS

"I hereby call the meeting to order," Louise said, pounding a small gavel she pulled out of her purse. "First order of business is the Spring Extravaganza Fundraiser."

For the next two hours, the women discussed fundraising, menus, venues, and guest lists. By the time the meeting ended, Amy was beat. She was happy that the monthly meeting was held at a different member's house each month. She wouldn't be able to do this if she had to host it more than once.

"Amy, you've done a fine job today. I am very proud of you dear. And please know that I am praying for you. I know how much you really want a baby."

"Thank you, Mother Cora. How kind of you to say. And thank you so much for the prayers. It's in God's hands now. I've done all I can do."

"Indeed, it is, Dear. Again, thank you so much. Get some rest darling."

Amy was stunned. Her mother-in-law was usually overly critical. Maybe she had softened because of her husband's passing. It felt good though hearing a compliment from her this time instead of judgment. Smiling, Amy bid farewell to the last guest and happily shut the door.

"Whew," she said wiping her forehead. "What a day." She walked slowly to the sunroom and looked out the window.

The garden that she was tending looked beautiful. The flowers were so vibrant in color and pretty. She received many compliments on it from the ladies. The garden looked one hundred percent better today than it did yesterday. Not because of Amy's green thumb but because she had planted silk flowers in place of the dead real ones. Tomorrow, she would try her hand at it again and pray that it grew this time.

It was only four-thirty in the afternoon, but Amy was pooped. She buzzed Ruthie and asked her to assemble all the other staff members in the main foyer.

"Yes, Ma'am, Miss Amy. We'll be right there."

Amy mustered up the strength to get up off the chaise lounge she had just sat down on and made her way to the front of the house. By the time she got there, everyone, including Marisol was waiting quietly.

"First, I just want to start off by saying thank you all so much and I appreciate you. You all made this the best day for me possible. The women raved about everything from the cleanliness of the house to the quality of the food. You all truly outdid yourselves. Give yourselves a hand."

The staff clapped and looked around at each other, smiling.

"Second, and lastly, since you all have done such a great job around the house, I would like to give you the weekend off, starting right now."

"But its Thursday," Jesse, the driver said.

"Yes, I know. But you all worked very hard and deserve the time off. Mister Meadows will be away for a week and it's just me here. If I get hungry, I can fix something small or go out. I see the concern on some of your faces and I realize you need the hours, so as an incentive to the hard work you all have been doing, I am giving you those days off with pay."

Cheers rang out across the room.

"Now that's what I'm talking about!" Ruthie shouted.

"My family will be so happy to see me. Can I be excused now? I have some calls to make."

"Sure, Ruthie. All of you are free to go. Have fun this weekend and I'll see you all back here Monday morning."

Amy could hear their excited chatter as they walked away down the hall. Preston wouldn't like the fact that they she gave them time off with pay but what he didn't know wouldn't hurt him. Hell, he did plenty of things that he knew she didn't like that hurt her far worse than this. What were a few measly bucks compared to having a faithful and loyal staff? In the Blessingale household, Amy's mother always made sure the staff was well compensated and happy. That way, they would perform better.

Smiling, she walked into the library and grabbed a book off the shelf to read and returned to the sunroom. One by one the staff all came to say their 'goodbyes' and to thank her for her generosity. Everyone except Marisol. That was fine with Amy. She didn't want to see her anyway. Amy opened the book where the bookmark was and began to read. Before she knew it, she was waking up and darkness had fallen. She glanced at her watch. It was ten o'clock.

"Wow. I was tired," she said out loud.

She yawned and stretched, then made her way upstairs. After the long week, she'd had, all she wanted to do was soak in the tub, listen to a little jazz, and relax. At the top of the stairs, Amy heard a noise.

"Hello? Is anyone there?" She called out. Nothing.

She stood on the landing for a moment and strained her ears to listen carefully for more sounds. It was completely quiet.

"Humph," she mumbled, shrugging her shoulders. Whatever the noise was, it stopped.

Amy made it to her room and walked over to her chifforobe to get a night gown. When she opened the doors to the cabinet the sweet smell of vanilla and lilacs tickled her nose. The scented hanging sachets made the closet and the clothes inside smell fresh and clean. It was Amy's plan to pamper her and sleep like the princess she was raised to be tonight. Even though Preston wasn't there, she wanted to look her best going to bed. It's not like it would have mattered if he were home anyway. They didn't have sex much and what she wore to sleep had very little to do with that. Hell, she could have come to bed stark naked and he would ignore her.

But tonight, wasn't about Preston. It was all about Amy and her happiness. Tonight, she was going to enjoy the peace and quiet of being home alone. For once, she was going to bask in the praises of her peers, knowing that finally, she could hear her mother-in-law say, "well done."

"Where did I hang the new gown?" She questioned herself. She was referring to a powder blue silk peignoir set she had purchased for herself when she traveled to Italy a couple of months ago. It was brand new.

"I know I hung it up, but where?"

Amy sauntered over to her closet and began searching the racks of clothes for the pretty gown. It wasn't in there either.

Scratching her head in confusion, Amy said out loud, "Now I know I am not going crazy. It has to be here somewhere."

"Are you looking for this?"

Amy's head turned so quickly there was a small gust of wind that followed. Standing in the middle of Amy and Preston's bedroom was Marisol. She was wearing the blue peignoir set.

"You! What in the hell are you doing here?"

"I wanted to bathe," she shrugged.

"You have your own home. I sent you all away for the weekend."

"Tsk…Tsk…You just don't get it, do you? You can't send me away like some commoner. I'm not the help. I'm your husband's lover. And I have every right to be here."

Amy's breathing began to get shallow and staggered as she tried to calm herself. Color flooded her cheeks.

"You need to leave, Marisol. Now!"

"Hmmm, when I'm ready. You and I need to talk first."

CRYING MEADOWS

"I have nothing to say to you. And I want you out of my gown immediately."

"If you insist." Marisol unlaced the ties that held the lace robe closed and spread it open slowly, revealing the naked curves of her full breast. It remained closed waist down. "Should I continue? I didn't need the gown. The robe was sufficient. Scottie likes me naked," she said wickedly. She used Preston's middle name purposely to show Amy just how familiar she was with the man.

"If you do not leave, I will call the police and have them remove you. YOU'RE FIRED!"

"I'm not the help. You can't fire me! The only one who can make me leave is Preston and he would never do that."

"You sound pretty confident for an undocumented woman. You're in this country illegally and when the cops get here, you will be sent to immigration."

Marisol laughed hysterically. "Undocumented? Silly bitch, don't you know I was born here? I'm a Grady baby." She laughed even harder when she saw the stunned expression on Amy's face. "I see you didn't know that. Well let me fill you in. I was born here in Atlanta. The only reason my accent is so thick is because I lived in Mexico most of my life. But I am as legal as you are honey."

Amy stammered, "Bbb-but Preston told me…"

"Lies, I'm sure. He's good at that. He lies to you and tells the truth to me. That's how I know he loves me. When he's lying in my bed at night, stroking my hot, wet pussy, with his tongue and hands, he tells me often how I am the only woman for him. The only one he loves now."

"You're crazy, Marisol. My husband loves me!"

"You're right. He does. He's just not in love with you. He told me. I know so much about you; I feel like we could have been friends if you weren't such a douche."

"You know nothing about me."

"On the contrary. My man keeps nothing from me. I know that you were a virgin when you two married and that you cried the first time, he fucked you. I know that you're a prude and you gag every time he asks you to suck his dick. That's one of the reasons he comes to me. I do it better."

Amy didn't speak. Instead, she let the tears that streamed down her face do the talking for her. She was hurt. There was no way that Marisol knew any of the things that she said unless Preston told her. She felt betrayed in so many ways. The man she shared her life with, was sharing his life with someone else.

"That's nothing," Amy said. "All women of my substance are virgins when we marry. Queens are raised with higher standards. Unlike peasants. Sex may not be enjoyable at first but believe me, I know how to please my husband and I give him everything he wants," she finished confidently.

"Everything except a baby."

At that exact moment, lightening cracked the sky and it began to rain hard.

"But don't worry," she continued, "because I've got that covered as well."

Slowly, Marisol untied the remaining laces and spread the silky robe open, revealing a very visible baby bump. Her small hands slowly caressed and massaged her tummy lovingly.

"I know you're not insinuating that the bastard you're carrying is my husband's child. He would have shared that morsel of information with me." Amy's voice shook with hurt and anger.

"He doesn't know yet. I'm waiting to surprise him when he returns from Maryland. He's not in Chicago like he told you. And he won't be a bastard. He will have his father's last name. I assure you. And yes, this is Scottie's baby. Because like you, I was a virgin when we first made love and I've fucked him every night for four years. Even while you were on your honeymoon."

"That's impossible. Preston and I honeymooned in Hawaii. We were all alone."

"Yes. It was quite beautiful. What suite were you in? Fifteen-thirty, right? Oh, don't look like that," she said referring to the ashen look that Amy had on her face. "The Halekulani Hotel is gorgeous. I was right across the hall. I gave Preston some sleeping pills to put in your drink so that he could stay with me and play in my wetness, all, night, long.

And oh, what a skilled and gentle lover he is. I love the way his tongue caresses my inner thigh when he's about to make love to me with his mouth. Does he do you like that, Amy? Of course, he doesn't. He fucks you doggy style, doesn't he? He told me he did so that he did not have to look at your face. He loves lying on top of me, looking at my sex faces. He loves how I purr like a kitten and call his name when I'm coming down his throat and he really loves it when I…."

Before Marisol could finish her sentence, Amy reached out and grabbed her throat with her hands, pushing the woman to the floor. Hot tears burned her cheeks as she screamed.

"Liar! Liar! Liar!" She screamed, banging her nemesis' head on the floor repeatedly.

Amy squeezed tighter and pounded harder, seeing nothing and hearing nothing. Oblivious to the small gasps of air that barely escaped Marisol's lips and the bluish purplish color of her oxygen deprived face, all Amy saw, was red. Slowly, she relinquished the hold she had on Marisol's neck.

"Oh my, God. What have I done?"

A frightened Amy looked down in horror as the housekeeper's body lay still on the ground, with lifeless eyes wide open. Shocked, she sat with her back against the wall, staring at Marisol for what seemed like hours before she got up.

Without wasting time to think about what she had done; Amy dragged the body out the room and down the steps. She cringed every time the dead woman's head slammed against the marble steps. It was like a bowling ball, rolling down the stairs, making a hideous thud. Once she was at the bottom, she dragged the body down the hallway out the kitchen door. Thunder clapped, and the rain began to fall in sheets.

Quickly, she ran to the garden shed and grabbed the shovel. It took a few minutes to dig up the garden where she had planted the silk flowers, but it took her almost two hours to dig a plot big enough to lay the corpse in. The rain pelts hit Amy hard as she struggled to move the woman in the hole. Mustering up all the strength that she had left in her body, Amy gave a final tug at Marisol's slippery wet legs and got her in the shallow grave.

Within minutes, the dirt had fully covered the body. Carefully, she planted the bulbs in the wet soil. No one would question the disturbed soil.

Exhausted Amy trudged into the house towards the laundry room. There she removed all her clothes and threw them into the washing machine. She pulled out the mop bucket and disinfectant, filled it half full of hot water and went to mop the foyer. Amy wanted to mop in case Marisol's head started bleeding as she was being bounced down the steps. She didn't want any traces of evidence left behind.

After she'd emptied the mop bucket, Amy went upstairs and ran some bath water. While the tub was filling, she picked up the robe her nemesis discarded earlier and placed it on her bed. There was a loud dong coming from downstairs. It was midnight per the antique grandfather clock.

Amy's legs felt like lead as she lifted them over the sides of the Jacuzzi tub. The hot water covered her like a blanket when she sank beneath it. She came up, water pouring down her face, just as a song by came on the jazz radio station.

CRYING MEADOWS

Carefully, she bathed herself, touching every area of her body. Her muscles were sore and tight, but the hot water helped soothe them. When the water began to cool down, she rinsed and got out.

She sat down in the small chair at her vanity table and began to lotion her body with the four-hundred-dollar Parisian lotion she had. Then she misted her naked body with the matching body spray. Next, she brushed her hair until it shined and fell softly over her shoulders. She stood eyeing herself admiringly in the mirror. She was beautiful, and she knew it.

Standing next to her bed, Amy donned the peignoir set that Marisol wore earlier. The silk was cool against her skin. The long gown flowed freely to her feet. She looked every bit a princess. It was a long day. Amy pulled the covers back and crawled into bed. She should have felt guilty, remorseful. But she didn't. Instead, she felt empowered, liberated, and self-assured. The old Amy was dead and buried with Marisol. She was a new woman and things were about to change.

CHAPTER 8
CHANGES...

A WEEK HAD PASSED SINCE Marisol's death. Amy was nervous and giddy the entire weekend but by the time Monday came about, she had made peace with what she did. Marisol was a thorn in her side and like any good gardener would do, she pruned it. When the other staff members returned to work, Amy called an early meeting.

"Good morning everyone, I hope all of your weekends were as relaxing and peaceful as mine was," she began.

They nodded.

"That's great! Well, I wanted to let you all know that Marisol is no longer with us. She has been terminated and left Meadows Manor."

"About damned time you came to your senses," Ruthie said. "She was all kinda disrespectful. I hated the way she sashayed her hot tail 'round the house, trying to get attention. It just wasn't right how she flirted so openly with Mister Preston. Not right at all."

"I agree, Miss Ruthie and that's why she is no longer with us. Unfortunately, because we are down one housekeeper, we all may have to pick up the extra slack until I find a suitable replacement."

"It's okay, Miss Amy. I've been cleaning this house by myself for a year now, I can continue til' someone else comes."

CRYING MEADOWS

"Damn, you only been here a year," Dale, the stable attendant said. "That's a damned shame."

"It is, but I'm cool."

"Thank you for being such a hard worker, Tabby," Amy said. "We are going to make sure that from now on anyone who comes on board to work here is a team player. It can be no other way."

Amy ended the meeting assuring the employees that she would work quickly to find another housekeeper. She was glad that no one asked her where Marisol went. None of them cared for the mean housekeeper. She had burned bridges with all of them. Everyone seemed very happy to see her go.

Since the "accident", Amy hadn't built up the courage to go out in her garden. It could be overgrown but she'd never know it because she hadn't so much as looked out of window. Even though she felt justified in killing Marisol, there was still a twinge of fear inside her. When the regular gardener asked Amy if she'd like him to tend it for her, she politely declined. The last thing she needed was him digging up her secret.

The desk phone in her office rang and she ran to answer it. Steadying her breath, she said, "hello." It was her cousin-in-law, Katherine Blessingale in Oklahoma City, affectionately known as "Kitty".

"This is Amy."

"Hey Amy Jo, how are you? This is Katherine."

"I'm well, Kit. How are you?"

"Fine as frog hair if I do say so myself. Where's that randy husband of yours?"

Preston's in Chicago on business. How's Cousin Richard?"

"Still as cheap as polyester pants but other'n that, he's doing well. Listen Hun, I ain't gon' keep ya'. Just wanted to ask a huge favor."

"What is it, Hun?" Amy asked, mimicking her country bumpkin relative.

"Well, I'm starting a non-profit organization called Blessed Hands and was told I needed a board of directors. Can I add your name to it since you have a degree in social services? You don't have to be present. You can be a silent member. It'll look good to the Internal Revenue Service though."

A degree I've never used, Amy thought to herself.

"Sure, Kit. What will you be doing?"

"Feeding and clothing the homeless. We've been doing it for some time now but just decided recently to give our cause a name."

"Wow, that's great Kit! It really is."

"With all of the homeless people you all have in Atlanta; I'm surprised you haven't thought about doing this."

"I'm busy enough as it is, Katherine. I don't need more on my plate."

"Are you still lolly gagging around with those saditty bitches? I thought you'd drop them like a hot potato fresh out the oven by now. Tsk. Such a shame."

"There's nothing shameful about the Distinguished Ladies of Leisure. We support many charitable organizations and perform noble service for our community."

Katherine laughed. "You sound just like a brochure. Look, there's nothing wrong with getting down in the trenches and doing something that makes a difference. Get up and help someone who's not in the position to help you for a change."

"What do you call the good works that we do now? We're not out there for our looks."

"Not a damned thing. You posh princesses do just enough to ease your guilty hearts. You entitled wealthy folks are a trip."

CRYING MEADOWS

"Kitty, you and Richard have boat loads more money than me and Preston. What are you talking about?"

"That's only because we sow good seeds. Me and Dick care about more than ourselves. Our mission is to give a voice to a community that people don't see."

"What do you mean, don't see? That's all that you run into here. In downtown Atlanta, especially. Just the other week Preston and I attended a musical at the Fox Theater, and I swear we weren't out of the car five minutes and two people came begging for money. It was frightening, too."

"Chil' you're about as dense as fog after a long, hard rain. Geesh! You may see them physically, but I know you wish they would all go away."

"No, I wish they would all get a job. That's what I wish."

"Don't you think they want that? A job? A stable place to lay their heads at night? Food? God, Amy they're just like us."

"I beg your pardon. *They* are NOTHING like me!" Amy yelled.

"You're right. They have hearts and care about others. I'm glad that Dick and I care enough to help. We're trying to get things started so we can start accounting for the people."

"What do you mean by that?" Amy asked, not caring much about the answer.

"The homeless are nameless, faceless people who are lost in the system. It's not like the government has a homeless registry. Some of their own families don't even know where they are and if they do, they don't care. They could be dead and buried and no one would even know it."

"How awful," Amy yawned.

Katherine got the point. "Well, I'll let you go so you can get back to playing socialite. Thanks for coming on board with my project."

"You're wel-," she began with the dial tone buzzed loudly in her ear. "How rude," Amy mumbled placing the receiver back in the cradle.

Not that she had anything else to do but Amy wondered why she stayed on the phone with her so long. Kitty was always trying to do something to appease her own guilty conscience since she found out one of her ancestors in South Carolina used to hunt and kill runaway slaves. Now every other month or so she was doing something to help *those* people.

In Amy's opinion, most of them were lazy bums who wanted to do nothing more than hang out on street corners, drink, and beg. The women sat around on their big behinds watching soap operas and talk shows all day. Many of them had multiple children with different, deadbeat men. It was a slap in the face to Amy that God would bless those types of people with kids and not her.

Amy didn't think that all of them were bad. There were some black people she liked. *Miss Ruthie, Tabby and Dale were nice to be colored folk and they worked very hard*, she thought. Then there were the amazing colored folks who played sports or entertained.

"Yes, I love that Queen B," she thought out loud. "She's the most beautiful ni-, colored girl I've ever seen. And boy can she sing."

Amy knew her views regarding black people came off as racist to some, but she would swear on a stack of Bibles that she wasn't. How could she be? After all, one of her closest friends in college was a black girl. It had been years since Amy laid eyes on Vivica Jeffries, but she still held her in the same high regard today as she did years ago. Shaking her head, Amy dismissed the conversation in her head. She knew that she was a good person, and she didn't need anyone trying to tell her differently. Especially Kitty's self-righteous, religious behind. She was the last person from whom Amy would take advice.

CRYING MEADOWS

"She's crazy. Pff, I'm nothing like them."

Amy walked around her desk and pulled out the top drawer to retrieve her checkbook. It wasn't payday, but she felt inclined to give her staff a bonus. Maybe the conversation with Katherine bothered her more than she thought. She opened the leather-bound binder that contained her sheets of personal checks. It only had one check left in it and that one was made out to the vintner who supplied the bottles of wine she gave as gifts after her garden party.

"Darn. I was supposed to mail this last week" Amy pulled the check out, placed it in an envelope and walked down the hall to Preston's office. There, she stamped the envelope and got Preston's checkbook out, writing a check for each of the employees.

It frustrated Amy knowing that her husband was such a poor manager of money. The bank called a couple of days ago advising her of a twenty-seven-thousand-dollar overdraft that needed to be paid. This was the fourth one in less than three months. Her mother, Larue, who was independently wealthy of her husband and Amy's father, George, gave all her daughters a monthly stipend.

"A woman needs to have her own," she told them many years ago.

Amy received almost one-hundred-fifty-thousand dollars a month in interest and dividends from some securities that she owned that had increased in value over the years plus a monthly allowance of thirty-five-thousand dollars that she received directly from her mom. Preston had no clue she had anything that sizeable outside of him. She planned to keep it that way. Preston blamed the brunt of their debt on Amy's spending.

The truth is, she spent very little of the Meadow's money and relied solely on Blessingale funds. Her family's wealth outnumbered the Meadow's almost five to one. The difference between the Blessingales and the Meadow's is that Amy's family lived well below their means while Preston's family lived lavishly.

Amy's father believed in paying cash for things he bought or if he financed it, the item had to be paid off within a years' time. Abbott, Sr., was nothing like her father though. He relied on his name and good credit to get him to the top and while that worked for him, he could have had even more money had he not owed so many creditors.

Thankfully, at the time of his passing, he was debt-free. Otherwise, that would have created a hardship for Cora Lee.

George, Amy's father, told her that Abbott, Sr., favored the marriage between her and Preston because she had her own money, and the older man was concerned that Preston would end up a pauper. She also knew that Abbott lusted after her because he was brazened enough to tell her to her face.

"Dirty bird," she laughed.

With the mail and checks in hand, Amy exited his office. Just as she was passing through the foyer, the doorbell chimed. No sooner than she got to the door did the heavy pounding begin.

"I'm right here. No need to beat my door down," she said, snatching the door open.

"Sorry Ma'am. The door is rather thick. I uh, have a delivery for Preston Meadows."

"That's my husband. I'll take it."

"Sign here, please."

Amy signed the slip on the clipboard and the courier was on his way. It was a standard white envelope marked 'confidential'. Unable to resist temptation, Amy opened the letter and read it.

CRYING MEADOWS

"Well, I'll be damned," she gawked at the letter and the other document that accompanied it.

Her mouth hung open in disbelief as she read it in its entirety, looking alternately from the letter to the other paper. The letter was from Abbott Sr., to Preston.

"Wait 'til Preston sees this," she said matter-of-factly. "On second thought, I'll keep this to myself. What he doesn't know won't hurt him."

Amy trotted upstairs to her closet. She moved her rack of dresses to the side and stepped in front of the wall safe she had secretly installed while Preston was away on business last summer. After the envelope was tucked away safely, Amy went back downstairs to finish what she began.

During the time that Preston was away, Amy transformed. Overnight, she matured. Marisol tried to do any and everything to devalue Amy as a woman, but instead made her realize her worth. She did much to help her husband whether he acknowledged it or not. Clearing up bank overdrafts was only a small fraction of it. Because of Preston's past bad boy reputation, many people did not want to invite him to their social functions. Although he calmed down significantly, his reputation preceded him.

But Amy was the epitome of charm and social grace and she was included in even the smallest of gatherings. It would be rude to exclude her husband. When Amy was a little girl, she had a big, black, buxom nanny named Maimey, who always quoted scripture to Amy and her sisters.

"I'm raising you girls to be Proverbs thirty-one women. The kind of women whose husbands are known just because of them. You girls will build-up your men and because of you, his name will be great in the streets."

After Marisol's death, Amy picked up the Bible and read it. That's when realization struck. Preston needed her. Not the other way around. And he always had.

In the twelve days Preston was away, he called Amy twice. Per Marisol that night, she claimed he was not in Chicago. Amy didn't know where he was nor, did she care. The time apart did them good.

Later, Amy sat alone in the dining room enjoying the meal Miss Ruthie prepared for her. Roasted quail, baked asparagus with Balsamic butter sauce, marinated tomato salad with herbs and a chocolate soufflé. Dinner for one. The cook was used to serving Amy alone and had stopped including Preston as part of her meal planning a long time ago. It was a waste of time and food.

The meal was delicious down to the last morsel. Amy picked up the linen napkin and wiped her mouth just as Preston walked into the dining room.

"Smells good in here. Tell Ruthie to bring me a plate," he demanded.

"This was service for one dear. Miss Ruthie had no idea you'd be home," she replied calmly. "And frankly, neither did I."

"This is bullshit Amy! Every night a man comes home he should have a hot meal waiting."

She slid her chair back and got up.

"Too bad you do not come every night. When a man comes home that is what he deserves. Let me know when one shows up, will you?"

Preston followed her upstairs to their room, complaining.

"What the hell has gotten into you?"

"Not you."

Ice cubes clinked loudly in the glass as Preston angrily fixed himself a drink at the wet bar.

"I swear sometimes I do not know why I married you!"

"Probably because I was the only one young and dumb enough to fall for your crap."

"You're getting disrespectful, Amy. Know your place."

"I'm your wife. My place is by your side. I'm not your whoring housekeeper, Marisol so DO NOT speak to me that way!" she said firmly.

"Hmm, she's exactly what I need right now," he said, trying to get a rise out of Amy. "Guess I'll go to her warm bed since it's so cold in yours."

"Go ahead. You'll find it empty. Unless you plan on sleeping alone."

"It's Wednesday. She should be here."

"Marisol is…. gone. She's no longer with us."

"What! You had no right to get rid of her."

"On the contrary, Preston. I had every right to do what I wanted to do in my house. The gate may read Meadows Manor, but it was bought with Blessingale money. Remember that!"

Preston walked over to the window, disgusted at the truth she spoke.

"You're such a screw up, Amy. Can't do shit right! It's your fault I can't get my inheritance."

"You will stop blaming me this instance, Preston. It's high time you man up and take responsibility for your actions. You were lazy and entitled and A.B. saw through your fake charm. And I'd probably have a child by now if you actually came in me."

Preston looked stunned.

"How stupid are you? A woman can feel the heat of her man's semen when he comes in her. I know you jack off in the shower after we have sex. You're pathetic."

He didn't deny the accusations. Instead, he said "Huh, the pot calling the kettle black. I'm pathetic?" He pointed to his chest. "Hell, you've failed at just about everything you've tried. Cooking, sewing, archery. Your ass can't even grow a fucking gar-. "

He blew out a whistle. "Well, I'll be damned. You finally did one thing right."

Amy watched Preston stare out of the window. His mouth was agape. Curiosity piqued, she walked over to the window and looked out.

"Whoa."

The couple stared at the garden below. It had flourished. Even by the soft glow of the garden lights, the colors were vibrant. The yellow Tulips were bright. The red Chrysanthemums were bold. And the green grass looked as soft and plush as new carpet.

"Are those flowers real?" Preston asked incredulously.

Amy nodded. This was her first time looking at the garden since...

"How the hell did you manage this?"

Instead of answering him right away, Amy went to the bed and grabbed her laptop.

"What are you doing?" Irritation rang his voice.

Amy put her hand up to silence him. The room was quiet except for her pecking on the keyboard. She stopped. A devious smile spread across her face.

"Honey, I have an idea how to make Lush Meadows beautiful again. But first, I have a confession to make."

CHAPTER 9

A MEADOWS MISSION...

BRIGHT LIGHTS. BIG HAIR. BALL gowns. Black Ties. It was the Fifty-Second Annual Georgia Cares Gala. This grand event recognized people, agencies and businesses that went above and beyond the call of duty with their public service.

The governor bestowed honors upon those who made significant change in their communities. And tonight, this stellar event was being held at Lush Meadows. Five years ago, this would not have been possible. The golf and country club had transitioned into the phenomenal, blue-chip place that it once was. No longer shunned by the elite, the club was now sought after.

Each year the gala was held at a prestigious venue. This was the first year being held at the country club, but Amy was hoping that it wouldn't be the last. She watched all the well-dressed nominees, socialites and who's who of Georgia, walk the red carpet, taking pictures on their way inside. As a nominee herself, Amy, beamed with pride. She was up for the Heart of Georgia Award that was given to the non-profit agency of the year. This was her second time being nominated. She did not win last year but had it on good authority that she was a strong contender this year.

Taking her cousin Katherine's advice, Amy started her own non-profit agency called Meadows Mission. Its purpose was to get the homeless off the streets, find employment and permanent housing. The goal was to help each person become self-sufficient again. Amy purchased a high-rise apartment building that needed repairs and renovated it. Some units were used for temporary shelter while others served as transitional housing units. Those who lived in the transitional housing units paid rent. The money they paid was held in trust to help them re-establish themselves when their time at the program ended. Proudly, Amy had served hundreds of people and outreach was working.

"Welcome to Lush Meadows," said the valet as he helped Governor Christie out her car.

She was one of the last people to arrive. Dinner was served after a short cocktail hour and then the award ceremony was underway. Meadows Mission was nominated for a few awards up front but did not win in those categories. Still, everyone congratulated her on her success and was genuinely happy for her. Well, almost everyone. Blayke Ladd of Off the Street Homeless Shelter was not a big fan of Amy's at all.

"Pssh, Meadows Mission. Sounds more like a military detail rather than a non-profit agency."

"Blayke Ladd, if I did not know any better, I would swear you were jealous. Looks like the green-eyed monster is rearing its ugly head," Blayke 's sister Bianca stated. She was also his escort for the evening.

"I should have left you at home," he joked. "Nobody's jealous this way, you hear? It's just that there's something fishy about the numbers they report."

"Humph, sounds like jealousy to me. You are mad because they served more people than your agency."

"We are partnered together to serve the community, Bianca. This isn't a competition. Many of the people from Off the Street went into the transitional housing program at

CRYING MEADOWS

Meadows Mission and ended up with jobs here at the golf and country club and other places around the city. You remember Steve? The guy who used to help in my kitchen who could cook his butt off?"

"Yeah, what about him?"

"He went through the Meadow's program. He worked here in the kitchen for two years as a prep cook and now he is a kitchen supervisor over at the Kennedy Hotel."

"Wow! That's a five-star hotel. Good for him."

"Yep. So, you see, I'm glad things are working out for the people in the program. I just hate it when agencies pad their numbers. They report higher outreach numbers to get more money from the government."

"But you do not know that she's doing that Blayke. Can you honestly say that since that program began that you don't see the homeless population dissipating?"

"It is but- "

"And that many of the very same residents are now gainfully employed here at Lush Meadows or other fine establishments? In addition, most of them are now one-hundred percent self-sufficient, living on their own."

"Okay, okay, I get your point. Meadows Mission is a great agency, and the program is effective. I just feel that something isn't quite right."

"I think that's the former police detective in you."

Blayke remained silent. He stared off into space, getting a faraway look into his eyes.

"Do you miss it?" His sister asked.

"Huh?"

"I said, do you miss it?"

"Miss what?"

"Being a cop."

"Nah., I love what I do. Opening this shelter was the best thing I have ever done."

"Yeah, it was. Do you miss her?"

Blayke knew his sister was referring to his former fiancé Tyra Gibson. She was partly the reason that Blayke quit the force and started the shelter. Both had volunteered for another agency and when they saw how corrupt it was, they wanted to do something that would help others more than themselves.

When they began dating, it became apparent to Blayke that Tyra was someone he could build with. Not one to waste time, he popped the question six months after their first date.

"Yes!" She said excitedly. "But let's not rush it. I think we should have a long engagement."

"How long?" He said, giving her the side eye.

"Don't look at me like that. A year. Maybe two. Not forever. I just think it will give us an opportunity to get to know one another even better. People tend to change once the ring is placed on a finger. This way, you will see if you know me or my 'representative'. Is that alright with you?"

Everything she said made perfect sense and he agreed. He loved her and did not have any reasons to question her motives. It did not even bother him that she rarely wore the five carat Princess-Cut diamond engagement ring he bought her. After all, they worked with transients on a day-to-day basis and the last thing he wanted was for her to get attacked and robbed.

One day, eight months into their engagement, Blayke received a phone call. Tyra had been in a car accident. Too anxious to drive and get behind the wheel of any moving vehicle, he called his sister to come rush him to the hospital. Once there, they saw that some of Tyra's family had already arrived. Some had been there for a couple of hours.

CRYING MEADOWS

"Why are they just now notifying you, Bro?" Bianca questioned.

"Beats me. I'm sure it's because everyone is stressed."

Blayke and Bianca sat quietly at the end of the large waiting room, choosing not to bother the family just yet. He only knew a few cousins and an aunt because she told him that she and her immediate family were not very close. However, he did know her parents and sibling's names and what they looked like. One day he invited her to dinner at his home and she had brought a photo album, containing tons of pictures of her family and friends.

"Who is that?" Bianca said, pointing to the waiting room entrance on the opposite end.

A man in a torn black suit was wheeled into the waiting room with the family. His right arm was in a sling and there was a bandage on his head.

"I am not sure. I've never seen him."

The man in the wheelchair was distraught.

"I never should have let her drive. It's all my fault," he wept.

"It's not your fault, Son. Don't blame yourself." The reassurance came from Tyra's dad.

"That's her brother," Bianca stated.

Blayke 's eyebrows furrowed together. Tyra did have a brother, but he had met him before. Her brother, Tyrone, attended a fundraiser they threw for the shelter. This man was not familiar to him, but he kept quiet.

"If anything happens to them, I don't know what I'd do," The man said.

He said it with conviction as if he could have been her lover. *I'll ask her about that later*, Blayke thought inwardly. A plump nurse walked into the room.

"Little Benjamin is out of surgery and doing well. He is going to make a full recovery."

The family cheered. Blayke remembered Tyra telling him about her eight-year-old nephew. He looked at the man in the wheelchair again. He had an uncanny resemblance to Tyra's little nephew. They were father and son.

"Wow," he mumbled under his breath. "That's her brother and here I am thinking the worst. And at such a time as this." He hung his head.

"What was that?"

"Nothing, Sis. Just trying to make sense of all this. "

An hour later a doctor came into the waiting room. Everyone, including Blayke and Bianca gathered around him.

"Mrs. Bell sustained traumatic injuries."

"Who's Mrs. Bell?" Bianca mouthed.

Blayke shrugged his shoulders.

"There was some internal bleeding," the doctor continued. "We did everything we could to stop it. Unfortunately…"

The wailing began before he finished. Cries of despair and heartbreak rang out in the room. The doctor removed the cap off his head and hung it low. Blayke noticed Rita, Tyra's mother looking at the doctor, concerned.

"What about Kimberly, doctor? Is she gonna be alright?"

The doctor exhaled slowly, wiped his brow, and shook his head.

"Kimberly succumbed to her injuries as well. We could not save her."

Another round of crying and hysterics rang out.

"This is so sad. Who's Kimberly?"

CRYING MEADOWS

"I don't know," Blayke said honestly. "Maybe a niece or a cousin. I want to find out how Tyra is doing. I will ask the doctor after he tells the family about Mrs. Bell."

"Oh God, not my baby, too! She was only three-years old. Why Lord? Why?" Screamed the man in the wheelchair who had just returned from the men's room.

The crying was so loud a hospital security guard ran to see what all the commotion was about. The doctor waved him off and told the immediate family that they could view the bodies. They were in adjacent operating rooms. Tyra's parents, her brother Tyrone and her brother in the wheelchair all followed the doctor out. Blayke saw one of Tyra's aunts he'd met before and went to speak.

"Mrs. Gipson, I'm so sorry for your family's losses today."

"Oh, baby thank you so much. It's such a shame for us all. But God is in control and we can't question that."

"No, we can't. I came as soon as I heard about the accident. Tyra means a lot to me."

"I know she did."

Did? Blayke picked up on that immediately but said nothing.

"Hello, Mrs. Gipson. I'm Bianca, Blayke 's sister. My condolences to you all. Was Mrs. Bell and Kimberly very close?"

"About as close as a mother and a daughter could be considering the short time they had together. Yes, Tyra loved her baby girl."

Tyra? Baby? Bianca blinked rapidly.

"Excuse me but is Tyra's last name Bell?"

"Oh, that's right, you two worked together," the aunt turned to Blayke.

We did more than that, he thought.

"I knew I recognized you. Yes, Bell is her married name. For business reasons, she just used her maiden name. I never understood that. Have you met her husband Benjamin? Here he comes now."

The man in the wheelchair.

Blayke composed himself enough to introduce himself.

"Mr. Bell, my name is Blayke Ladd. I, uh, worked, with your wife at the shelter."

"Oh, wow. Hey Blayke. Tyra spoke very highly of you and the work you do. I asked her to invite you for dinner thousands of times, but you were always busy. Then when she told me about your engagement, I asked her to invite you and your fiancé over."

That would've been kinda interesting considering your wife was my fiancée.

"Is this her?" Benjamin continued, looking towards Bianca.

"Uh no this is uh, um…"

"I'm his sister, Bianca, Mr. Bell. You have my deepest sympathy."

"Thank you. How very kind. If the two of you will excuse me, I must go check on my son. He's all I have left."

Tyra's parents came at that moment and rolled the man away. Blayke and Bianca walked out of the hospital and didn't say one word to one another until they were in the car.

"Before you ask, the answer is no. I had no clue she was married. Not one iota."

"I know you didn't bro. You're not that type of man. I was just going to ask how you are holding up. You got hit with a lot back there."

"I am stunned to tell you the truth. I'm hurt. That's for damned sure. Sad, angry and pissed-off are not too far behind either. I'm mad at her for lying to me and him and I'm mad at myself for being mad at her knowing she just died."

"Your feelings are valid big brother. Just know that I'm here for you til' the end."

The funeral services were a week later. Blayke and Bianca attended the double service. At the repast, Blayke discovered that most of Tyra's family knew of his business relationship with her but nothing more. One of her cousin's, Todd, did not have a problem, talking with Blayke.

"Yeah man, me and Ty were pretty close. She used to tell us how hard you worked and all that. Told me that maybe I could come work down there with y'all as well."

"We can always use great volunteers," Blayke said, knowing the man was talking about a paid position.

"Anyway, they were out having a celebratory meal. Ol' Benjamin just made partner in his law firm. Won them a fifteen-million-dollar client. They gave him a bonus. A brand new twenty-fifteen Aston Martin Rapide S. That joint was fancy."

Not quite a family car, Blayke thought pettily.

"They were at a red light leaving the restaurant when a drunk driver lost control of his car and slammed into the driver side. Tyra and baby Kim were on that side."

"All of this," Blayke waved his hand in an ushering motion. "It all seems so surreal."

"Who are you telling? My cousin had just given Ben some good news, too."

"Oh, she told him that we got the grant to expand the shelter?"

"Nah., She told him that she was pregnant."

Blayke remembered almost choking on his water after the cousin told him that. He was devastated. It was a strong possibility that the child she carried was his and he would never know. Thankfully, Bianca was talking to another one of Tyra's relatives across the room and was out of earshot. Blayke would be left to mourn two losses and grieve for the unknown. Although he never fully got over what happened, he did learn to deal with it in his own way.

"Hello? Did you hear me?" Bianca spoke firmly, waving her hand in his face.

"I said do you miss her? You checked out on me for a minute there."

"Sorry. I do at times. I miss the person I knew. I didn't know the woman who died."

With that, Bianca dropped the conversation and turned her attention back to the ceremony.

"And here to present the Heart of Georgia Award is none other than Preston Meadows who so graciously allowed us to host the event here at his club this evening. Preston."

Preston stood gallantly at the podium. "Thank you, Governor Christie. Let's give her a round of applause for the wonderful job she's doing in our great state, shall we?"

When the applause subsided, Preston began the presentation.

"It brings me great honor to present this award tonight. Normally the governor is the one doing this but because of the recipient, she allowed me this great honor. I'm proud, not just because the tremendous works this agency performed this past year, but also because the recipient is none other than my wife, Amy Meadows."

From her seat, Amy basked in Preston's praises. Things had improved significantly in their relationship in the past few years. She still hadn't conceived but she sure enjoyed trying with him. She threw out the fertility clocks and ovulation schedules and decided to let nature take its course. Before Marisol's 'accident', everyone in Preston and Amy's social circle knew about his infidelities. No one knew who his mistress was, but they knew he had one.

Now Preston appeared to be the picture-perfect husband. If he was cheating, he was hiding it very well. Amy had been so enthralled with her thoughts that she hadn't noticed Preston calling her name.

"He's calling you dear," Cora Lee said, tapping Amy on the elbow.

"Oh, my." She got up and made her way to the podium to accept her award and to deliver the speech she'd been working on for two years.

"I'm speechless," she lied. "The journey of a thousand miles must first begin with a single step, a great man said. I wouldn't be standing here today; Meadows Mission wouldn't be recognized tonight if I hadn't taken that first step. Every nominee has worked their tail ends off to achieve great goals. Please, join me in praising them.

Together, we have worked towards one common goal and that's to help build up our neighbors who are just like us."

Applause rang out across the room.

Amy continued her speech, "borrowing" some words from her cousin, Katherine.

"They are people who want jobs; a stable place to live; food. Tonight, I share this honor with Blayke Ladd and Off the Street Shelter, Ellen Woods and Georgia Restores, Mitchell Reed and Second Chance Furniture and Pamela Grinnell at Learn to Earn. Each of these powerful organizations have partnered with the Meadows Mission Transitional program. Together we have helped over sixteen-hundred-seventy-five people get off the streets and out of the cold in the past year. Of which, over five-hundred people have regained self-sufficiency through employment, education and stable housing."

"Yikes," Bianca asked Blayke as she clapped at the astounding numbers. "There are that many homeless people here in Atlanta?"

"More probably. We don't have an exact number. We can only count those who come in for help. There are many who won't."

"In closing, I want to thank Governor Christie for working so closely with all of us to meet the needs of the people and reach our common goal to restore Georgia. Thank you!"

Amy floated off the stage with grace. Blayke watched her as she posed for the camera. He had to admit that she was a stunning beauty. Still, there was something inside that kept gnawing at him, telling him that something just wasn't right about Amy Meadows.

CHAPTER 10
HARD HABITS TO BREAK...

WINNING THAT SINGLE AWARD BROUGHT
Amy and Meadows Mission more notoriety and free press than her entire two-hundred-fifty-thousand-dollar annual advertising and marketing budget had. The awards ceremony was two months ago, but the press was still clamoring for interviews.

Today, the host and crew from Atlanta Live was coming to Amy and Preston's home to interview the couple about the phenomenal success of Meadows Mission. Upstairs while Amy and her stylists primped and prepped to get television ready, Preston got ready downstairs.

"Ride this stallion, baby. You know how I like it," Preston said, thrusting his hips upwards.

"Mmm, yes daddy. I know how you like it," his lover said, grinding her hips on his pelvis.

She eased up just a tad and moved her feet so that she was now in a frog-style sitting position. She rolled her hips in a circular motion for a moment and then she began to rise and lower on his hard member. Slow, teasing glides she made until a heat began to form in her core and then she bounced, clinching her walls as she did so.

"Don't you like the way I stroke you with my tight, sugar walls, Daddy?"

"Mmm hmm."

"Can't you feel my pussy snapping on this hard dick? It feels good, doesn't it?"

"Oh yes, baby. I love it. I'm about to come."

"Come in this tight pussy! I need it. I'm about to come all over your dick," she purred.

Preston thrusted once, twice, and then her erupted inside her.

"That was amazing, Daddy. It always is."

"I agree," he said trying to control his breathing.

"Did you do what you said you were going to do the other day?"

"Yes, babe. It is there. I did it the same day. You didn't check?"

"No. I've been so busy I haven't had time to call the bank. I trust you."

"As well you should. Have I ever lied to you?"

"No."

"And I don't plan on it."

She laughed.

"What's so funny?" He said rising on his elbow.

"I never thought that I'd like cream in my coffee."

"You never thought you'd meet cream this good looking, did you?"

Chuckling, she said, "never."

"It didn't hurt that the cream was wealthy and packing all this heat either, did it?" Preston rubbed his limp, thick manhood.

"Nah, that made it even better. I hate to leave you, but I got to go," she spoke as she dressed quickly. "See ya' tonight?"

"Absolutely. I'll be over at nine. Before bedtime."

"Cool."

Preston kissed her on the lips and watched her ass bounce as she walked out of his office.

There was a knock on the front door when she passed it and she answered. It was the reporter and her crew. She seated the guests and went to the powder room to adjust her uniform and wipe herself off before heading upstairs. She walked into Amy and Preston's room with a huge smile on her face and spoke to everyone.

"Oh good, you're here." Amy was relieved. "Do you know where I put my diamond earrings I bought in Dubai?"

"Yes. They're right here." The young woman walked to Amy's chifforobe, reached in, opened a drawer, and pulled out a small velvet box.

"Ann Lange and the Atlanta Live crew just arrived. Miss Ruthie had them set up in the library."

"Thank you so much. What would I do without you?"

The young lady smiled but didn't answer.

"Oh, you know Sloan is on vacation, so you may want to run downstairs and service Mr. Meadows."

Tabby turned around, swung her hair, and said, "I already did."

·ͼ Ϭ·

"Preston," the reporter began. "Tell me about Amy."

"Amy is…loving, generous and warm." Preston rubbed his wife's hand.

"Oh, come now, there's got to be more to her than that. You make her sound like a loyal pet."

"My wife works harder than anyone I know and has the tenacity of a bulldog."

"You seem quite proud of her."

"I am."

"Some men would be intimidated by the level of success your wife has achieved. Are you?"

"Of course not, Ann." Lie. "I've been Amy's biggest fan since her debutante ball. This woman here has shown me that she's capable of anything." That was the truth. "I've been in the limelight for many years and at the forefront of major corporations. Now it's my wife's time to shine."

"Wonderful. Amy, tell us about Meadows Mission. What made you establish such an advantageous organization?"

"I saw a need, Ann and I wanted to be able to meet it. I am a member of an amazing group with other women here in Atlanta whose main purpose is helping others. However, I always felt like I needed to do more. I didn't want to just feed the hungry one day. I wanted to teach them how to grow a garden so that they eat every day."

"What a powerful statement. Tell us how Meadows Mission operates."

"Certainly. We operate purely on a referral basis. Meadows Mission is a temporary shelter with a transitional housing component. Our focus is to assist with job placement and job training. We hire many of the staff at Lush Meadows, our golf and country club, directly from our program. If a client needs adult basic education, we assist with that as well. Our partner organizations refer clients to us who they feel would benefit from the services we offer. Those they refer already have the mindset to do better."

"Is there a screening process?"

CRYING MEADOWS

"Yes, there is. While it's our desire to help as many people as we can, we know that's not possible. All residents of Meadows Mission must be drug and alcohol free or willing to become so within 30 days of entering the program. We also do a background check. We're not looking at a person's past to exclude them, but we do need to know who we have in the confines of our walls. Safety is a priority. The referring agency forwards a letter of reference to us and the client also writes a letter to us telling why they would make a good fit to the program. That's about it."

"Sounds like a doable process if you're serious about changing your life. What happens to the people you can't help or have to turn away?"

"In those rare cases, I find a special place for them, Ann. Everybody counts at Meadows Mission."

There was something about the way she said body that made Blayke's skin crawl. He turned off the television in his office and turned around in his chair.

"Are you sure you want to apply for this program?" He asked his client.

"Yes, Sir. I have seen so many people go there and end with jobs and a place to live. I want that, too. I'm smart and have been drug-free for over two years. I should at least try. All they can tell me is no. I hope that's not the case though. Lord knows I've had enough rejection to last a lifetime."

"True. Alright. I'll submit your application today."

"Thanks. You never did finish telling me about the gala. Who was all there? Did you take a date? Sorry if I'm being too nosey."

"You're fine. Let's see, where do I begin."

"At the beginning."

"Okay," he chuckled. "It seems like the entire Who's who of Atlanta came out. The governor, mayor and about ten other elected officials were in attendance."

"I don't care anything about them. Tell me which stars were there."

"Hmm, Grand Hustle and his wife were there, Skyler Perry, The Willis sisters…"

"Stacy and Veronica? The tennis stars? Oh, wow…it was star studded huh?"

"It really was. John Connery came and presented an award, and the entire cast of the movie Speed Demons were in the building. They sat at the table next to ours."

"Okay. Now we're getting somewhere. Tell me about your date."

"Look at you all in my business."

"Oh boy. I already know what that means. Bianca again? Dude, I don't mean to overstep my boundaries, but you really need to meet a nice woman and settle down."

"Have you been talking to my sister?"

"Nope."

"You know she's always happy to go with me."

"Yes, I do. But it's time you get out there and start dating again. It's like riding a bike."

"Oh, is that, right? Well, if it's so simple, why aren't you dating?"

"Mister Ladd, I live in a shelter. Do you know how embarrassing it would be to meet a man and have him pick me up here? Come on now. Plus, that's all out of order. I need to get my life back on track before I can worry about that."

"Your life is not as unmanageable as you make it out to be. I know people who are worse off than you."

CRYING MEADOWS

"Worrying about other people and what they do or don't have is not a luxury I can afford right now. That's how I ended up in this mess in the first place."

"Keep your head up. You may get into this program and then your luck will change."

If it weren't for bad, Jasmine Aster felt as if she wouldn't have any luck at all. At thirty, the bronzed beauty had seen her fair share of heartache.

"Enough about the gala and my personal life, tell me about Jasmine."

"Well, I'm from Memphis, Tennessee. Grew up in an area they call Ward Two-Thirty-Two. It had the highest crime rate in the city. Burglaries, assaults, rapes, you name it, it happened."

"I'm familiar with that area."

"That's right. You used to be a cop."

"Yep. Any siblings?"

"I have a brother, Hollis and two sisters, Heather and Iris. He's the oldest at forty-three. He lives in Chicago and is a college English professor. Married with three children. My oldest sister, Heather is forty, in the military and is stationed in Hawaii. She's single. No kids. Then there's Iris, thirty-eight. Works as an aid for the governor of Tennessee. She's married and she and her husband, Ronald are about to welcome their first baby boy in December."

"And your parent's? Are they still living?"

"Yes. My Dad is a retired teacher from Memphis Public Schools and my mom owns and runs a small flower shop. My dad helps her out with that now."

"I gathered your mom loved flowers. She must, to name all of her children after one."

"You caught that, huh?"

"Yes, I did. For your guys to have grown up in such a rough area, you all seem to be doing pretty well."

"We did. Don't get me wrong. It was rough in Ward Two-Thirty-Two, but our immediate neighborhood wasn't that bad. It was quiet for the most part and when crime would come our way, the neighbors banded together to keep it off our doorsteps."

"That's the way it should be. How did you come to be in Atlanta?"

"It's a long story."

"I've got time."

"Well, when I was a student at Tennessee State University, I met this guy who wanted to sing and rap. He wanted to be famous."

"I can see where this is going."

Jasmine laughed. "Right. Well, he claimed to know someone who could get him a deal with Man of Steele Records. We were getting serious and he said he didn't want to leave me. When school ended that summer, we packed up and moved here. That was in two-thousand-eleven."

"How long did you have until you graduated college?"

"I have a bachelor's Degree in Horticulture Science. I was working on graduate studies. I know. Don't look at me like that. I'm still kicking myself."

"So, what happened to your boyfriend? Did the friend get him the deal?"

"Please. The only thing the guy did get him was an audition. He probably would have had a chance if the audio on his demo was better. It sounded garbled and when he tried to sing over it, he sounded as if he was underwater."

"That's a bad break."

"It was. Before we left Memphis, I told him to get another engineer or find another recording studio altogether. He didn't listen. After the failed audition, I made the mistake of telling him that he should have listened to me."

"Uh, oh."

"Uh, oh is right. He hauled off and hit me so hard I saw stars for two days." Jasmine's voice softened. "That day set the tone of our relationship for the next two years. One fight ended with me having a broken wrist and fractured thumb on my left hand. The doctor gave me a prescription for pain..." her voice trailed off.

"Is that what drugs you were taking?"

"Yes. I began self-medicating, so I wouldn't feel the pain. I was taking Tramadol and drinking heavily. Half the time he and I would fight, I would be so out of it I wouldn't feel a thing or remember the next day. I'd just wake up with bruises."

"I can't imagine what that was like. Why didn't you go home?"

"Pride, I guess. I was too embarrassed to admit that my family was right. After I graduated high school, I took a couple of years off to explore the United States and try to figure out what I wanted to do. I started working with my mom in her shop and found that I loved flowers and plants as much as she did."

"I'm sure she was proud of you when you told her you wanted to be a horticulturist."

"She was. Both of my parents were. My dad thought it would be a good thing with me coming on board. I could help her expand her business and then eventually take over. I wanted to do that, but Cory came into the picture and I lost sight of what was important. My dad kept telling me he was no good. But like a child, the more they said he was wrong, the more I convinced myself that he was right."

"We've all been there. Don't beat yourself up."

"Meh," she shrugged her shoulders. "I've always wondered what made a woman stay with a man when he was beating her. Now I know."

"How did you get out? What was the final straw?"

"I ran out of pills one day and couldn't get anymore. Cory beat me up and gave me a black eye. The next morning, for the first time in a long time, I had to face myself. Literally. I looked in the mirror and saw what I looked like. My eye was swollen shut. Blue and purple bruises were all on the side of my face. I had a busted lip and scratches all over my neck. It was awful. Drugs alter your perception. I didn't realize it was as bad as it was because I was doped up most of that time. I looked horrible, Mr. Ladd."

"Blayke, please."

"Okay, Blayke but I looked a mess. My hair was disheveled. It hadn't seen a beautician since I came to Atlanta. It still hasn't," she said, finger combing her tresses.

"Your hair is fine."

"If you say so. Anyway, I walked into the bedroom, saw him lying in bed and asked myself what in the hell was I doing. I packed my bag with what little stuff I had and left."

"Wait, what happened to your things?"

"He poured bleach on my clothes and cut them up. I'm lucky I had anything to pack. I walked around for a while and then ended up in Centennial Park. I met a cop walking through there and he saw my face. It was meant for me to meet him. He asked me if I wanted help and I said yes. That's how I got to the domestic violence shelter."

"I understand now. So, you stayed over there until they were shut down and now, you're here."

"Pretty much."

CRYING MEADOWS

"Do you have any regrets?"

"Concerning him? Not really. Those were very expensive life lessons. I was in love with him and believed in his dreams. He hurt me to the core. Pain like that is uncommon. I trusted him and thought that we were going to build something solid together. I was very wrong."

Blayke knew of pain and trust like that from his previous relationship but did not speak on it. It was common that clients shared their life stories with him but not the other way around. It would not be professional of him to talk about his failed relationships. Listening to her speak so openly and honestly about her failures made Blayke evaluate his own. All these years since Tyra's death, he held on to the anger of her betrayal.

He leaned back in his chair and placed his chin on his hand. He had dated some great women since her death, but he was punishing them all for her mistakes. They bore the blame that belonged to her. While he was not hurtful or mean to any of them, he was guarded and aloof. No one could get past the impenetrable, invisible wall he had built around his heart. Blayke knew that it was time to lay Tyra's betrayal to rest once and for all and to let his guard down.

"Anyway, that's Jasmine in a nutshell."

He leaned back and stared at her for a bit. She had big, brown eyes that sparkled; with eyelashes so long, they looked like feathers. Her high cheekbones appeared to blush naturally and Blayke could not help to notice how kissable her full luscious lips looked. He shook his head to refocus on their conversation.

"Not all of her, but that'll do for now. Listen, I have some calls to make and some paperwork to prepare if you plan on getting into that program. I'll get with your advocate and we'll get the ball rolling for you."

"Thank you so much. You have no idea how much this means to me."

"Trust me, I do. I'll let you know as soon as I hear something."

Two weeks later, Blayke received a fax from the intake coordinator at Meadows Mission, scheduling Jasmine for an interview appointment.

"You've got an appointment," he told her reluctantly. Inside he was genuinely happy for her, but he did not want to see her leave. They had managed to talk every day for hours in the past two weeks. The more he talked to her, the more he wanted to. She was an awesome woman. Smart, kind and even in the cheap t-shirts and jeans, Blayke admired her shapely figure. What's more is that Bianca was crazy about her and his sister didn't like just anyone. Especially the opposite sex.

"Yippee!! This is great! Now I can put some things in place and get my raggedy life on track."

"Stop it. Your appointment is October tenth at nine o'clock."

"That's next week. I have got to find me something to wear. Can I go to the clothing closet?"

"I don't think we have anything appropriate for an interview in there. I will send over a referral for you to Dress to Impress. They have nice suits and dresses for women who are job hunting and I'm sure they'll have something nice."

"Thank you! Thank you! Thank you!" Jasmine threw her arms around Blayke and gave him a tight hug. He hugged her back, reluctant to let her go.

"My pleasure. Just go in there and knock'em dead. Show them the woman that I've come to know over the past few weeks, and you'll be a shoo-in."

"What a great day! Thanks, again."

Jasmine ran out of his office waving her appointment paper in her hand. Secretly, Blayke prayed that the program was too full to accept her. Unfortunately, his prayers went unanswered.

⸎⸎⸎

Amy Meadows had not met a black girl that intelligent since her college roommate. Jasmine Aster was impressive on every level. She had above average intelligence, was extremely articulate and well spoken. It was obvious to Amy that the young lady had a post-secondary education. Even if it was from one of their schools.

When she looked at Jasmine's application, she knew that the woman would be an asset to the golf and country club. It did not hurt that she was also beautiful. Her milk-chocolate complexion was smooth and clear of any blemishes and she had long, wavy hair, that Amy learned was real and not weave.

"Jasmine, I am excited about the possibility of working with you. I would like a Rose garden just beyond a sculptured maze walkway on the club grounds but none of the landscapers I brought on have been able to see my vision. I thought I found someone, and he did a small maze for me, but the grass kept growing back along the path."

"Mmm, sounds like he was using regular dirt. Course dirt is needed for a non-grassy path. I can prepare a few mock-up designs for you to look at on my iPad. I minored in landscape design and architecture."

"Excellent. You just may be the savior my gardens need. Now, I'll prepare your apartment at once and email you your new-hire packet as well. Do you have any questions?"

"Not now, no."

"If you think of anything, please feel free to call or email me." Amy handed Jasmine her business card.

"Thank you, Mrs. Meadows. I really appreciate this opportunity."

"Call me Amy, Jasmine. We dispense with formalities around here."

"Yes Ma'am, I mean, Amy."

"Well, if there's nothing else, I would like to formally welcome you to Lush Meadows."

CHAPTER 11
WELCOME TO CRYING MEADOWS...

IT WAS A BRISK FALL morning. The sun shined brightly over the Georgia sky. The air was cool with just a hint of warmth from the sun's rays. Leaves of many colors floated softly to the ground in the gentle breeze. It was the perfect day for an autumn walk. Peachtree Street was lit by the first rays of the day, shining through the last remaining grey clouds of the night before.

Aromatic scents of brewing coffee hitched a ride on the invisible wind and traveled down the streets. It was inhaled by the early birds who headed to work. Clicking heels of walkers and muffled cell phone chatter could be heard, disturbing the quiet of morning. Atlanta was awake. And so was Jasmine.

Today was her first day at Lush Meadows Golf and Country Club. That morning, she had taken great care, preparing for work. She paid more attention to her hair and her make-up. Even ironing took a little longer than usual as she labored to get every wrinkle out of her slacks and press them like a professional. Excitement and nerves both filled her. This was her first job in almost three years. She wanted to make a good impression on the staff and new bosses.

Jasmine had been in the Meadows Mission program for almost two weeks. It felt good to have an apartment again. Even if it was transitional and temporary. At Off the Street Shelter, it was more communal living and she shared space with seven other women in the room. There were four sets of bunkbeds, four desks at the end of each bed that the bunk mates shared and eight footlockers, two under each bunk for the ladies to store and secure their valuables. Each woman may not have had much but what she did have she wanted to hold on to.

It wasn't a bad situation. Sharing a room allowed Jasmine to meet new people. Most nights, she and the other women would sit and talk. They shared their stories of how they became homeless and of their past lives. They even revealed their hopes and dreams for the future. Out of the eight ladies in the room, five of them applied to the Meadow's program. Three were accepted.

The two ladies, Chris, and Tina, who were not immediately accepted, were wait-listed. They were not fit for the program. Not in Jasmine's opinion anyway. Amy's either, for that matter. Both ladies were still actively using recreational drugs and drinking heavily. Neither showed a desire to get clean. The only reason Mr. Ladd did not kick them out of his program is because it was getting cold outside.

But their lives and what they both had going on did not have anything to do with Jasmine. She made it a point to mind her own business. A person lived longer that way. She was no longer their roommate. They were Mr. Ladd's problem, not hers.

Now, her only issue was getting her hair to do what she wanted it to. Only thing is, she did not know what style to comb it. In all her planning, she forgot to decide what she was going to do with the unruly mane that sat atop her head. It was too late in the hour to try and straighten or curl it. Her only recourse was to pull it back into a ponytail and make a bun at the nape of her neck.

"Drat! And I wanted to make a great impression all the way around today. Oh, well."

CRYING MEADOWS

Jasmine gave herself the once over in the full-length mirror that hung over her bedroom door.

"Not bad, little lady. You clean up quite well."

Before she left the small apartment, Jasmine grabbed a jacket. It was a bit chilly outside. She walked the few short blocks towards the train station where she boarded the northbound train towards her new job. A few stops on the train and a couple of blocks walking and she had arrived.

"Welcome to Crying Meadows," a valet said to her as she walked past him in the parking lot.

"Huh?" She spoke. But the young man walked off and did not hear her.

"Welcome to Lush Meadows," a thin lady of Asian descent said, extending her hand towards Jasmine. "I'm Yuki Wong, head of Buildings and Grounds. I will be your immediate supervisor. Did you have any trouble getting in the gate?"

"Not at all. I just told the guard this was my first day and he told me where to come."

"Excellent. We will take a picture for your identification badge a little later today. You will be able to use it to tap in and out of the gate when you arrive and leave for the day. Employee parking is on the left side and back of the building. I'll make sure you have a sticker for your car as well."

"I don't...own a car right now," Jasmine hesitated. "I take the train."

"Really? So, do I. Atlanta traffic is bananas. MARTA is smarta."

Jasmine smiled. She immediately took a liking to the stylish woman. Yuki seemed easy to get along with and very friendly. The two women spoke of Jasmine's experience with flowers and gardening as Yuki gave her a tour of the club.

"I see why Mrs. Meadows was so excited to have you come aboard, your experience is vast. Our new maze of Roses and botanical gardens will be the talk of the town after you're done with them."

"I hope so. You have no idea how anxious I am to get started."

"Be anxious for nothing, but I understand. Come, let's get that picture taken."

Two hours later, Jasmine had completed her new-hire paperwork and was shown the newly built greenhouse. It was an impressive state-of-the-art structure that was extremely energy efficient. What impressed Jasmine the most was the fact that it had its own restroom. That was a relief. The last thing she wanted to do was trek across the vast expanse of lawn in the rain or cold to use the facilities.

"What do you think?" Yuki smiled appreciatively.

"Great, huh?"

"Yes, it is. They went all out it seems. I haven't seen greenhouse technology like this in person. I've only read about a few places in Alaska with houses of this magnitude. They're built for sustainability. I'm impressed."

"I'll give you a moment to familiarize yourself with your new workspace. There should be some paper and pens in your office over here. Walk through and make sure that you have everything, and I do mean everything that you need to do your job. Should you lack even the smallest item, please do not hesitate to let me know. Our desire is to make our gardens a tourist attraction here in the State of Georgia."

"I believe I can help you with that," Jasmine admitted confidently.

Yuki nodded her agreement. "Call me if you need me. My extension is next to the phone" and exited the greenhouse.

CRYING MEADOWS

This is going to be an interesting experience, Jasmine thought, watching her walk away. It didn't take her long to assess the needs of the greenhouse. Amy didn't miss a beat when it came to the basic things, she would need but it was clear that the owner knew little about gardening. That much was evident by the quality of seed grass she had chosen.

"I'll have this place in top notch shape in a couple of months. Just watch."

Fifteen minutes after one o'clock, Jasmine took her lunch break. She remembered where the employee dining room was from the tour earlier. It was just as lavish as the one for guests and a far cry from the one at the shelter.

"I can get used to a place like this," she whispered.

A tall, lanky man stood beside Jasmine as she weighed her options for dessert in the display cooler.

"You new here?"

"Yes. Today is my first day."

"Right on, young lady. Welcome to Crying Meadows. I'm Zell Jacobs, I cook here." he said.

"Jasmine Aster. I'm the new landscape designer."

Jasmine made an entrée selection after choosing a dessert and followed the man to the beverage station.

"You are like the third or fourth person who's said that to me today. I thought this club was called Lush Meadows?"

The man set his tray on an empty table and sat down.

"It is."

"Then why do you call it Crying Meadows?"

"We call it that because sometimes, when the wind blows, it sounds like a woman is crying."

"Crying?"

"Yep. It is creepy sometimes. But we've all heard it at one point or another. The cries seem to float on the wind. It's creepy like I said but beautiful at the same time."

"Hmm, I wonder what that's about."

"None of us know. Some of us thought it was a ghost."

Jasmine let out a loud laugh. "You're not serious, are you?" She hoped not. Her new co-worker seemed like an intelligent man. It would be unfortunate to learn that he was stupid.

"Yes, I'm serious that that's what we thought, although I don't believe in ghosts. But it's so strange that it's the only thing that seemed to make sense."

"Wow."

"I recognize that look, young sister, and it's okay. None of us believed it until we heard it for ourselves. Jeff, a mower who used to work here, used to say that he saw a woman in the trees, but no one else ever did."

"You said he used to work here. Where'd he go?"

"Who knows? He relapsed. Got back on that shit. Excuse my French. He's probably back on the streets. I'm praying for him, though."

Jasmine sat and reflected on what he said before speaking. "I'm not trying to be in anyone's business but are all of us from a homeless shelter?"

"Many of us are. The Meadows wanted to give us a second chance. Lord knows I am thankful to have this job. Because of them and Blayke at Off the Street Shelter, I have been gainfully employed and drug free for almost five years. I even got my family back."

"Good for you! I think that's great. I was at Off the Street, too. Blayke was a blessing to me and very instrumental about getting me into this program."

CRYING MEADOWS

"Listen, the Meadows are some pretty cool people. If you show them that you want to move up and do better, they will stand behind you. Mr. Meadows is helping to pay for my college right now. I got my GED when I started working here and expressed interest in furthering my education. He told me that all I had to do was come to him when I was ready. Well, two years ago, I knocked on his door, sat down with him and we came up with a plan. He said that if I graduate, I don't have to pay one red cent back but if I drop out and don't get my degree, I have to pay it all back. And he put it in writing."

"Hearing this reaffirms that I made the best decision coming here."

"Indeed, you did. Tell me about yourself, young sister."

The two of them exchanged light conversation, getting to know one another. Zell was a distinguished gentleman who reminded her of a younger Morgan Freeman. He was in school working on his business degree. His plan was to start a catering company. They talked until their lunch break was over and had to return to work. Before her shift ended, Yuki came to the greenhouse to check on Jasmine.

"So, how was your first day?"

"It was wonderful, Yuki. The staff is amazing and has made me feel very welcome. I think I'm going to like it here a lot."

"Great! That's what I was hoping to hear. Do you have everything you need?"

"No, actually. I made a list of things I'll need, and this is the design I drew for the maze."

"Impressive," Yuki said, admiring the design that Jasmine presented her with. "It would be even more beautiful if we added a fountain in the center."

"I was thinking the same thing. If you look here, I made notes reflecting that but wasn't sure what my budget was."

"You have a budget, but then again you don't. Does that make any sense? Amy wants us to spare no expense with these gardens. You're the designer here. I trust your judgment. I have to sign off on your requests but if you say you need it, you got it."

"Thank you very much. I appreciate your vote of confidence. I'm going to make it a showstopper."

"I believe you. Now let's get out of here. It's been a long day."

The two women clocked out and walked to the train station together. Jasmine couldn't have been happier. Working at Lush Meadows was a blessing, and she was going to do everything she could to make the gardens everything she dreamed of and then some. With a smile on her face, she rode the train to her stop and walked to her apartment basking in sheer joy. Her life was finally on the right track and she reveled in the direction it was going.

Over the next few weeks, she got acclimated with the staff at Lush Meadows and began to settle into a routine. Amy had come by on a few occasions to check the progress of the gardens when the landscaping team began digging and replanting.

"Hiring you was one of the best things I could have done for this club. You are an absolute Godsend, Jasmine," Amy gushed.

"Thank you. It's easy to do a good job when I have all the equipment I need. If you like what you see now, you'll love the finished product."

"I'm sure I will."

"Are you sure you don't want to see the design? Yuki said that you hadn't seen them yet."

"No. I want it to be a surprise for me also when we do the big reveal."

CRYING MEADOWS

"If you say so," Jasmine shrugged.

Amy excused herself and left Jasmine with her crew. It was nice to be trusted and even nicer not to be micromanaged, the lovely gardener mused appreciatively. Jasmine had had her fair share of jobs where she couldn't breathe without her supervisor's permission. Lush Meadows was by far the best job she had so far. Not only were her bosses great, so were her co-workers. It was nice having friends and people she could hang out with after work hours.

Friday night was payday and Jasmine was invited by a few co-workers to have dinner at a local restaurant and lounge in Midtown Atlanta. Peaches' was a popular place and Jasmine had longed to dine there since moving to Georgia.

"I can't believe you've never been here," Terry, a Lush Meadows server told Jasmine.

"Girl, it's a lot of things that I haven't done. But I have you guys now to get me out of the house so I'm sure all of that will change soon."

"You got that right," Angie, the club's receptionist, high-fived them. "It's about to be on and popping. Since you've never eaten here, do you want me to tell you what's good on the menu?"

Terry leaned her head over to the side and said, "ain't nothing on this menu as delectable as the fine piece of meat that's walking this way."

All the ladies turned their heads in the direction that Terry was looking.

"Yes Lord," Angie agreed.

"Ladies how are you this evening?"

"Thirsty," Terry said, salivating.

"I don't mean to interrupt; I just wanted to know if Jasmine would like to dance?"

"Jasmine? You know this man?" Terry questioned. The look on her face clearly stated that he looked too good to associate with the likes of her.

"Uh, yes. Blayke, I'd like to introduce you to my co-workers, Angie, and Terry. Ladies, Blayke Ladd."

"Nice to meet you."

"What's up?" They both said.

"So, are you going to dance or what?" He persisted.

"Sure. Excuse me guys."

"You have to forgive me, Jasmine. When I saw you across the room, you looked familiar. I didn't realize it was you until I was almost to your table."

"You didn't recognize me? I've only been gone for a few weeks. I'm hurt," she feigned, clutching her chest.

"I could never forget you. But I've never seen you like this. You have on make-up and your hair is down. I'm used to the long ponytail and lip gloss." He wanted to tell her how sexy her body looked in the tight jeans and form-fitting top she wore but did not want to let on that he had been checking her out.

"Oh. Is that good or bad?"

"It's definitely good. How is the new job and apartment?"

"Oh, wow. Where do I begin? It's everything I hoped it would be. The Meadow's are great, and my supervisor Yuki is the bomb. I mean really cool. And don't get me started on my apartment. For it to be transitional housing, they made sure that each unit was up to par. I love living in Midtown."

"Sounds like things are really great. I'm happy for you. You deserve this."

"Thank you. At first I didn't know if I was going to like some of my co-workers because they seemed strange."

"Why do you say that?"

CRYING MEADOWS

"Well, when I first started working there, most of the employees used to call the country club 'Crying Meadows' instead of Lush Meadow. I thought I was coming to work at a loony bin. Hell, you know most of us were on drugs," she laughed.

"Did they tell you why they call it that?"

"Oh, yeah. This one man said that when the wind blew sometimes, it sounded like someone was crying. Like I said, I thought they were all fruits and nuts until I started hearing it for myself a few weeks ago."

"Really?"

"Yes. It was spooky. It sounds like a woman crying. It really may be someone crying, too because the other day, when I was walking the maze, I could have sworn I saw one of the guests walking through the trees and it seemed as if she were sobbing. Forgive me, but I was more concerned about her getting her white dress dirty than her reasons for crying."

"Did you say something to her?"

"Of course not. I don't interact with the members like that. I answer their questions if they ask but other than that I just greet them, smile and keep it moving."

"You know it is okay to talk to people."

She shook her head. "Not these people, Blayke. These are billionaires and trillionaires and…"

"And they are just like us. They all put their pants on one leg at a time and pull their pants down to shit," he spoke.

"Thanks for the visual. The song ended; you know?"

"Did it? I hadn't noticed. But you and I are the only ones on the dance floor. Listen, I'm not trying to keep you from your friends, so I'll let you go but would you like to grab a cup of coffee after work one day? I'd love to continue catching up with you?" He asked.

"Sure. I'd really like that. You'll have to tell me how everyone at Off the Street is doing."

"I will. You still have my number, right?"

"Of course. Other than my parent's yours is the only number I know by heart."

"Great. Let's talk tomorrow. Call me on your lunch break."

"Yes, Sir."

Jasmine wasn't sure her feet touched the floor as she floated back to the table where her friends sat.

"Now honey child you know you are going to have to spill the beans about that tall drink of water."

"Terry, you are crazy," Jasmine giggled. "Well, his name is Blayke and he runs Off the Street Shelter."

For the next hour, the trio discussed men, money, men again and sex. Jasmine couldn't remember the last time she had had that much fun. She couldn't wait to call home and tell her mom all the good things that were happening to her. And seeing Blayke tonight was the icing on the cake. She was glad after all that she had taken the time to do a little more to herself before coming to the lounge.

"Always look your best, Jazzy," her grandmother used to say. "You never know who you will run into. And make sure your panties are clean every day in case you are in an accident. You do not want the paramedics to think you are one of those nasty women."

When she laid her head down that night, Jasmine wasn't concerned what any man thought about her except for one. Blayke Ladd.

CHAPTER 12
THE REPLENISHING...

WHAT **DO YOU MEAN DEAD?"** Amy was livid. Victor, the landscaping supervisor, had just delivered some horrible news. Some of the grass near the eighteenth hole was dead.

"Senora Meadows, maybe dead was the wrong word but it is dying. Come, I'll show you."

They hopped into the golf cart and drove to the troubled area. Amy pulled out her phone and pounded on the touch screen rapidly. This was the last thing Lush Meadows needed. From a distance, Amy could see that the grass was yellowing and knew what that meant. Dread filled her stomach. When the golf cart came to a halt, the two got out and walked over to the damaged grass to assess the issue.

"My word, Victor! This is awful," Amy gasped in horror. "Do you have any idea how this happened?"

"Right now, no. I've questioned the guys to find out when they first noticed this. Of course, no one has any idea. Unfortunately, it could be a number of things and this time of year brings about disease for grass."

"Disease? But I thought this was turf grass. It shouldn't die."

"This is turf grass, Senora Meadows. Not Astroturf. This is real grass. Bermuda grass to be specific. It could get like this if we mowed too low."

"Well did you?" She demanded.

"No, Ma'am. All mowers are set to a certain level to prevent that from happening. I believe this may be a disease called Dollar Spot. See here, these small silver dollar-sized spots that are tan and brown appear over the lawn. The spots may merge into large, affected areas. If it's Dollar Spot Disease, it will. Thankfully, it won't cause permanent damage."

"How can we fix this? It needs to be done immediately. You know we are being considered to host the IGA Championship. I can't have one of their representatives coming and finding this atrocity. They'd reconsider. We could lose so much and all that I've done will have been for naught!"

Amy threw her arms in the air at the last statement and began pacing. Victor observed her neck beginning to turn an unnatural shade of red and hurried to calm his flustered boss.

"Senora, please. It's okay. We can fix this, and it won't spread to the other grass. I have a powerful fungicide in the warehouse that will treat the area. It sprays on green and will camouflage all discolorations. Before I apply it, we will cut out all this affected area that you see here and then after its healthy, I'll just apply some of that awesome fertilizer that you bought for us."

Slightly relieved, Amy spoke. "And you think that's all that we need to do the trick?"

"I assure you, Senora. It will be perfect."

"Phew," Amy exhaled deeply. "I thought we were in big trouble. I'll send over the fertilizer in a few hours. Thank you, Victor. I appreciate you."

"It's my pleasure."

It didn't take long for Amy to get back to her office. She had just sat behind her desk when her husband walked in.

"I got your text. It said it was an emergency. What's so important that you pulled me from a meeting?"

CRYING MEADOWS

While Preston was pleased that Amy had helped him turn things around at Lush Meadows and save his inheritance, he still was not as happily married as he knew his wife would have liked. In fact, he was about ready to call it quits.

Hell, the only thing that's holding us together is this club. I can leave when I get ready. Fuck, 'til death do us part. Preston was smiling at the thought of leaving until the last part of his thought struck a nerve. Til' death do us part. Death. Then he remembered. It all came rushing back to him like a tidal wave. He couldn't leave. His family would be ruined. Deflated, he sat in the chair across from hers and let her explain what was going on.

"Victor said that the grass at the eighteenth hole may be diseased. I went to look at it and it's a yellowish tan and brown."

"What? How did this happen?"

"According to Victor, the grass is susceptible to it. He told me that he can have it back green in no time. I'm going to take him some fertilizer. I know that'll help," she finished confidently.

"Ah, your 'miracle' grow. Yes, I'm sure that will do the trick. It better!" He added sternly. "I just got word that the International Golf Association selection committee is planning on touring the top three clubs within the next two weeks. I'm counting on winning that bid. I need it. The IGA brings millions to the club it selects. Before and after the tournament."

"Don't you mean, we?"

"You heard me. If you manage to screw this up for me, Amy I swear I'll…"

"If *I* screw this up. I didn't give the grass a disease. Hell, if it weren't for me, none of this would be possible." She waved her hand around her lavish office. "That car you drive, our home. All of it would have been gone. It was my forward thinking and research that got us to where we are today so don't you go blaming any of this on me, Mister!"

"You're right. I apologize. The gravity of the situation has me up in arms and now I'm stressed out. You know how I get when I'm stressed."

"Yes honey, I do. Let me take a little of that pressure off you."

Amy didn't wait for her husband's reply. Instead, she walked to her office door and locked it and then strutted to where her husband sat. Stepping out of her sling back heels, Amy kneeled in front of him. He exhaled and leaned his head back against the big, comfortable leather executive chair.

Without wasting time, Amy unzipped his pants and maneuvered his anxious member from the confines of his boxers through the small slit in front. Her hot mouth covered the head and Preston rubbed the back of her head in pleasure. She sucked and wet it before allowing her tongue to travel the length of it.

Alternating between sucks, slurps and squeezing, Amy worked hard to extract every bit of tension out of her man's body. As her head bobbed up and down, she could hear his breathing intensify. His thighs tightened, and a slow quake began at his feet. An almost guttural howl began to escape past his lips.

"Oh shit, Ames! I'm coming!"

Preston lifted his hips off the chair and gripped Amy by both ears, holding her head steady. Fire coursed through his veins and then shot out of the small opening in his penis. Amy could feel the heat of him as his thick cream slid down her throat. Once he was back in a seated position, he released Amy and she sat back on her haunches.

His eyes were closed but the corners of his lips were slightly turned upwards. He was well satisfied.

CRYING MEADOWS

She got up and made her way back to her desk and sat down. The smile hadn't left his face. Slowly her head nodded, and she smiled as if congratulating herself on a job well done. Amy knew that she was the only woman who could satisfy her man like that. And if she kept doing it like that, Preston was not going to ever go anywhere.

"Thank you for that. I feel like a thousand-pound weight was removed from my shoulders."

"It's always my pleasure," she confessed honestly. "I was wondering if you and I co-."

"One moment babe, I gotta take this," he interrupted her as the shrill ring of his cellular phone pierced the air. "Preston," he said, holding up one finger towards his wife, non-verbally asking her to give him a moment to handle the call.

"Of course, we're still on for dinner this evening. You're going to love the presentation we put together for you. Excellent. See you at eight."

"Another business dinner?" Disappointment filled her voice, yet he didn't notice.

"Yes, and a big one. We're meeting with Brock Standish, the Cowboys wide receiver. He wants to host a celebrity golf tournament here at the club and I've put together some marketing ideas for him. What was it you were saying before he called?"

"I was going to ask if we could have a nice, quiet candlelight dinner at home, but you have other plans."

"Yeah, tonight is bad for me. I'll look at my calendar and see when my next free night is. My secretary has meetings booked for the next month and a half it seems but it's cool. You know how I feel about making money."

Dejected, Amy said, "I know all too well how you feel about money period."

116

Preston walked behind Amy's chair and kissed her on the top of the head.

"I'm heading to Sandy Springs, Ames. I'll see ya' later. And oh, thanks again." And with that, he was gone.

Amy sat looking dumbfounded. She still hadn't figured out how Preston could treat her like he loved her one moment and like a piece of shit the next. She didn't understand him at all. A sob caught in her throat. Just then, her secretary buzzed her, interrupting her pity party.

"Mrs. Meadows, Sturgis Blessingale is on line one for you."

She cleared her throat before responding, "Put him through."

The light flashed to her direct private line. This was a call she had been waiting for.

"Sturgis, how are you?" She inquired genuinely. Sturgis was her second cousin who she had grown close to over the past five years. The two of them had a unique relationship.

"I'm well. God is able. I take it that you need me again?"

"You don't beat around the bush, do you? Very well, yes I need you."

"Do you have any candidates yet?"

"I do actually, although they haven't been formally accepted into the program."

"Well, you have work to do. My wife wants to take a vacation. You know that I deny her nothing. You have two weeks. Fourteen days exactly to get them in and out. My reservations for Greece are already made."

"Two weeks. That's not enough time to get everything done."

"Make it enough. When I leave, Truitt will oversee Restful Blessings and he won't be able to help you."

CRYING MEADOWS

"But Sturgis I- "

"Don't 'but Sturgis me. All the time we've wasted on this phone you could have been handling your business. You have fourteen days, Amy. Not a minute longer. I have a massage to give." Click.

"Ugh!" She shrieked, grabbing the sides of her head. "I swear that man is so exasperating sometimes."

Exhaling slowly, Amy tried to calm herself. If the putting green needed more fertilizer to ensure it was the most pristine in the nation, she would make sure it had it. Deep down she knew that Sturgis was right. They had wasted time on the phone she could have made a couple of calls and been working on a third.

Sturgis was serious about his work at Restful Blessings, the funeral home and mortuary he owned and operated. Although he had several morticians on payroll, Sturgis liked to personally massage the bodies himself to prepare them for the embalming process.

"They need a gentle, loving touch," he once told her. "My massages help relieve them of rigor mortis. It pleases me when I caress them."

Sturgis was a necrophiliac. He found sexual gratification from corpses. Everyone in the Blessingale family knew it and yet, no one ever said anything about it.

"Another buried Blessingale secret," she mumbled out loud.

Regardless of how creepy that made him, he was the only one in her family she trusted to help her and the fact that he owned a mortuary made it all the better.

"I've got to kick it into high gear." She pressed a button on her office phone.

"Yes, Mrs. Meadows," her secretary answered.

"Mildred please come in here and have your notepad with you."

Amy was gathering some files when the secretary came into the office.

"Yes, Ma'am?"

"Have a seat, please. I'm going to be out of the office for a week. I have some pressing business with Meadows Mission that needs to be handled. While I'm gone, I'd like you to handle a few things for me."

The secretary jotted down the instructions as fast as Amy rattled them off.

"When you get back to your desk, please get Blayke Ladd on the line for me."

Knowing she was dismissed; the older lady nodded and then left the office.

"I have Mr. Ladd for you."

"Thank you. Blayke, darling. How are you?"

Blayke rolled his eyes in the top of his head. "I'm well, Amy. How are you?"

"Smashing. Listen, I'm on my way to the mission. I'll be working there for the next few weeks."

"What? You're going to trust Preston to actually run his country club."

She noticed the jab but didn't respond.

"The reason I'm calling is that I interviewed a couple of young ladies at your shelter and they were wait listed. I wanted to know if they were still in your program because I have room for them in mine. A Miss Tina Robinson and Miss Chris Porter."

Thank you, Jesus! Blayke didn't want to put the two out on the streets again, but they were working his last nerve with their constant drinking and drug use. Neither wanted the help he offered so he stopped trying. He tried to contain his excitement when he spoke.

"Oh, um, yes. Both Tina and Chris are still here. Would you like to schedule an interview with them?"

"No."

She said it so abruptly he thought he was hearing things and waited for her to explain. She didn't.

Crestfallen, Blayke asked, "Did you reconsider all of a sudden?"

"What? Oh, no. Please forgive me. I received an urgent text just as I was about to answer you and it distracted me. I meant to say, no that won't be necessary. I've already interviewed both women before. A second one is unnecessary. I'm heading over to Meadows Mission now. I can call you with their intake date and times as soon as I check the schedule."

"Sounds great. Is there anything I can do to expedite the process on this end?"

"Anxious to get rid of them, huh?"

Busted.

"Uh, no. It's just..." Blayke got warm under his collar from embarrassment.

"No worries, Blayke. I gathered from their interviews that both were firecrackers. I understand women like them and believe me; I have the perfect place for them at Meadows Mission. Just let them know that the on-boarding process will go rather quickly. With the holidays coming up it's going to be hectic."

"Gotcha! Thank you very much. I'll let them know."

"My pleasure. Talk to you soon."

Both Blayke and Amy got off the phone with a great sense of relief but for very different reasons. While Blayke tracked down the two unruly residents, Amy got on her cell phone and called a few other shelter managers to speak to them about clients of theirs who were wait-listed also. By the time she made it to Meadows Mission, she had ten new people.

Two days later, Amy hosted an orientation for the new residents. They were seated in the dining room of the shelter, enjoying a delicious meal of pot roast and spring vegetables.

"I know you all were expecting to be in your new apartments immediately, but our maintenance staff is a bit overwhelmed and behind schedule. If you all will bear with this communal living situation for a short while I assure you, we will have you all settled in no time."

"Shit, this place is like a mansion. I have never seen a shelter that looked like this."

"Me, neither."

"Uhn uhn."

Amy purposely made it seem like the shelter was less than stellar when in all actuality, it was top notch. This temporary residence was not a shelter at all, but a home owned by Amy and her cousin Sturgis that was used for special clients. The ones who they had alternative uses for other than legitimate business. Eventually, all of them would be used to replenish the Earth.

"Thank you all for being so understanding. Now I know that none of us like to discuss our business in front of strangers but as you all know; Meadows Mission is a drug and alcohol-free program. None of you passed your urinalysis but your shelter managers spoke so highly of you that I couldn't keep you out of the program.

With that being said, you will begin to detox here before you begin working. Unfortunately, when you stop using drugs or alcohol it's like taking the weight off the spring, and your brain rebounds by producing a surge of adrenaline that causes withdrawal symptoms. You may experience insomnia, headaches, nausea and vomiting, irritability, and even muscle aches just to name a few."

"Got damn," one of the male residents exclaimed.

"My sentiments exactly. However, to help you manage the pain, the doctor in our clinic has prescribed some medicine for you all. In the white boxes inside of you all's bags are ten patches called Scopolamine transdermal patches," she paused to smile at the looks on their faces. She had them, hook, line, and sinker.

"Normally they are used to treat motion sickness and reduce nausea and vomiting in patients having surgery who get sick from anesthesia, but research has shown that it helps reduces withdrawal symptoms in people addicted to heroin or other narcotic drugs and alcohol without causing the "high" associated with the drug addiction."

"They always coming up with some shit," the vocal man from earlier stated.

"Indeed, they do," Amy grinned.

"It kinda sounds like Methadone," an older man who appeared to be of Native American descent said.

"Yes, it is. And like Methadone, it is habit forming. Even in small, regular doses, which is why I warn you all to use it only as directed," Amy informed them all.

"What's transdermal?" Chris Porter asked.

"That means you apply it to your skin. Let me demonstrate." Amy used a small Band-Aid to show the residents how to properly affix the patch to their skin. She also warned them about using too many at one time.

"If you use more than one it will make your mouth dry and you will have to drink an excessive amount of water to get rid of the feeling. Like I just said before, you can become addicted to it so use with caution. It's our goal to get you off all drugs, not substitute one for another."

She downplayed the severity of the drug and lied about its effect on people.

"One last thing. Because you all are new to the program, you won't be allowed to leave out this evening or have your cell phones on you for twenty-four hours. Please pass them up." The group of misfits complied.

"Thank you. You may not be able to leave but you all do have televisions with cable in your rooms, a computer room with internet access and there's a game room. It's equipped with a pool table and retro arcade video games like Mrs. Pac Man, Donkey Kong and Pole Position."

"What? Now you're talking my language," Tina chimed in. "Those games are from back in the day. I didn't even think they still made them anymore."

"I hope you enjoy it, Tina. Well, if you all will excuse me; I must rush home to cook for my husband. This is your new home. Please take care of it. Also, please don't forget what I said about the patches. You only need one."

A slow, sly smile crept over her face. Her studies in psychology taught her that adults, when warned not to do something, did just the opposite. By looking at the residents, she could tell that each one of them were going to try the patches to find out what they did.

With pep in her step and joy in her heart, Amy left the house. She knew that if she were able to help Lush Meadows cinch the IGA bid, she and Preston would begin planning their family. He promised her that. If she kept up her end, so would he.

The next day, Sturgis called Amy at the home she shared with Preston. He had news for her.

"Hey, Sturgis. How are you?"

CRYING MEADOWS

"I am blessed and highly favored by the Lord, dear cousin. And so are you. The Almighty has shown His face and eradicated our enemies."

Excited, she asked, "Are you at the house now?"

"Indeed. I must commend you on handling things so quickly. Bravo."

"I can do all things through Christ who strengthens me," she declared.

"That you can, my dear. How ingenious of you to have the basement of this house connected to the basement of the mortuary. The Chamber is a blessing and a necessity to the work we are doing. You do the Blessingale name proud."

"Thank you."

"I will take care of this tonight. You've done well. Take some time with that randy young husband of yours and relax. I'll call you if I need you."

Amy was so happy she wanted to shout. Things were coming together for her once again. Instead of resting or even trying to make love to Preston, she went to the house where her new residents were. She walked the house and smiled as she saw each one. Tina was seated at the Pole Position game, Chris was laying in front of the screen in the movie room, a couple of them were at the dining room table and everyone else was in their beds. They were all just like Amy wanted them.

Dead.

CHAPTER 13
FINDING A LIFE...

THERE'S NO BETTER FEELING THAN being self-sufficient after being homeless. Jasmine was proud of herself and the strides that she was making in her life. Everything was going well for her. She had a good job, a nice apartment, and the relationship with her family and siblings was improving with each passing day. But the icing on the cake was Blayke Ladd.

Ever since they saw one another at the lounge, they talked or text daily. Their friendship was developing into something more. And she liked it. The light from the fall Atlanta sun shone through her window, casting a beautiful glow on her bronze skin. Stretching, she sat up and smiled.

"Well Jasmine, this is gonna be a lazy Saturday. So glad I checked out lots of books from the library."

She reached over on her nightstand and picked up a book, preparing to read it. Just as she relaxed into her pillow, her cell phone rang. Without looking at the caller I.D., she answered it.

"Hello."

"Hey, lady. You sound like you're sleeping. Did I wake you?"

It was Blayke. She smiled.

"Nope. I was just sitting here in bed reading a book. What's up?"

"Nothing much. Bianca is having a day party at her new place and wants me to bring you. It starts at three o'clock. Would you like to come?"

Quickly she weighed her options; sit in the bed and read or spend time with a sexy, single man. This was a no brainer.

"I'd love to come. What time should I be ready?"

"If it's not too much trouble, could you be ready as early as one-ish? I'd like to talk to you, and I know once we get to my sister's she's going to monopolize you."

"Yeah, sure. That's not a problem. What's the dress code?"

"Cute and casual according to Bianca. Whatever you decide will be fine with me. You always look good."

She blushed at the compliment.

"Thank you."

"You're welcome. Well, I'll let you get back to reading. Talk to you soon."

"Yes, Sir," and she clicked the end button.

"Woohoo! Looks like this won't be a lazy Saturday after all. I'm going out."

A few hours later, Blayke arrived looking dapper. He had on a pair of Levi jeans, a vibrant, yellow t-shirt, and a pair of high-end athletic shoes.

"Hey now. Don't you look great," Jasmine praised.

"So, do you. Love the hair. I didn't realize it was that long. It must've taken you hours to get it straight like that."

"Nah, not long at all," she laughed. "I'm lying. It did take a couple of hours, but I really wanted to look nice for you," she admitted bashfully.

"You always look great, Jas. Even when you were at the shelter. Shall we go?"

"Sure. Where are we headed?" She asked once inside the car.

"I thought we'd take a stroll through the Atlanta Botanical Gardens and talk if that's okay. I know how much you love flowers."

It took a moment for her to respond so he continued.

"If you don't want to, I understand. We can grab a coffee or do whatever you like until it's time to head to Bianca's."

Finding her voice, she said, "I'd love to go. No one has ever taken my likes into consideration when planning a date. I mean, this may not be a date but...damn."

Blayke placed his right hand over Jasmine's and gave it a gentle nudge.

"This is very much a date and had my sister not invited you to her party, trust and believe you were always going to be there."

Reassured, she relaxed into the heated leather seat and made small talk until they arrived at the botanical gardens. He escorted her inside and she gasped in sheer delight.

"Wow. This place is impressive. I would have loved to work here."

"I imagine so. Come this way, there are some gorgeous flowers over here I'd like you to tell me about."

The two began their own self-guided tour. Along the way, Blayke pointed out flowers and shrubbery and questioned Jasmine about each one. He loved how her eyes lit up as she spoke about the greenery and plants. Once they made it through a scenic harvest area, they sat down on a concrete bench.

"How's work?" He began after a moment of silence.

CRYING MEADOWS

"Wonderful. Thank you for bringing me here. This place has given me a few ideas I'd like to implement at Lush Meadows."

"Figured you would enjoy it. How're Tina and Chris doing?"

Pssh, how am I supposed to know? You're the one who sees them every day."

"I meant how are they doing at work?"

"Uh, how am I supposed to know?"

"I know you guys may not see one another often since the kitchen is so busy, but does it look like they are doing okay?"

"What kitchen? Lush Meadows?"

"Yeah. Both Tina and Chris were accepted into the program. Didn't they tell you?"

"Blayke, I haven't seen either of them since I left Off the Street."

"Stop playing, Jas. They've been at Meadows Mission for almost two weeks. They got there two days before Thanksgiving."

"I'm not playing. I haven't seen them. But the high-rise is a big place and there are lots of people I don't see. Once I get off work, I go home, and I don't come out until it's time for work again."

"True, but I thought you would have run into them at the club by now. Especially Chris. You know how outgoing she is. Before she left the shelter, she told me that she was going to do right because she wanted to get her kids back. "

"Hmm, well, I'll ask around, but I haven't seen'em."

"Thanks."

Time flew, and they headed to Bianca's. There were cars lining the street in front of her house when they pulled up. It was a good turnout inside.

"Jasmine, I am so glad you're here." Bianca hugged the young lady, and they began talking at once.

"Your brother doesn't get any love?"

"Oh, hush it," she said, playfully swatting his arm.

Bianca went around the room, introducing Jasmine to all her friends as Blayke's girlfriend. He was right there and did not bother correcting his sister so Jasmine felt like she did not have to either. A few of the women there gave her some sketchy looks but she shrugged it off. That was to be expected. After all, Blayke was a handsome, single man with a lot of great things going for him making him a great catch.

The day party turned into a night party and kicked into high gear. Some of Blayke's college buddies came and they had a wonderful time catching up. One of Bianca's friends suggested they play a game called Substitution.

"How do you play that?" Jasmine asked. "It sounds interesting."

"Well, someone asks you a question about what you'd rather do, say or be and you have to choose one and explain why," April one of Bianca's friends explained. "I'll go first. Blayke, would you rather be the prostitute or the pimp?"

"What! Come on," he laughed.

"He's a man, he'd have to be a gigolo," Bianca guffawed.

"I'd rather be the pimp of course because I'm in control; I get paid the most for doing the least and can have as much sex as I want."

"Good answer!"

"Hi-five on that one, Bro," A few of his frat brothers yelled out.

The game continued in that manner and the questions and answers got sillier as the game progressed. When it was

Jasmine's turn to ask a question, she directed it to Blayke's best friend, Aaron.

"Aaron, would you rather be in jail for three months or homeless for a month?"

"That's a no-brainer. I'd rather be in jail for obvious reasons. Three hots and a cot." The men all slapped high fives. "Man, I'd hate to be homeless because I could be dead, and no one would ever know it. Who would come looking for me?"

Laughter rang out in the room, but Blayke didn't see anything funny about that. In fact, that last statement really made him think about some things. They played a game of Twister after that and he tried hard to appear as if he was having a good time, but he had a lot on his mind.

Later, he helped his sister clean the kitchen as guests began to leave. He was rinsing dishes and talking to his sister about how much fun he had and how proud of her he was. From the other room, Jasmine looked at Blayke as if she were seeing him for the first time. Tonight, he had included her in the conversation and made her feel as if her opinion mattered. That night when he dropped her off in front of her building, he kissed her square on the mouth.

His tongue wrestled with hers and he pulled her close enough to let her feel how much she turned him on. As much as she wanted to invite him upstairs, it was against program rules. Later, lying in bed alone, hot, and horny, Jasmine made a life decision.

"It's time to get my own apartment," she said into the night.

For Blayke, he was consumed by something else.

"It's time for me to do some investigating."

ঙেঙ ঙৈৎ

"Impressive," Paul Whittaker, chairman of the International Golf Association selection committee said of the putting greens at Lush Meadows. "I don't think I've ever seen grass this green, or soft" he remarked, kneeling, rubbing his hand across the silky blades.

"Thank you. But my wife gets all the credit there. She's worked relentlessly to restore the grounds to their former luster," Preston informed him.

Smiling, Amy stated, "Actually Paul, what I've done has surpassed the grounds former beauty. Lush Meadows is immaculate."

"It is that. What's your secret?"

Amy stone faced, then a smile formed at the corners of her mouth. "Now if I told you that Paul, I'd have to kill you."

Everyone chuckled.

"Seriously though," she continued. "We employ great landscapers. As a matter of fact, just recently we brought on a horticulturist as our lead landscape designer. She is building a Rose garden and maze for us that will rival the likes of the one at the Atlanta Botanical Gardens. Shall we get in the golf cart and take a look? I'm sure you will find that equally impressive."

The trio got back into the golf cart and toured the remainder of the grounds. Victor had called Amy to let her know the fertilizer that he used had worked and the grass was looking healthier than ever. Amy was relieved that it did because her special formula was not done yet and this morning, the IGA rep popped in to do a surprise inspection of their club and grounds. If he would have come last week, it would have been horrible for them.

They dined in the formal dining room at the club after they saw the Rose garden and maze. Jasmine had her crew working overtime and Amy was astonished at the quality and quantity of work they managed to produce.

"I must say, Preston and Amy, that you all will definitely give the other clubs a run for their money. Your club is well run. The staff is courteous and professional, and your putting greens are pristine. I am pleased to announce that you all have secured the third and final spot of clubs we must select from. Congratulations!"

Preston hugged Amy tightly and shook Paul's hand at the same time. Abbott Meadows, Sr., tried to screw Preston over with his inheritance but now he would have the last laugh. He could not wait to throw this victory up in his sibling's faces either.

None of them thought that he would make a go of the once run-down club, but he had. Correction, Amy had. Looking at his wife with the beautiful smile on her face, Preston knew that she had made this all possible and he owed her so much.

"The tournament isn't until August, but we will be making our final selection no later than March first. This will allow us to begin an aggressive marketing campaign for the tournament as well as your club. Here is a list of things we will need faxed or emailed over as soon as possible. Should you all win the selection; these things will need to be in place prior to signing the final contract."

Both Preston and Amy looked over the document that Paul gave them. They would need to provide local hotel information, menu selections and have planned activities outside of the tournament. Nothing too difficult for them to prepare and send back. They walked Paul to the front of the club and made small talk until the valet appeared with his car, then headed to Preston's office.

"You did it, Ames!" He yelled, picking her up and swinging her around. "You're the best, babe."

"Oh, Preston, we did it! This was a team effort."

"Sweetheart, I know I can be an asshole at times but please know that you are the best thing that has ever happened to me. I'm sorry for taking you for granted."

"I love you, honey. There's no need to apologize. God placed us in one another's lives for a reason. I'm your rib."

"Yes, you are. Come here, woman."

Preston pulled Amy close to him and kissed her passionately. With his left arm, he swiped everything off his desk and pushed her forward on it.

"It's time to uphold my end of the bargain," he said gruffly.

He lifted her skirt, pulled her hose and panties down and impaled his hard shaft into her wet center. She cried out in pleasure as she gripped the polished mahogany desk. He plunged his throbbing penis into her trembling core.

"Ooohhh, Preston!" She screamed, her body jerked and spasmed with each thrust. She clenched his penis with her lips, and he pumped madly, finally groaning with pleasure, spilling his seed inside her. He withdrew and before she could even stop tingling, his tongue replaced his member. Lapping up her sweet nectar, Preston brought his wife to fulfillment once more. Their breathing steadied, and Amy spoke as she peeled herself from the desktop.

"You tasted me. Now it's time I do the same."

And she did exactly that.

⋆✧⋆

Jasmine was so pleased that Amy and her husband came to see the progress they were making on the maze and Rose garden. They worked tirelessly to get things in order. Amy called to tell her that they were a finalist with the IGA, and she believed that it was the garden that made the difference.

"If we win this bid, Jasmine, you are in for a huge bonus," Amy told her.

She had already put in her notice at the transitional house and found an apartment. A bonus was right up her alley because now Jasmine wanted to purchase a car. Her new place would be ready right before Christmas, and she was excited. That was her gift to herself. Amy had been supportive when Jasmine told her she was ready to move.

"I think you are as well, my dear. You have done quite well and frankly; we could not have asked for a better client. If there is anything, we can do to help you transition into the next phase of your life, please let me know."

"I sure will," she told Amy before they ended their conversation. Oh, she most definitely would.

The phone in the greenhouse rang. It was Victor letting her know the flowers she ordered had arrived.

"Have them brought to the greenhouse please. I need to inspect them. The last batch had too many dying leaves."

Jasmine walked through the maze to check the work of the crew. Things looked good. She walked further out and began to hear crying.

"She's here," she whispered out loud.

Quietly, Jasmine followed the sound and stood and watched the woman walking slowly and crying.

I wonder what's wrong. She thought.

The woman never turned around, so Jasmine did not see her face. She was of medium height and had long, stark white hair. From the distance, the white dress she wore looked very pretty. Expensive.

Yeah, she's definitely a member of the club, she assumed.

Regardless of the woman's social class, the lovely gardener felt the need to help her. Blayke was right, wealthy, or not, they were still just people. But no matter how many times Jasmine told herself that, she still couldn't muster up enough courage to go over and talk to the woman. The woman began walking towards the trees.

Just beyond the meadow there was a newly built, gated subdivision that backed up to the country club. Jasmine figured that the woman lived over there and that there was a path through the trees. Just as she was about to follow the woman her cell phone rang. It was Blayke.

"Hey, you," she said to him. "How are you?"

"I'm fine. Are you busy?"

"Nah, not really. I was about to go and talk to… Damn, she's gone."

"Who's gone?"

"The woman in the white dress I was telling you about. She was over by the maze but now she's gone. She must have walked back to her house."

"Wow. She lives in *that* subdivision?" Blayke said referring to the million-dollar community on the other side of the club.

"I think so, yeah. Anyway, what's up?"

"I know you move into your new place next week and I was wondering if you would allow me to buy you a housewarming gift."

"Oh of course, of course. I am not turning down anything, but my collar and my bed covers at night. But you didn't have to ask me."

"Yeah, I did. Because I want to take you to pick it out. Tonight. Let's say I pick you up around seven and we can head to Bed, Bath and Beyond. I love that place."

"Me too. Seven it is. See ya' tonight."

CRYING MEADOWS

"Cool."

Jasmine turned around and looked back at the trees. She let the woman get away again.

"The next time I see her and have an opportunity to talk to her, I promise I'm going to take it."

CHAPTER 14
UNLIKELY FRIENDS...

THE FOG IN ATLANTA WAS so dense, an advisory was issued. Fog or not when she woke up that morning, she felt it was going to be an extraordinary day. Nothing spectacular had happened overnight or even the day before, but there was something inside telling her that it would be great. As she walked along the platform waiting on her train to arrive, she found a crisp twenty-dollar bill.

"Hot damn! I knew it was going to be a good day. It's starting off awesome already."

Once she boarded the train, she noticed that it was unusually crowded for that time of morning. There were no seats available. And even though she only went up a few blocks, she liked to be able to sit and read. A handsome older gentleman who bore a close resemblance to Sean Connery, offered her his seat.

"Why, thank you, Sir. How very kind of you."

And that's the way the day progressed. At work, the crew did what they were told without questioning her every command. The new flowers that arrived were all healthy. The fountain that she ordered came in on schedule and her steak at lunch was cooked to perfection. Medium, just how she liked it.

CRYING MEADOWS

"I think we need more foggy days like this. There's something in the air that's bringing about good fortune for me."

Shortly after lunch, Jasmine went to plant the new flowers in a certain corner of the maze installation. She passed the ones she'd planted days ago, and they were thriving. Even in the foggy mist she could see their vibrant colors. She could also see the woman in the white dress, admiring the Roses that she planted last week.

"Okay, Jas. Here's your chance."

Quietly, she walked over to where the woman stood and struck up a conversation.

"Interesting weather we're having here, huh?" She began.

The woman was startled and turned to leave.

"No, please don't go!" Jasmine begged. "I've wanted to talk to you for a while but never had the courage. I've seen you crying. Are you alright?"

The woman did not turn around, but she did answer Jasmine. "No, I'm not alright. I've ruined my life and now it's too late."

"Don't say that. It's never too late. Trust me, I know," she tried to encourage the stranger.

"No! It's too late for me I said!" The woman turned abruptly and stared at Jasmine with the evilest glare.

Frightened, Jasmine backed up.

"Listen, I'm not trying to overstep my boundaries here. You just looked like you needed a friend, is all. I'm sorry."

The woman did not say anything. Getting the point, Jasmine walked back to the maze, picked up the flowers she hadn't planted and headed back towards the greenhouse.

"Well, there goes my good day," she said sadly.

She busied herself potting plants, pruning the Bonsai trees, and cleaning up her workspace until it was time for her to leave. The fines hairs on the back of her neck stood up and she felt as if she was being watched. When she turned around, she saw the woman in the white dress looking into the greenhouse. Jasmine motioned for her to come in, but the woman turned and ran away.

"Wait!" Jasmine called after her when she got to the door, but the woman was gone. The fog was still too thick to tell which direction she headed so Jasmine shut the door and finished her work for the day.

"I'm sure I'll have another chance to talk to her."

For the next few days, Jasmine did not see the young lady and then out of the blue, she appeared in the window of the greenhouse once again. She motioned for the woman to come in, but she refused. This time though, she did not run away.

Not knowing what to expect, Jasmine walked out the door and over to the trees where the young lady stood.

"I know you're probably used to this whether, but you really should think about wearing a coat. It's getting cold out here," she admonished.

The woman remained silent. Jasmine continued.

"I used to be on drugs," she began. "I screwed my life up. Chased a man who had a dream that turned out to be a nightmare. I've been homeless, abused, and hungry. My family stopped speaking to me. My friends left me out in the cold. I was alone. I said all that to say that you are not alone. This is a no judgment zone here. I'm not trying to be in your business. I'm just trying to be your friend."

Neither woman spoke. They just stood there in silence, listening to the breeze. Jasmine went to sit on the white cement bench outside of the greenhouse. The woman followed suit.

CRYING MEADOWS

"I'll be right back. It's almost time for me to leave for the day and I need to reset the automatic indoor sprinkler in my plant watering room."

"Hannah."

"Excuse me?" Jasmine stopped short, thinking she was hearing things."

"My name is Hannah. Hanna Whitlock."

"It's a pleasure to meet you, Hannah. I'm Jasmine Aster. All my friends call me Jas and since you are my new friend, you can too. Be right back."

She went inside and did what she came to do. Five minutes later, everything was done and ready for the start of a new workday.

"Whew, sorry it took so long but I had to...Hannah? Hannah," she yelled out. "Damn, she disappeared quickly. Oh, well. Guess I'll head home."

For the next few weeks, Jasmine would come out and sit on the bench when she saw the woman outside the greenhouse. The first few days Hannah did not say much. And Jasmine did not push her. Instead, she let her warmup to her and speak when she was ready. But day by day, Jasmine learned more about her.

The two women had more in common than Jasmine realized. They both loved CSI Miami, The People's Court and Chocolate Chip Cookie Dough ice cream. Hannah also confessed that she was a drug addict as well. That was not something that Jasmine could see looking at her.

When she used to hang out with her ex-boyfriend, she had heard his friends use a term 'closet smoker'. This was a person who was addicted to drugs but functioned like he was clean and sober, and no one knew about the drug use. Jasmine figured that Hannah's drug use was the reason things were not so great between she and her family.

It was hard to tell since Hannah was a bit guarded about certain details in her life. As nice as Jasmine found her to be, she also noticed that her new friend was a bit strange.

For instance, Hannah did not like to be touched. Anytime Jasmine would reach out to her, she would back away. She also never shared where she lived. All Jasmine knew is that it was through the meadow behind the maze and Rose garden. Wherever it was, it was not with her family.

"Hannah, you know I get to move into my new apartment this weekend. Just in time for Christmas. That's my gift to myself."

"How wonderful for you, Jasmine. I wish I could have done something like that."

"You can. People start over all the time."

Hannah got a faraway look in her eyes. "No, it really is too late for me. I've accepted that. But I am very happy for you. Make every day count, Jasmine. Do not take anything or anyone for granted. You never know when your time is up."

The warning was so subtle yet stern, that it sent chills up Jasmine's spine. Hannah had a way of doing that. Some of the things she said were spoken with such conviction a person would think that she was speaking from experience.

"I'm learning that. Thank you for the advice." To keep the conversation upbeat, Jasmine changed the subject.

"Did I tell you that my boss, Amy bought me a housewarming gift? I haven't opened it yet, but the wrapping looks very expensive. I'm giddy with excitement. One day you should come by and let me introduce you to her."

"I know Amy Meadows!" Hannah snapped, and then softened. "I met her years ago."

"Duh, silly me. Of course, you know her. Most wealthy people run in the same social circles. Why aren't you a member of the club? It's great. The Meadows have done a great job building it back up. I saw pictures of it before they did. The place was quickly becoming a dump."

"I'm aware of what it looked like. Me and a few others are the reason this place looks the way it does."

"Wow! You are an investor here at Lush Meadows? It must have cost you an arm and a leg to get involved."

"More than you'll ever know. I must go. Be careful with Amy Meadows. She's not what she seems."

"Wait, what do you mean by that?" Jasmine asked, standing up.

Hannah continued to walk away. She moved fast. Jasmine picked up her pace to follow her friend.

"Hannah, wait!"

Bzzzz. Bzzzz. The phone in her pocket vibrated. She took it out of jacket pocket but kept moving quickly. There was a stone in the path and Jasmine's right foot hit it causing her to stumble, sending her cell phone flying into the bushes.

"Ouch, Dammit!"

She reached over to the left and retrieved her phone prepared to continue pursuit but when she stood up, Hannah was gone.

"How does she do that, shit?" She said, shaking her head. "She must be used to running from the cops or something because she knows how to get out of Dodge quick, fast and in a hurry."

Shrugging her shoulders, Jasmine made her way back to the greenhouse. She only took a couple of steps before she stepped on a big tree branch.

"I have got to have Victor and the guys come out here and clear this out."

Looking down she saw something sparkle in the grass.

"What's this?" She said out loud, stooping to pick it up. It was a ring. A gold four leaf clover with a small diamond like stone placed in the center. It sat next to the prettiest, most unique stick Jasmine had ever seen.

"Looks like my luck continues," she smiled. She put the items in her pocket and began walking again. Once she was back at the greenhouse, she pulled out a cedar box that she bought at a thrift store from under her work bench. This is where she kept all the trinkets and bobbles, she found.

"I wonder if this ring is real," she uttered, then shook her head. "I doubt it."

The soft chime from the clock in her office alerted her that it was four o'clock. She only had a half hour left. Passing the time, Jasmine cleaned and swept the greenhouse and made a 'to-do' list of things she needed done in the upcoming days. At exactly four thirty she packed her things up, grabbed her cute box and made her way to the main building where she ran into Terry.

"Hey, lady. Long time no see," Terry said, hugging Jasmine.

"I know it's been a while. I've been busy in the fields."

"Uhn uhn. Don't even say it like that. You sound like you are a slave who has been picking cotton."

"Tell my body that I'm not. I'm so tired."

"Awe, poor baby. I guess that means you don't want to hit Wings and Whiskey night at the pub tonight with me and Ang?"

"I wish I could. Even if my body were not sore, I'd have to pass. I still have so much packing to do. You know I'm moving into my new place this Saturday, right?"

"Yes. Angie was telling me about that. Congrats, girl! I remember when I moved out of the high-rise and into my own spot. I couldn't wait to get me a man, so I could screw him silly."

Jasmine laughed until her eyes were teary. "I know exactly how you feel. Me and Blayke went out a few weeks ago and girl he kissed me so good I had to run upstairs and finish what he started."

"How is that fine specimen doing? You better be lucky I didn't have on my good bra that night otherwise he'd be mine right now."

"He's well. I guess we talked him up. This is him calling me now."

She swiped the screen to the right, answering her phone.

"Hey, you," she smiled happily.

"Well girl I'm gonna let you have some privacy. I still have an hour left on my shift. I'll call tonight. And don't forget me and Angie are both down to help you move."

"Thank you so much. I'll talk to you tonight."

"Huh?" Blayke said on the other end.

"Sorry. That was Terry's crazy butt. You off work yet?"

"Not yet. I have one more meeting and then I'm headed home. May I take you to dinner tonight?"

"Sure, as long as it's not Wings and Whiskey."

"That must be where Angie and Terry are going tonight, huh? But don't knock it 'til you've tried it. It's a crazy combination but somehow it works."

"I'll take your word for it. Just think, this time next week, if you call and ask me out to dinner, I can say no and offer to cook for you at home."

"Sounds so good. I'll pick you up at seven. I gotta go, Charlie is here. He's trying to get into Meadow Mission."

"Really? Good for him. Okay. Give him my love and tell him I'm praying for him to get in. See ya' tonight."

AVERY GOODE

"Hey Charlie, come on in," Blayke ushered the older gentleman in. "What have you decided?"

"I want in, Blayke. It's time for me to get my family back. I'm too old to be out here in these streets. My kids may be grown but they need me. Since Lana died, I've been on the path to destruction. Couldn't see myself living without her so I figured I'd drink myself to death."

"I've never heard you speak with such resolve. You're serious now?"

"Yes Sir, I am. Charlie Jr. and his wife are going to have a baby. I wanna be there. I'm going to be the best grandpa ever. Watch!"

"I believe you. Okay, then. I'll get your packet put together and submitted and we'll see what happens. I'm proud of you Charlie Turner."

"Thanks, Blayke. I'd be dead already if it weren't for you and Off the Street. You're a blessing to Atlanta. A real blessing."

It was clients like Charlie who made Blayke's job worthwhile. He encountered people from different walks of life daily. From Bankhead to Buckhead and everything in between, Blayke had met them all. He wanted to see all his client's drug and alcohol-free and self-sufficient.

Not all the clients at Off the Street had substance abuse issues. Some were people who had lost their jobs and homes and had no place to go after being evicted. He serviced everyone there and turned no one away. Off the Street even had a family unit. Most shelters didn't allow the family to stay together but it was necessary for success. Tyra helped him see that.

CRYING MEADOWS

Tyra. He had not thought about her in a while. She was the reason that he established Off the Street in the first place. It was a joint effort with them. That's when he thought that they were building a life *and* a business together. Before he found out she was married with children.

He shook his head at the bad memory and then quickly realized something. He was not angry like he normally would be after thinking about what she did. Had he forgiven her? If so, when did this happen? Then it hit him.

Jasmine was the reason he finally let go of the past. As much as he thought that he loved Tyra, he knew deep down inside that she was not the woman for him. Their views on important things like church and family were too different. Well, the views that she shared with him were different than his. It was apparent he did not know her at all. When they would talk, she mostly asked him about himself, avoiding opportunities to share things about herself. With Jasmine, things were the opposite.

It was if she wanted him to know all about her. With Jasmine, there were no secrets or pretenses. What you saw was what you got with her and Blayke loved it and her.

"I love her?" The reality of that truth made him sit back in his chair. "Damn, when did this happen? I've forgiven Tyra *and* fallen in love with Jas? Whoa."

Shaking his head, Blayke returned to work. This was too much for him to deal with right now and he was not sure he was ready. He had work to finish. A few hours later, paperwork complete and faxed to Amy, Blayke was in his car headed to Meadows Mission to pick up Jasmine.

He could not wait to see her. When he pulled up in front of her building, he called her to let her know he was downstairs in front of the building. He could not wait for her to move because he hated not being able to go get her and escort her to the car.

He opened the door for her when she got near the passenger door.

"You look wonderful. Is that a new dress?" He observed.

It was new to her but old to someone else. She bought it at the thrift store last week.

"It is. Thanks for noticing. You look great. I see you wearing the sweater I knitted for you. Great fit."

"Man, I got so many compliments on this today it was crazy. By the way, Charlie said you promised you'd make him one, too."

"Darn it. I did, didn't I? No problem, after I move, I'm gonna get on it. It doesn't take long."

"You are an amazing woman, Jasmine Aster. Has anyone told you that?"

"Nope. Thank you. I try. So where are we headed?"

"I figured we'd do a chain restaurant. How about the Cheesecake Factory?"

"Yippee!" She exclaimed. "White Chocolate Caramel Macadamia Nut Cheesecake here I come."

"I take it that means you're cool with going there?"

"Very cool."

One of the many things that Blayke loved about her is that she was so easy to please. Not too many women he dated before would care to walk the botanical gardens or hang out with his little sister. No, they wanted fine dining at an upscale restaurant where they could be 'seen'.

She was the type of woman his parent's and his sister wanted to see him hitch his wagon to. The type of woman he could see himself spending a couple of forever's with.

On the ride back to her place she chattered away.

CRYING MEADOWS

"Oh my gosh I am looking forward to Saturday. Please make sure your cousin and his moving van in here at eight in the morning sharp. Who's not trying to dally is me."

"I will."

"Man, I'm excited. And did I tell you that I've been speaking to Hannah every day?"

"Who?"

"Hannah. The woman in the white dress I was telling you about. Remember?"

"Yeah, I do but you always refer to her as the woman in the white dress. You never told me her name."

"Oh. Hmm, you know what I just realized?" She didn't wait for him to respond. "She always has on the same white dress. Strange thing is that it's just as clean as it was when I first saw her. You'd think walking through the meadow and the trees that it would get dirty on the bottom but it's not."

"Maybe she uses Oxy Clean or something."

"It's possible."

And the conversation continued in that fashion through dinner until he pulled up in front of her building after the date ended.

"I know I can't walk you up, but I'm going to walk you to the door."

"I had a great time tonight, as usual. Thank you so much."

"It's my pleasure. Um, I'm not going to kiss you goodnight because I uh…I mean to say, the last time I was…"

"Don't even worry about it. I totally understand. I know what you're saying. It happened to me too."

"Really?"

She rolled her eyes in the top of her head. "Geesh. Every part of my body was on high alert. That was some kiss."

"I promise you, the next time I heat you up like that, I'll be able to cool you down."

"I'm going to hold you to that, Mr. Ladd."

"Make sure you do."

He stepped closer, hugged her, bid her goodnight, and then left.

The next day, Blayke got a call from Amy Meadows. Charlie Turner was granted an interview for Meadows Mission.

"You sure are moving quickly, Amy. What is the rush? Normally I must wait at least two weeks to hear back from your office about an interview? What gives?"

"Process improvement, Blayke. I've hired some people here who've helped me streamline the intake process. You should try finding someone to help you. Off the Street could really use a revamping."

The dig did not escape his notice. "We're fine over here but thanks for the suggestion."

"As you know, we are transitioning clients all the time. We have four people moving out of the high rise this weekend so that clears up bed space for new clients."

She always had an answer for everything, Blayke thought, irritated.

"Fax over the appointment and I'll make sure Charlie gets it. I've gotta run, I have a meeting I am already late for. Talk to you soon."

He did not wait for her answer before he hung up the phone. There was something about her and that damned program of hers that did not sit well with him. Call him paranoid but something was not right. When he talked to Jasmine later, he was going to make sure to tell her to watch herself at the club. He could not put his finger on it, but he felt like Amy Meadows was up to something.

CHAPTER 15
GOOD HOUSEKEEPING...

THANK GOD IT'S FRIDAY, PRESTON thought, heading home. He loved the fact that Amy was working at Meadows Mission again instead of at the country club. Having her underfoot was bothersome to him. Every time he turned around; she was in his office begging.

"Let's have lunch together or babe let's sneak into the sauna and make love."

And more requests along that line. With her at the club, he could not come and go freely the way he wanted to because she was always checking up on him. He could not leave midday to enjoy other activities or people. Or seeing one person in particular; Tabby. The buxom housekeeper who had bewitched him.

Today, he came home early because he was expecting a delivery. He ordered a few suits, and they were supposed to arrive today. Until they came, he sat in his home office going over some financial records that looked dismal. Amy did not know it, but Preston was back to his old ways, cheating and spending. Not that he ever stopped cheating on her, but he had managed to curtail his excessive spending. Although Lush Meadows was profitable, the club was not making money faster than he could spend it.

He slammed the leather-bound book shut. Thankfully, the club was going to host the IGA Championship and that would take care of all the debt he was accruing. The championship would net millions for the club. And he would finally be able to do something he had been longing for, for years. Divorce Amy. The very thought of that brought a smile to his face.

"You must have gotten some good news or is that smile for me?" Tabby, the housekeeper asked, sashaying into his office, closing the door behind her.

"Lock the door and it's for you."

"Can't. The tailor is here with your suits. Should I escort him in?"

"No. Get them and bring'em to me. You can assist me with my fitting."

"Yes, Sir."

Tabby stepped out for a few minutes and then returned carrying a garment bag of Preston's new suits.

"Let's see how you look in these," she smiled, draping the garment bag over the back of the sofa, bidding him to stand up.

"These are the ones you picked out for me," he acknowledged proudly.

"Well, I have to have my man looking good, don't I?"

When he was in front of her, she began undoing his belt, and then unzipped his fly. Feeling her fingers so close to his manhood gave him a massive hard-on she noticed.

"I can see I've been missed. It's been too long," she spoke as she pulled his jeans down to his ankles.

"Indeed, it has."

On her command he stepped out of them obediently and stood in the middle of the room in nothing but his starched, white dress shirt and his boxer briefs. She picked up a pair of slacks off the sofa for him to try on but then had a change of heart.

CRYING MEADOWS

"I think I need to take care of this first," she said, pointing to the rock in his shorts that was on the verge of busting through the material.

Preston swallowed hard as Tabby came up close to him and put her arms around his waist as she slowly lowered herself down to her knees in front of him.

"Time to remove these bad boys," she teased, referring to his shorts.

His legs began to shake slightly as she slid them down ever so slowly and then gently began fondling his balls with both of her small hands. He closed his eyes as she ran her fingers around his groin area. Then suddenly, without warning, she took the head of his dick between her big, luscious lips and slid it into her mouth as far as it would go. Preston took a big deep breath that almost deprived the room of oxygen. Feeling an overwhelming desire to begin fucking her face, it took every bit of will power in Preston to remain still.

With one hand at the base of his hard shaft and the other massaging his engorged balls, she began to move his penis in and out of her mouth, occasionally stopping and then continuing to suck it with increased enthusiasm. Preston put his fingers in her hair and held on tight as she quickened the pace, knowing that she intended to make him come. Faster and faster, she went, with her tongue moving around in her mouth as she did so.

He started to breathe heavy and groan as the action got wilder and wilder. Tabby could feel he was about to come, and she gave him everything she had until he shot his load into her mouth, releasing a muffled groan as he did so. Exhausted he sat on the sofa and just looked at her. She wiped her mouth with her hand and began to take off her clothes. The black and white maid's uniform slipped down around her ankles followed by her panties.

Her pussy was partially shaved and exquisitely formed, and his dick began to rise as if it could not wait to explore her inner-most depths. Tabby took off her bra last, revealing tits to die for, nicely shaped and with nipples already hard and waiting to be sucked.

"Yum, it looks as if they're getting fuller," he said, licking one nipple then the other as she stood before him.

"They are. And it's all because of you. Again."

With only her heels on she moved to the sofa and sat on the edge inviting Preston to kneel before her, so he could lick her moist center. His right knee hurt from banging it against the desk the day before, but he soon forgot about that as he separated the lips of her hot box and began to run his tongue up and down her crack.

She responded by grabbing his shoulders and leaning backwards. As he gently licked her petals, he moved his hands up to her breasts and rubbed the nipples between his fingers. It didn't take long before her body began to quiver and then to shake furiously.

"I'm coming, I'm coming," she cried, "Keep doing it – keep doing it – I'm coming."

Preston continued his tongue assault and Tabby went berserk and fell on the top of him causing him to fall back onto the carpet and she landed on top of him. Her round breasts conveniently dangled near his mouth for his lips to absorb. He grasped onto them with his fingers and started to suck on the large erect nipples as she groaned and attempted to lower herself onto his dick.

When she managed to insert it, she gasped, preparing to ride her lover when he grabbed her slender waist and quickly turned her over. With his throbbing member still buried deep inside of her he proceeded to thrust it in and out as she dug her nails into his back and wrapped her long legs around him.

CRYING MEADOWS

He increased the pace until his ass was going up and down at a furious speed and their colliding bodies were making slapping sounds that echoed in the rafters of the large office.

"Preston. Preston," she cried out, as he pounded her flesh.

Again, her body started to shake uncontrollably and he, dripping with perspiration, was desperate to shoot his load deep inside of her. When he did, she let out a low-pitched scream, moved her ass up and down and pounded on his shoulders with her fists. When they regained their composure, they lay in each other's arms for a while and then sat naked on the sofa together and he sipped another brandy.

"I love you, Tabitha Nicole Long," said Preston, still a little bit out of breath.

"You're using my whole name. Is everything okay?" She looked concerned.

"It's good. I was just thinking about how happy you make me. My life is full because of you."

"Awe, baby. You have no idea how happy you make me. We are blessed to have you in our lives. I love you, too."

"Soon, we're not going to have to sneak around. No more secret rendezvous. And you'll finally be able to share my bed all night. One day," he added, waving his hand around, referring to Meadows Manor, "all of this will belong to you and our family."

Tabby faked a sad face and pouted.

"What's wrong love?"

"I was just thinking that as many times as you've made love to me, I've never shared your bed. Not once."

" I'd love to have you in my bed. Come on, let's go."

"Wait. I don't have on any clothes," she said, picking her things up off the floor.

"You don't need'em. Follow me."

Preston walked to the other side of his office and pulled a book off the shelf that had a button behind it. Suddenly, the bookcase opened and revealed a wrought iron staircase.

"This leads to the master bedroom. Come."

"Wow. This is sweet. I never knew this existed."

"Amy doesn't either. It's our secret."

"Well, what are you waiting for?" she cried rushing out of the room. Still naked she took the stairs two steps at a time with Preston hot on her heels.

Preston stood in front of her admiring her figure before sitting her on the edge of his and Amy's massive king-sized poster bed. He kneeled, placing his head between her legs and gently pressed the tip of his tongue against her clit. As he touched her, he felt her take a few short sharp gasps and then relax. As he continued, he could hear her starting to moan and pant. From the amount of juices now flowing from her, he could tell that she was enjoying his tongue's exploration.

Her legs began to quake around his ears as her body released its flowing nectar into his mouth. Satiated, Tabby fell back on the bed and Preston stood up and positioned himself between her thighs. He leaned over and sucked on each nipple, gently biting as he went along. Her legs spread in pleasure until she was wide open for him. Scooting back to the center of the bed, she welcomed her lover inside once more. Together she and Preston, writhed, bucked, and enjoyed one another. Light moans and groans filled the room.

Up and down, in and out, he created a rhythm their bodies danced to. With her legs wrapped tightly around his, she took him inside her fully, savoring every touch and every kiss he gave planted on her heated body. He sat up on his haunches and pulled her hips onto his lap without removing himself. The sight of his hard manhood sliding in and out of her was almost his undoing.

Wetting both of her index fingers, Tabby began making circles around her hard nipples and he felt himself tighten almost instantly. He tried to hold out if he could, but she contracted her vaginal muscles, sending him to ecstasy and she screamed out as her orgasm crested as well.

"Amazing," she complimented him when her breathing steadied.

"Yes, it was."

Preston rolled over onto his side and propped his head up on his hand.

"I know this may not be the best time to talk about this, but I want you to know that I have put some things in place to make sure that you all are taken care of."

"What do you mean? And why are you talking like this? You act as if something is about to happen."

"It's nothing like that. But if I ever learned anything from my father is was to make sure things are in order no matter what."

"Okay. What have you done?" She asked, sitting up to look him in the eyes.

"For starters, I purchased a home for you. I know that you would have liked to have found your own place, but this a gift and we never have a say in what people buy for us."

"I am sure if you chose it, it's beautiful. Tell me about it. Where is it?"

"It's not too far from where you are now. Cascade Glen. It's a gated community. The house has six bedrooms and eight bathrooms. There's a pool but I had it drained for now, because the little ones may go out and get into trouble. It's not furnished yet though. I figured you and your mom could do that."

"That's great but I don't have the money to furnish a house of that size. You all do not pay me that much. Not even with my extracurricular activities." She laughed but was very serious.

"I know. There is an account set up for you at Contemporary Furniture and Design. All you have to do is show your identification and begin picking out the things you want."

"Seems like you covered all the bases. Thank you, baby. I really appreciate you and I hope you know that I would love you rich or poor." She was telling the truth.

"I know and that's why you have my heart forever."

"So how much is my mortgage?"

"That's the best part. The house is paid off free and clear. I even paid the taxes up for two years. All you have to do is go to my attorney's office Monday and he will help you with the transfer of the deed."

"What! Are you serious? You paid for us a house?" Tears filled her eyes.

"Yes. And that's only the beginning. I told you when we first hooked up that I was going to take care of you for the rest of your life and I meant that. There are some other things I put in place but they're all trivial right now. We'll discuss them when the need arises."

"Okay love. But since you have done all this stuff for me, I need to show you my proper appreciation," she said as she began to straddle his hips. "I'm about to take you on the ride of your life."

CHAPTER 16
LAYING PIPE...

IT HAD BEEN A WEEK since Jasmine moved into her new apartment. Tonight, she was going to host the first dinner party of her life and she was nervous. There were only five people coming over, but she wanted to make a good showing, nevertheless. Bianca and her new beau, Miles; Terry and a guy she met on Marta named Xavier; and of course, Blayke.

Angie couldn't make it because her baby was sick, so it was just the six of them. This was the first time she had ever cooked for Blayke, so it was important for her to impress him more than anyone. There was a knock at the door, and she went to answer it.

"Hey, B. You're early," she said, hugging him and planting a kiss on his cheek.

"I know. I figured I would come offer my services if you needed any help."

"Awe, how sweet. As a matter of fact, you can set the table for me. The place settings are on the buffet."

"Look at this place. You've done a great job. Remind me to have you help me move the next time I decide to relocate. You're completely unpacked."

"I'm not really. I just put the last few boxes in the closet. I'll finish putting things away maybe tonight. The important stuff was unpacked first."

"Jasmine, do me a favor."

"Sure, what is it?"

"When I compliment you and your achievements, please just accept it. Don't always downplay the great job you're doing. Can you do that for me?"

"Absolutely. And thank you. I'm excited about this new journey. My parents, brothers and sisters will be up for here for All-Star Weekend. I'm looking forward to seeing them. More importantly, I'm looking forward to them seeing me."

"It's been that long?"

"Yep. And the last time they saw me it wasn't pretty. Me and stupid had just had a fight. I had a bruise on my eye, my hair was all over my head and I was skinnier than I was in grade school."

"Yikes. Must have been some visit."

"It was the worst ever. I'm praying that I never return to that person again."

"You won't. I won't let you." Blayke felt like things were getting too intense, so he changed the subject. "It smells great in here. What's for dinner?"

The quick change of subject didn't escape her. "Since the holiday is upon us, I prepared Cornish game hens with garlic and rosemary, roasted red potatoes, glazed long Chinese green beans, crusty garlic bread and a light Chianti wine."

"Girl, who taught you how to cook like that?"

"My dad. He wanted us all to know how to take care of ourselves. Especially my brother's. He didn't want them looking to a woman to feed them."

"Can't wait to meet him. Sounds like a great man."

"He is. You're a lot like him." After she said that, she blushed.

CRYING MEADOWS

He helped her with the final touches of dinner before the other guests arrived. Terry and Xavier were the first to arrive and Jasmine was shocked to see that he was white.

"Girl you didn't tell me that you were down with the swirl. What gives?"

"Jas, I told you that I liked milk in my coffee. Obviously, you weren't listening."

"I heard you, but I thought you meant, real coffee. Hell, how was I supposed to know?"

"Rest assured that I love men. All men. Particularly those who treat me like the queen my mama raised me to be."

"I know that's right. Well, he's fine, I know that much."

"And you know this. Is there anything I can do to help?"

"Sure. Will you pour the wine for me? It should be chilled by now."

Xavier and Blayke were sitting in the living room getting to know one another when Bianca and Miles arrived.

"Jasmine I love the décor of your apartment. You have such an eye for color and patterns. I like it."

"Thanks, Bianca. I'm trying to get it together."

"This picture is awesome. Where'd you get it?"

"From the GW Couture."

"Where's that at? I've never heard of it before."

Both Jasmine and Terry looked at one another and said at the same time, "the Goodwill," then burst into laughter.

"Okay, GW Couture. Funny. But seriously, this is a cool lithograph. It looks like it cost a fortune. And this vase. It looks like it's a Lalique. Did you get it from the Goodwill, too?"

"It is Lalique Crystal and no, Amy bought that for me for my housewarming gift."

"Well then I'm sure it did cost a fortune," Bianca affirmed.

"You damned, skippy it did," Terry said, walking into the kitchen.

Jasmine made the introductions.

"It's a pleasure to meet you, Terry. Do you work at Lush Meadows as well?"

"Child' yes, I work at the nut house."

Laughing, Bianca asked why.

"Them damned Meadow's be doing too much. They act like people don't have eyes. We can see them screwing up."

"What do you mean by that?" Jasmine asked, wiping her hands on a dish towel.

"Both of them are weird as fuck but Mr. Meadows fucks everything with a twat and then Amy walks around acting like they have the perfect marriage. Her head is so far in the clouds when it comes to that man."

"Preston is cheating on her?"

"Bianca, I heard that he's been cheating on her since before they got married and that he's never stopped."

"Terry don't be spreading rumors. We don't know this to be true."

"See Bianca, Amy bought her loyalty, so she won't be able to see anything wrong with her esteemed boss, but trust me, I know. And it's all true."

"Nobody has bought me and how do you know it's true?"

"Because my mother works for them at their estate, Meadows Manor and she tells me everything that goes on there."

"Are you women in here gossiping?" Miles walked in, interrupting their good conversation.

"Yes, we sure are," admitted Terry. "We'll finish this discussion later," she assured them.

CRYING MEADOWS

"Baby, yes we will. Let's eat everyone. I'm starved."

The group of friends enjoyed the meal that Jasmine cooked for them, often complimenting her on her culinary skills. After dinner, they had a battle of the sexes game of Scrabble and feasted on mini lemon tarts and coffee. By the time the two couples left, it was after midnight.

"Let me help you with the dishes," Blayke offered.

"You wash, I'll rinse, dry and put away."

"You said that fast."

"Do you think that I'm going to turn down an offer to help clean? As if."

Together they made quick work of putting away the leftovers and cleaning the kitchen. Pooped, they collapsed on the sofa and began watching a late-night weekend talk show.

"Do you remember when television stations used to go off?" Jasmine quizzed.

"Sure do. Remember how it used to play the Star-Spangled Banner and would show a waving flag. Then after the song ended it was nothing but snow?"

"Oh my gosh, I hated that. And my parents refused to get cable television for the longest. They told us if we're still up by the time the channel goes off then we needed to read a book."

"Reading is fundamental," he added playfully.

She socked him lightly in the arm.

"Someone call nine-one-one, I've just been assaulted by a pint-sized, horticulturist."

"Ooh, I'm impressed. I didn't think you knew words that big."

"You got jokes; I see."

"Just call me Wanda Sykes 'because I can keep'em coming all night."

"I'll bet you can. How about this then?"

Blayke picked up a throw pillow and swatted her on the back of the head.

"So, you wanna play dirty, huh? Alright then, take that," She reciprocated.

The pillow fight went back and forth until they were out of breath.

"This is the most fun I've had in ages," she confessed.

"Same here."

It got quiet in the room.

"Blayke," Jasmine said quietly.

"Yeah, Jas."

"Will you kiss me?"

He replied by leaning in and pulling her against his hard chest. Slowly, his tongue probed her mouth then began to wrestle with her own. Relaxing into the sofa cushions, Jasmine pulled Blayke into her until he was almost on top. Gently he nibbled down the side of her neck.

Sensations from her brain transmitted signals to awaken her sleeping womanhood. Moisture began to form in her center. She was glad she wore a skirt. The more he kissed her, the further she leaned back until they were both lying down flat on the extra wide sofa.

With her free hand, she discreetly eased her skirt up, revealing her well-toned, naked thighs. Absentmindedly, Blayke 's hand began to rub her legs and travel upwards. The heat emitting from her core served as a force field and his fingers were the magnet it attracted. The closer he got to her wetness, the more her legs opened. Gently he eased two fingers inside her.

The soft moan that escaped past her lips made him rock hard. His lips traveled lower until they rested on the thin material of her blouse. She could feel the heat from his mouth as he sucked her nipple through the gauze-like material. Out of her mind with passion, Jasmine lifted her left leg, resting it on the back of the sofa. Somewhere between her moving and Blayke's nibbling, he managed to get his member free.

His big hands slid under her, each one cupping a buttock. Without removing his lips from hers, he lifted her hips and eased his penis towards her opening. When Jasmine felt the head at the entrance, she gasped.

"I'm sorry," he said. "I can stop if you want me to."

"No, please don't. I need this. I need you."

Taking the time to reach into his wallet, Blayke sheathed himself with protection before picking up where he left off. Back in position, he plunged as deep as he could go inside of her.

"Yes," she cried out as he worked her over slowly.

Somehow, the two of them moved from the couch to the bed and he loved her as completely and thoroughly as he could.

The next morning, he showed her his skills in the kitchen when he prepared breakfast for the two of them. They ate, watched a movie, and then made love again. Later that day, he took her to the Kroger grocery store not too far from where she lived so he could pick up something special to cook for dinner.

"You're not the only one who can get down in the kitchen," he boasted.

"You showed me that this morning when you had me all up on the counter," she ribbed.

"My skills span far and wide."

"Oh, yes they do," she reminisced. From now on, breakfast would be her favorite meal of the day.

The two of them exited the store and headed towards his car. There was a flyer on the windshield, and he yanked it off.

"I can't stand when people put stuff on my car. Half the time I don't realize it's there until I'm going down the street. By that time, it blows off."

He was about to wad the paper up and throw it in the trash by the shopping cart station when Jasmine spotted something familiar.

"No!" She yelled. "Let me see that, please." She reached for the flyer. "Good Lord," she breathed.

"What is it? What does it say?"

He took the flyer. *Have you seen this woman?* It said and had a picture of a pretty, blond woman on it.

"That's Hannah, babe."

"Who?"

"The woman in the white dress who lives next to Lush Meadows."

While they talked, he put the groceries in the trunk, and they got in the car.

"I don't get it. If she lives by the club, then why are they putting out missing persons posters?"

"Beats me. But she doesn't think that her family wants her around anymore. Every time I talk to her, she tells me how badly she screwed up and how it's too late for her to go home. I can't wait to show her this. She's going to be so excited."

Monday dawned a new day and Jasmine was happier than ever. Her weekend ended as wonderfully as it started. Blayke had pampered her with good food and good loving. Both of which she could never get enough of. Stretching, she got out of bed. She couldn't wait to get to work to find Hannah. Her friend was going to finally reunite with her family.

Usually when she arrived at the club, Jasmine headed to the employee dining room and had breakfast. This morning she wanted to get to the greenhouse as quickly as possible. Her stomach had other plans, rolling to announce its hunger.

"I am hungry," she agreed.

The cooks always set up a breakfast buffet for the staff members that rivaled that of what they prepared for the guests. Only until she had fixed a plate did Jasmine realize that she was as hungry as she was.

"You look like a woman who is well satisfied," observed Terry.

Giggling, Jasmine nodded.

"I knew it. Girl I could tell when I walked into your house Saturday night that that fine ass, Omari Hardwick looking man wanted to snatch you up and just ravage you. Those big ol' arms of his were made for picking you up and just taking the cookie while standing against the wall. Did he do you like that?"

"Look at you all in my business. Did Xavier do you like that?"

"Yes, he did. Let me tell you, he t- "

"No!" Jas interrupted. "Spare me the details. Please."

"Whatever. Did you have a good time at least"?

"Did I? That man is one-of-a-kind. I've got to be careful with him though because he's so great, he'll have me falling in love and I'm not trying to do that."

"Why not? You two look great together."

"Looking great together and being great together are two different things. I am not trying to fall in love with him when he doesn't feel the same about me. Been there done that and don't wanna do it again."

"How do you know how he feels? Have you asked him?"

"No. Not yet anyway. Look, this weekend was our first-time making love. I'll wait and see what happens."

"Jasmine, sex and love don't have anything to do with one another. You can have one without the other and vice versa."

"Thank you, Dr. Phil. I'm going to take it slow, is that okay with you?"

"Perfectly fine, Ma'am."

"Good. Have you talked to Angela?"

"Yep. She's here today. Let's meet up for lunch around one o'clock."

"Cool. I gotta get to the greenhouse. I have something important to do. Talk to you later."

"Bye."

She could not wait to see Hannah and show her the flyer, but by the looks of things, she was going to have to. Jasmine walked through the maze of roses, calling out to Hannah but she did not see her. She had even gone so far where the gardens ended, and the meadows began but there was still no sign of her. This was her first time being that far out during the daytime, so she never noticed the fence that separated the meadow and the trees from the golf and country club.

"Hmm, that's strange. I wonder how Hannah gets through here then." Shrugging her shoulders, she made her way back to the greenhouse. Once inside she took the flyer out and laid it on her workbench and began pruning some flowers.

After lunch, Amy Meadows happened by to discuss a couple of things with Jasmine.

"Hey, Amy. How are you?" Jasmine acknowledged.

"I'm well thanks for asking. Since you are doing such a great job here, I was wondering if you would be willing to come to my home and help me get my garden on track. I'd pay you of course."

CRYING MEADOWS

"Yes. That would be great. Nothing better than getting paid for something that I love to do. When would you like me to start?"

"Let's shoot for after the holidays. There's no rush. I'll let you know. Also, I know I'm being a pest," she began. "But I'd like to start planning a ceremony around this."

"It's cool. I understand. Victor and I were just talking about that. Although we've made considerable progress with the design, we still need to have the sprinkler system repaired. Apparently the old one that was installed has some rusted pipes and we may need to replace them."

"Replace them?" Amy was alarmed. "But the hedges are already in place. Would we have to uproot them to fix the pipes?"

"I doubt it. We're going to go over the blueprint to see where the pipes are installed and then figure out our plan of action. But to answer your question, we're looking at about eight to twelve weeks. So sometime around February or March."

"Not what I was expecting, but that gives me a little time to make the necessary arrangements. Consult me before digging. Did you remember to remind Victor to bag the leaves and place them in the warehouse? I really need them."

"Yes. He said there are over twenty bags already. Why do you need so many leaves?"

"A project."

"Really? What kind?"

"Is there any scratch paper nearby? I need to jot down some notes," Amy completely ignored the question.

"Check on my workbench. It's a stack of it there."

Jasmine's office phone rang. "That may be the irrigation company now. Excuse me while I take this call."

Amy walked to the workbench and picked up a folded piece of marigold paper. She was about to write on it but opened it up to make sure it was not something Jasmine needed. Her eyes got big like saucers when she saw the face on the flyer. It was Hannah Whitlock. This was the last face she expected to see. It had been five years since she last laid eyes on her.

"That was the irrigation man, but he wanted to talk about the fountain. He'll be out after Christmas to assess the piping."

"Very good. Where did you get this?" Amy asked, holding up the flyer.

"It was on the windshield of a friend's car when we came out of Kroger in Buckhead. I was going to tell H- "

Ring.

"Drat's. I promise this phone has never rang this much. I'll be back."

Amy folded the flyer back up and discreetly slid it into her back pocket. Before Jasmine got off the phone, she slipped out of the greenhouse.

"Thanks for...Amy? Well damn. I swear these white women know how to disappear around here."

Jasmine looked on her workbench for the flyer and didn't see it. She leaned over to look under the table, searched the trash and her pockets. Nothing.

"Dammit. I've lost the flyer. Now how am I supposed to convince this woman that her family still loves her?"

A couple of things that Jasmine paid close attention to, were the way Amy ignored her question and how she reacted seeing the flyer. She was visibly shaken. Clearly, she was the one who took the paper, but why? Maybe Terry was right. Maybe the Meadows' were not all what they wanted people to believe. She would find out once she started working at their home. People were different outside of work. Blayke told her on several occasions to be careful around them. From now on, she would.

CHAPTER 17
WIN SOME, LOSE SOME...

AMY MEADOWS WAS MANY THINGS but stupid was not one of them. She knew that Preston was cheating on her again, but she did not know with whom. The very thought of him lying with another woman after all she did for him, for them, made her blood boil. If it were not for her, Lush Meadows would have closed its doors five years ago. It was on the verge of bankruptcy and the membership was down in the low hundreds. Now the club boasted thousands of members and under her direction it had expanded.

She is the one who came up with the idea to revamp the club. And the fertilizer that was used to treat the greens, making them the most pristine in the nation, was her formula, down to the last ingredient. He would have nothing if it were not for her.

"He's a selfish bastard just like Abbott, Sr.," she fumed, comparing him to his father. Indeed, they were alike in ways that Preston did not even know about. But Amy did. And one day, she would get the opportunity to tell him. Not today though. She had more pressing matters to deal with other than her philandering husband.

In less than an hour, her cousin Sturgis was supposed to deliver a new batch of fertilizer and she was excited. She and

CRYING MEADOWS

Preston were also hosting a dinner party at their home to celebrate them winning the IGA bid. There were still so many last-minute details to iron out that Amy did not know if she was coming or going. Thankfully, Miss Ruthie and Tabby were there to help lighten the load.

Having a party was a bit premature since the announcement had not been formally made but Paul Whitaker told her the other day that Lush Meadows was guaranteed the bid. Well, maybe those were not his exact words, but it was in the bag. Preston really was not on board to host an event until he was for sure they'd won, but Amy was ever the optimist and she could feel something big about to transpire.

The guests were set to arrive at seven that evening. That was only a few short hours away. Out of all the people who were invited, Amy was most looking forward to her in-laws coming over. She wanted all his family present, so they could see how great the club was doing. Really, she wanted to rub their noses in it for once. She had waited a long time for an opportunity like this to come. A very long time.

Usually around the holidays, the days moved quickly. But since Amy had been waiting for this huge announcement, the days crept by. Thankfully, the holidays were behind them. It seemed to take forever for this day to come. Patience was not one of her strong suits. She was a product of rich parent's and the microwave generation. Wanting what she wanted when she wanted it.

Winning the bid meant that Amy would finally get the chance to work on having her baby. When she tried to talk to Preston a few months ago about them trying to have a family again he brushed her off. Before the club was as successful as it was, he promised her that if she helped him win the IGA bid they would start their family.

Therefore, she had been rushing the days along. She could care less about hosting the national golf championship. All she wanted was to be swollen with her husband's seed.

Miss Ruthie knocked on her open door and asked if she could come in.

"Of course, Miss Ruthie, how are you? Happy New Year! I haven't seen you since last year."

"Happy New Year, Mrs. Amy! I sure do appreciate the vacation. That was the best Christmas present ever. That is what I came in here for, to tell you thank you."

"It was our pleasure. You have worked so hard and never took a proper one. I can't think of anyone more deserving than you."

"As long as I lived and breathed, I never thought that my husband and me would have seen Hawaii anywhere other than on the television. And for three luxurious weeks. You really blessed us."

"Awe, Miss Ruthie, you know how we feel about you and Hamilton. Come give me a hug. I don't know what I'd do without you."

Amy embraced her cook tightly. She really did love the aged woman. When it was time to hand out Christmas bonuses, she wanted to do something extra special for the lady who had cooked and served them for the past decade. One day she stopped Ruthie's daughter, Terry, who worked at the country club and picked her brain about what her mother might like.

"Honestly, Miss Amy, Mama would like some time alone with her husband. Every time she looks up her house is crawling with people. I know she loves us, but she needs to get away from all of us, stop serving others and get served herself."

"Thank you, Terry. You've given me a great idea."

CRYING MEADOWS

Amy knew how much Miss Ruthie loved Hawaii because that is all she ever talked about. Sending her on a dream vacation was the least she could do for her.

"Excuse me, Mrs. Meadows, here's the mail."

"Thanks, Tabby. You are looking wonderful. I forgot to ask how your New Year was?"

"It was great. I spent it...relaxing. How were yours and Mr. Meadow's?"

"Mine was great. Preston was out of town on business. He had something important he had to get into."

Yeah me, the naughty housekeeper smiled.

"Awe, such a shame," she whined.

"That's what I said. But hey, life happens and things like that are to be expected when you're dealing with a successful businessman like him."

"I couldn't agree with you more. Oh, here's the mail. I was about to walk out with it in my apron."

"Thanks. I need to look at these credit card bills and see what kind of damage we did over the holidays. I am so glad all of that is over. Thanks again," she said dismissively.

"You're welcome," and Tabby walked slowly away.

"Tabby, why do you wear heals to work with your uniform?"

Because my man loves the way my legs look in them.

"My mother always said, the better you look the better you feel. Just because I'm a housekeeper doesn't mean that I have to look like one."

"Good for you! I love the positive attitude that you people have."

Shaking her head on the way out of the room, Tabby thought, *lady, you have no clue.* Tabby had not taken five steps when she heard Amy yell.

"Sixty-eight thousand dollars! What the hell did he buy?"

Tabby whispered, "My new twenty-sixteen black on black Jeep Rubicon Unlimited," as she walked away whistling.

Immediately after her heart rate returned to normal, Amy picked up the phone to call the credit card company. She needed to get to the bottom of such an astronomical charge. Especially considering that Preston had not spent it on her. She followed the automated prompts until she was able to get a live representative on the line.

"Thank you for calling Platinum Express, this is Sharon, may I have your account number please?"

Amy rattled off the long list of numbers.

"How may I assist you today, Mrs. Meadows?"

"Yes, Sharon, I just received my statement and saw that there's a charge on it for over sixty-eight thousand dollars. Where was this purchase made?"

"One moment. That was not a purchase. It was a cash advance which was processed at the Atlanta State Bank."

"A cash advance?" Amy mumbled, not realizing she had said it out loud.

"Yes, Ma'am. The transaction was made on Mr. Meadow's card."

Was the rep supposed to be divulging this much information? Either way, Amy did not care. She needed as many facts as she could gather.

"Thank you so much for your help."

"Have I answered your questions to your satisfaction?"

"Yes, you did. More than you know. Have a nice day."

Angrily, she drummed her fingers on the desk. For every step Preston and Amy took forward, he did something that caused them to go back at least four.

CRYING MEADOWS

"Fuck!" She was pissed off.

"Blessings and curses should not come out of the same mouth. The Lord our God has decreed that."

"Hello, Sturgis. I wasn't aware that you'd arrived, I wouldn't have said that."

"It matters not if I am here or not, our Savior who sits high and looks low is always watching. He is omnipresent."

"Yes, cousin." Amy was tiring of this conversation before it began. "Did you bring the fertilizer?" That is all she wanted. If he did, he was free to go.

"Whoever keeps his word, in him truly the love of God is perfected."

"A simple yes would have sufficed, Sturgis. Thank you very much."

"It is always my pleasure to do the work of the Lord. Have you gathered leaves for the storehouse?"

"Yes. I will bring them next week. Are the drums in the stable?"

"Yes. Be careful, though. The lid on one of them is bent," he said.

She snapped her fingers. "I forgot that one fell off the truck when it was being delivered. I'll have a new one by next week."

"Good. May the Lord God of our fathers be with you." Sturgis spoke the blessing over his cousin and then he left.

"I swear that man exasperates me to no end."

One thing down a million more to go. Somehow, Amy and the staff got the last-minute things done and she was able to dress for the party. Preston managed to creep in just before the first guest arrived. Not wanting to start a fight and ruin the evening, Amy let it go. They would have plenty of time to discuss his whereabouts and that large bill she received earlier.

"Dear, I'm so proud of the fine job you've done at the club. It's simply amazing."

Amy turned around expecting to thank her mother-in-law for the compliment but saw that the woman was talking to Preston.

"Your father would be so proud of you," Cora Lee continued. "Great work."

"Thank you, Mother. It's been a long, trying road but I stayed the course."

"Fine job, Pres. That's the Meadow's way."

"Thanks A.J.," Preston said, shaking his older brother's hand with one hand and patting him on the back with the other.

Stunned that he was taking all the credit for the growth and improvement of the golf and country club, Amy stood there, staring in disbelief. A loud boom outside, shook her out of her trance.

"What on Earth?" Bella Rose, asked.

"Sounds like it came from the estate next door. I'll call Dale at the stables and find out what's going on."

Preston called his horse trainer to find out what was going on.

"Dale, what's the commotion?" He paused, listening to the man's response. "Oh, really? Well, thank you." He was about to end the call when the trainer said something else to him.

"She did what?" Preston asked, baffled. "I don't know, but it couldn't have been too important. Anything can be replaced. Goodbye."

"What's happening, dude?" Robert questioned.

CRYING MEADOWS

"The Jones' son is having a party and they made a bonfire. Some genius threw a kerosene lamp into the fire, thinking it was empty, but it wasn't."

"How dangerous. Kids these days are simply awful."

"Not all of them, Mother," Jennifer said. "We've got some pretty good ones."

Amy stood on the sideline and watched the exchange between Preston and his family. This is the best that they have treated one another in ages. She would allow her husband to take the credit for the club. He needed this validation from his family. It had been a long time coming. Too bad, Abbott, Sr., was not around to see it.

After dinner, everyone adjourned to the drawing room to watch the IGA announcement. It was an exciting time. Amy watched in slow motion as Paul Whitaker walked up to the podium. A hush fell over the room.

"Good evening. After months of touring clubs around the U.S., the selection committee has selected the golf and country club that will host the twenty-sixteen IGA Championship. It was not easy picking a winner because every entry had something great to offer. Our winning club had something special. The grounds were pristine, the staff warm and friendly…"

Amy got so excited because she knew he was talking about Lush Meadows. Those are the exact words that he used when referencing their club. This was it.

"We're pleased to announce that the twenty-sixteen IGA Championship will be held at Lu- "

Unable to contain herself, Amy screamed out in excitement.

"You dolt. What the hell are you cheering for? You didn't win."

"Wait, what?" She had not heard correctly.

"Paul said that Luxe Gardens won, Ames," Preston said, rubbing the small of her back to comfort her.

"Wow. I got so excited when I heard the 'L' come out of his mouth that I tuned out the rest." Hurt and disappointment filled her.

"Hey, why the long faces? Lush Meadows made a great showing and there's always next year. You all should be proud. The club was in the top three out of 300 clubs nationwide. That should tell you all something."

"Thanks, Bella," Amy said, hugging her sister-in-law. "You're right."

They resumed having a good time for another couple of hours and all the guests, except for the Meadows clan left. The women had gotten comfortable, removing their heels, and sitting around chatting. The men had pulled out Preston's cigars and began smoking and talking about sports.

"Well Preston, old chap. Since you all didn't win the bid, looks like you and Amy over there are going to have to get started on those kids so that you can get the rest of your inheritance," Robert remarked.

Everyone laughed, except Preston. There was nothing funny about that, but he knew his brother spoke the truth.

"You're right, Rob. Let's go, Ames. The bed is calling." More raucous laughter rang out across the room.

"Alright now children, settle down. Speaking of inheritance, Preston we need to talk when I return from Greece."

"Yes, Mother. Taking a little jaunt, are you?"

"Hardly," Jennifer began. "Mom will be gone for a whole month."

CRYING MEADOWS

"When do you leave?" He was interested in what she had to say about the inheritance and waiting a whole month would be hell.

"In a couple of days. I need the rest. My sister will accompany me, so you all don't have to worry about me being alone."

The conversation shifted, and the family enjoyed more laughs, drinks, and cigars until they all finally went home.

"That was a successful evening, don't you think?" Preston commented when they got to their bedroom.

"How can you say that? We lost the damned bid. You of all people should be upset considering."

"Considering what?"

"With your excessive spending you'll bankrupt us and the club in less time than it took for us to rebuild the damned thing. I don't know what whore you're keeping now but she must have some powerful pussy to make you spend over sixty-thousand dollars on her."

Angrily, he walked over to Amy, grabbed her tightly by both arms and pulled her close to him.

"Listen here you spoiled little bitch. What I do and what I spend is my fucking business. Yes, she has powerful pussy and she has my ch-.... she's many things to me, but she's not a whore!" He ended, pushing her onto the bed.

Tears poured down her face, "You need me Preston. A.B. said that for you to receive your inheritance we had to have a baby of our own loins. We have to make love for that to happen."

"I'm aware of what my father's will said. He put that in there, so we could not adopt children. He never said we couldn't use artificial insemination."

The air was knocked out of Amy's lungs.

"And by the way, Dale said whatever was in one of those drums was spilled in the stable. Meadows Blessing kicked it over. She was startled by the blast from the bonfire. I was actually considering sticking my dick in you tonight, but I changed my mind."

This night could not get any worse. If one of the drums was empty, Amy would need more fertilizer for the putting greens. For them to stay beautiful, she had to treat them twice a year. It was almost overdue.

The next morning, Amy woke up with a hangover sized headache. By the time she made it downstairs, Preston had eaten breakfast and left.

That's even if he slept here last night.

Things were not going as she planned. Right now, the only good thing that was going to plan was Meadows Mission. The shelter was doing everything that she intended it to and then some. Fed, dressed, and feeling somewhat better, Amy made her way to the house where her new clients were. She needed to check to ensure all was well herself because Sturgis had not called to give her an update.

She opened the door and turned off the alarm. As she made her way through the house, she was pleased that the scopolamine had worked again. Several dead bodies lay in the last place they occupied.

"Good, good. I can replenish my fertilizer soon."

A loud noise came from upstairs and she went to see what it was. Once she reached the top of the staircase, the sound of children singing about Band-Aids filled the hallway. It was the television. Amy walked into the room where the set was left on to see that Charlie Turner was laying serenely in his final resting place.

"Such a sweet man," she said out loud.

Charlie stirred.

CRYING MEADOWS

"Good morning, young lady. I did not know you came to check on us. Real nice of ya'."

"Charlie, you're ali-…I mean awake. What happened last night?"

"Well, the others wanted to watch movies and play games, but I'm an old man and I was plumb tuckered out. I needed my rest. Thinking about taking the bus to see my kids. When do you think we'll be able to use our cell phones again?"

Astounded, she said nothing. Instead, she wracked her brain trying to come up with a plan. This could not be happening. Her life was turning into a comedy of errors.

"Mrs. Meadows did ya' hear me?"

"Oh, yes, sorry, Charlie. Um, you can use your phone today. Follow me, I'll show you where we keep them, and you can show me which one is yours?"

A trusting Charlie followed Amy towards a back staircase. They walked down the steps until they approached the basement landing. There was a heavy metal door just ahead and the two of them walked towards it.

"You guys keep the phones in this room? This door looks like a vault."

"It is actually, we keep you all's valuables in here, so no one can steal them."

"Wow, this is such a great place. I can't wait to tell my kids how you all treated me."

"Come. I'll show you the phones and you can grab which one is yours."

Amy pointed to a table and told Charlie to look inside the box.

"You may find it in that box."

The old man began digging through the box as Amy got something out of the drawer next to her. Slowly, she walked up behind him and raised her arms. It was about to come down just as he turned around to face her.

"Argh!" He screamed as the butcher's knife came down, slicing him on the shoulder. "Help! P-please don't! This is my phone. I wasn't stealing anyone else's. I promise. Don't hurt me. My-my kids need me."

"They needed you when you were out drinking and doing drugs but that didn't concern you then so they certainly don't concern me now," she said angrily.

Wildly she wielded the blade, making small cuts in his hands and face as he backed away from her. There was a box in the floor, and he fell backwards. Seizing the moment, Amy quickly plunged the knife into Charlie's chest disabling him. Repeatedly she thrust the blade into him, puncturing his lungs in the process. Blood began to trickle out of his mouth. One final push and he was dead.

"Oh my God! What have you done?"

Amy jumped so quickly the knife flew from her hand and slid across the floor.

"Sturgis, you have got to stop sneaking up on me like that. Geesh."

"What is the meaning of this?"

"I came to check on our seeds and Charlie was alive. He didn't use any of his patches, he just went to sleep."

An angry Sturgis paced the floor.

"The devil has walked the Earth looking for a place to rest and I'm afraid he's found it."

"What are you talking about now?"

"First you curse and now this. The Word of our Lord says, 'Thou Shalt Not Kill.'"

CRYING MEADOWS

Amy knew exactly what Exodus, twenty-thirteen said but the deed was done. But this was not her first time. Nor would it be her last.

CHAPTER 18
RAIN, SLEET & SNOW...

WHEN IT RAINED IT POURED. Unless you were Amy, then it stormed. Lush Meadows had lost the International Golf Association bid and Preston was seeing someone else. Again. And he appeared to be in love with this one, too.

Usually, he would throw the affair up in her face as soon as it began, but not this time. He was also quick to tell her who the 'lucky' woman was, but he protected the identity of his new mistress. This woman, he was willing to fight for.

In all the years the two of them had been married, Preston had never manhandled her the way he had the other night. There was a small, visible bruise on her left arm caused by the death grip he had on her. But the bruise that could not be seen, the one she had on her heart, was much bigger.

Preston was everything to her and even though he was annoying at times, she really did love him. When they got married, she envisioned them having a relationship like her parents and her siblings. Instead, her marriage was exactly like the one Abbott and Cora Lee had. Dysfunctional and lacking.

Exhaling, she shook her head. Only if her marital woes were the worst of it. The icing on the cake was the fact that the green space just beyond the golf course was turning brown and she only had a little fertilizer. What's more is that she didn't have any clients on the waiting list for Meadows Mission.

The other shelters that she partnered with sent their clients to other rehabilitation centers since they could not get them into hers. Frustrated, she needed to figure things out and fast. Losing the bid would not hurt the club but an unplayable course would ruin it.

It was days like this that Amy wished she and Preston had children by the time Abbott, Sr., died. Living off his one-hundred-twenty-million-dollar inheritance would have been so much easier than trying to maintain this club. But Amy coveted wealth and status and would do anything to keep it. So, if that meant eradicating a few worthless druggies, then so be it. Nothing or no one could stand in the way of that happening.

Hopping in a golf cart, Amy drove to the area where Jasmine and Victor waited for her. This was going to be a long day.

"Hola, boss. How are you?" Victor greeted her.

"Hello you guys. What's going on?"

"Hey, Amy. I am just trying to get a handle on what's going on here. I've never seen anything like this before," Jasmine admitted.

"Do you think that we'll be able correct it? I do not want this to spread to the putting green. That'll ruin us."

"I don't think it will get that bad but honestly I'm not sure. There is still some of the fertilizer left that I used on the patches by the back nine, left. I can try that."

"Thanks, Victor. That was some good stuff."

"Did you get any more of that fertilizer that I love?"

"I'm working on it, Victor."

"Yes, I agree with him. Whatever we used before is way better than what we're using now."

"I know Jasmine. I have some at home, but it is only a small amount. The large drum was spilled accidentally, and I haven't been able to replace it yet."

"Bummer."

"You can say that again, Sir."

The trio continued to hash out a plan of action to restore the grass after they returned to the greenhouse. They were focused on the blueprints on the workbench in front of them that they did not see the woman looking in at them.

This was the first time that Hannah visited Jasmine in weeks. However, she had not laid eyes on Amy in almost five years. Without taking her eyes off the greenhouse, Hannah walked backwards back into the meadow and returned to where she came from.

While Amy was meeting in the greenhouse, Preston showed up at the club. He had just had the best morning with Tabby. That was one woman who really knew how to make him feel like a man. They had not had sex, but it was something about the way she spoke to him that edified him.

After he left his and Amy's home, he went to her house. She prepared breakfast for him and brought him his plate. And she complimented him on how good he looked in his suit. Although the sex was mind-blowing, her manner towards him was more intimate than even her lips around his member.

He hated to leave her, but duty called. The marketing department was supposed to be running ideas by him this morning that would help increase membership and drive higher paying events to the club. The club and Preston needed the money. Hopefully, his mother would tell him something good about his inheritance when she returned. A loud buzz interrupted his train of thought.

"What is it Dorothy?" He asked his secretary gruffly.

"You have a call on line one. She says it's personal."

CRYING MEADOWS

Tabby. Smiling, he told her to put the call through.

Staying in professional mode so she would not know that he knew it was her, he answered the phone.

"This is Preston Meadows; how may I help you."

"Hello, Preston."

He did not recognize the voice. Definitely not Tabby.

"This is Pat from Nations Bank regarding your past due credit card account. Before we proceed, I need to inform you that this is an attempt to collect a debt and any information obtained will be used for that purpose. You have an outstanding balance of thirty-one thousand dollars. How would you like to handle that today?"

Click.

"That's how I plan on handling it, bitch."

Another loud buzz.

"You have a visitor to see you. A Mister Blayke Ladd."

"Send him in."

The secretary escorted him inside the office.

"Blayke. It has been too long. How have you been?" Preston questioned, extending his hand for a shake.

Blayke reached out and shook the man's hand.

"I'm well. Busy. But I know you know all about that."

"Absolutely. What's going on?"

"As you know, non-profits have to have measurable results. I wanted to talk to you about some of the people who came from Off the Street and are now employed here."

"That's really Amy's area of expertise."

"Meh, for what I need, you may be able to help me or someone from human resources. I just need to know how they're working out here."

"Oh, well if that's all, I can pull up their last evaluation. Would that help?"

"Sure. First person is Tina Robinson."

Preston typed in the name.

"She's not in our system. Are you sure she works here?"

"I was told she did. Let's move on. Chris Porter."

"He's not in here either."

"He's a she, and are you sure?"

"Yeah."

Blayke rattled of a few other names. Nell Giggers, Ellis Landers, Joe Borden. None of them were in there. Preston got a sinking feeling in the pit of his stomach but tried not to let it show on his face.

"Maybe the system isn't updated yet. Can I make a copy of that list and get with human resources about them? I'm sure they have the updated information."

"That would be great. Get back to me as soon as possible. I need to send the information to the state."

"Will do. It was nice seeing you again, man. Come by sometime and play a round of golf with me."

"You got it."

As soon as Blayke was gone, Preston buzzed his secretary.

"Dorothy, call Doug in marketing and reschedule our meeting. Something pressing came up."

He grabbed his suit jacket and left. Once he got home, he went to his office and found the spare key to Amy's desk then went to her office. The records for Meadows Mission were kept there. The desk was neat and orderly, so he made sure to keep it that way, so she would not know that he had been snooping.

CRYING MEADOWS

Because he was so sneaky, Preston did not put it past Amy that she was as well, so he looked in every nook and cranny of her desk. She had some financial records that he knew nothing about. Apparently, Amy received a monthly stipend of over one hundred thousand dollars from her mother.

"Hmm, so that's how she was able to clear up so many of my overdrafts. Interesting."

In the bottom drawer, Preston noticed that the size of the drawer was larger than the depth of the drawer. There had to be a hollow compartment present. He knocked around until the sound was different.

"Bingo."

There was a small chain inside and when he pulled it, a thin piece of wood lifted.

"What's this?"

He lifted a leather-bound book out of the drawer and set it on the desk. The letter's E-B-C was etched into it. The book was thick. Preston opened it and saw that it contained a list of names with dates next to them. Nothing else. There were pages and pages of them. So many names that Preston lost count. As he flipped further back, a name stuck out.

"Why do I know that name?" He racked his brain for a few minutes. "Son-of-a-bitch!"

Swiftly he ran back to his office and opened his briefcase.

"Glad I threw this in here."

It was the copy he had made of the list of names that Blayke inquired about. Browsing the list, he recognized every name on the list except for one. His stomach revolted, and he spewed his breakfast in the wastebasket next to the desk.

This could not be happening. Slowly he made his way back to her office and finished looking at the book. It did not say anything about the people, but he knew whatever was going on, it was not good.

"I should have stopped this long ago when I first found out about..."

Grief-stricken, he placed the book back where he found it and put the other items back inside the desk and closed it up. Without locking it back, he slid the key into his pocket and went back to his office. He fixed himself a drink and sat on the sofa. The more he drank, the easier it was for him to hear Marisol's voice. He loved Tabby, but he did miss his Jalapeno Mami.

The night he returned from his business trip all those years ago to find out that Marisol was gone was one he would never forget. At first, Amy told him that she had fired the housekeeper until he began to lay into her. That is the night when he discovered her garden was thriving. And then the truth came out.

"Honey, I have an idea how to make Lush Meadows beautiful again. But first, I have a confession to make."

He remembered her saying those fateful words to him just like it was yesterday.

"I'm listening." He was very short with her. The trip was unsuccessful. No one would loan him any money to fix up the club. He was pissed off and horny and the one person he longed for was not there for him.

"I killed Marisol."

She said it so calmly that he thought she was kidding.

"Stop joshing me and tell me how we're going to get Lush Meadows up and running."

"I'm not kidding. She said some things to me that I did not like. I got angry, pushed her down and snapped. My hands wrapped around her throat and I squeezed the life out of her. I dragged her body to my garden, uprooted my flowers and buried her underneath. She's been dead for almost two weeks."

CRYING MEADOWS

"You did what!" He was livid. "I'm calling the cops. You're fucking crazy!" He grabbed his cell phone and pressed the number nine.

"Call them. If they arrest me for murder you won't get the baby your father insists that you and I must conceive to receive your inheritance, nor will you hear my idea on how to save the club. Either way, you will end up broke. So, what's it gonna be?"

Shamefully, he put the phone down.

"Good choice. I know my idea is going to work. Plus, no wetback is worth my freedom or our happiness, right?"

He said nothing. She was at her computer typing rapidly and taking notes.

"Have you ever heard of a green burial?"

He shook his head.

"Neither had I. Anyway, as a part of the green movement, people are opting to bury their relatives without caskets. Once they put them in the ground, they plant a tree or bush on top the of the body and the decomp fertilizes it. That is why my flowers are so vibrant. Marisol did it. She was finally good for something other than fucking my husband."

"So, what are you proposing?"

"I'm going to start a non-profit to help the homeless. For those who really want help, I will. For those who do not, I'll simply kill them." Amy shrugged her shoulders like what she had just said was normal.

"Are you nuts? What in the hell has gotten into you?"

"No, I am not nuts, I am wealthy and would like to remain that way."

Preston should have stopped her then. He could have but his love of money would not allow him to. Now, if the list of names were people she had killed, he had unwittingly created a monster. In a drunken stupor, Preston made his way outside to the flower garden where this mess had all begun and kneeled on the ground.

"Mari. Mari. I am so sorry. Please forgive me. Marisol!" He shouted to the sky and then the rain came down. As he was wallowing in self-pity, his wife was arriving home.

It had been a long day at the country club and all Amy wanted to do when she walked into the house was eat, shower and crawl into bed. Unfortunately, that would have to wait.

"Madam," Sloan, who is Preston's man servant, began. "Master Meadows is in a bit of a pickle."

"What do you mean?"

What is it now?

"Follow me, Madam."

They walked outside in the pouring rain and there was Preston, lying on the ground by the flower garden.

"Help me get him inside please, Sloan. Come on, babe. Let's get you to bed," she said lovingly.

"Mari, I love you. I am so sorry. Oh, Marisol. You were my air."

Anger consumed her so quickly that she let go of him and he almost fell to the ground. She did not hold the door open for the butler when he got near. Thankfully, he was strong enough to deal with his drunken employer alone. Once he got him upstairs, he changed him into some dry pajamas and put the man to bed.

"Thank you, Sloan. Go get dry clothes on yourself. Goodnight."

Amy looked at her husband in disgust. How dare he call out for another woman while she was trying to help him.

"Bastard."

The next morning, the Spring sun shined through, waking Preston. His head pounded like a drum.

CRYING MEADOWS

"What happened?" He drawled. "I haven't felt like this since college."

"You got drunk last night. You were thinking about Marisol."

Yes. He remembered much of yesterday. Marisol was indeed on his mind.

"Sad to say but the gravity of the whole situation, hit me all at once."

"Really? So much so that you went out to lie down by her grave? Sloan had to carry you in and put you to bed. You were a sodden drunkard."

"That bad, huh? I'll have to thank the old man."

"Thank him? Are you fucking kidding me? That is all you do is thank others and show them appreciation when I am the one who does the most for you. But what do I get? Not a damned thing. I'm sick of this shit and honey, I'm fucking sick of you."

"Oh, here we go with the woe is me bullshit. Face it Ames, you and I are never going to be the type of couple you want us to be. Point blank period!"

"Boy do I know it. I will never have the love I deserve if I am married to a man who will fuck anything with a skirt. Including his own fucking sister. Pervert!"

"Pssh, what are talking about. I have never fucked Jen or Bella. That's ludicrous."

"No, but you did fuck Marisol."

"Mari wasn't my sister you psycho. We were just close like brother and sister because I could confide in her. She understood me."

Amy walked to her closet and came back a couple of minutes later.

"I've waited a long time to give you this. Now is as good a time as any."

She opened the envelope and gave it to Preston and watched in pleasure as he read it.

Son,

If you're reading this letter that means I'm dead and gone. I'm sure you're ecstatic about that. Can't say as I blame you. Regardless of what you think, please know that I loved you and was proud of you. Out of all my boys you've always been the strongest. Guess I shoulda told you that while I was breathing. I was rather hard on you while you were coming up. Kinda felt like I had to be. I saw too much of myself in you. With that being said, I need to tell you about Marisol.

I know you've been sleeping with her and I know she's pregnant. But the fact is, well Son, she's your half-sister.

I know you find that hard to believe but that's why I enclosed the birth certificate as proof. And yes, your mother knows. Why do you think the little girl grew up in Puerto Rico? She lived with her grandmother until she died and then I sent her to boarding school.

Marisol didn't know that I was her father. I made her mother, Guadalupe, keep that a secret. So, she wasn't aware that she was banging her brother any more than you knew that you were banging your sister. Funny how history seems to repeat itself. I knocked up my housekeeper. You knocked up yours. See? Told ya we were just alike. Good luck, Son.

Abbott, Sr.

CRYING MEADOWS

Preston looked up from the letter to see Amy's arm extended with another sheet of paper. It was the birth certificate of Marisol Yesenia Ortega Hernandez. Her parents were listed as Guadalupe Hernandez and Abbott Charles Meadows, Sr. His head began to spin. He did not know if it was because of the hangover or what he had just found out. All these years. No one told him. Not even his parents. His father knew everything. He knew Marisol was pregnant and Preston did not.

"Did you know she was pregnant?" He yelled.

"Of course. Why do you think I killed her?" She said smiling.

Rage filled Preston. At that moment, he wanted to wrap his hands around Amy's throat just like she had Marisol's. He wanted to kill her. But he could not. He had to keep his wits about him. Marisol was gone. But now he had Tabitha and he would be damned if he allowed anything to happen to her. To either of them. Through squinted eyes he looked at her and wondered had she always been this crazy.

"You sound proud that you killed a child."

"No other woman will give my husband a baby."

His beautiful angelic looking wife was the devil. She was going to hell and when she did, he needed to make sure that he did not go with her.

"And if I do get another woman pregnant?" He challenged.

"I'll just kill her, too," she shrugged nonchalantly. "Since you're so proud of the affair you're currently having, I advise you to keep your dick under wraps because I promise that I will find out who this woman is and eliminate her and the bastard she carries if you impregnate her. Got it? I could make great use of them. Trust me. E. B. C."

AVERY GOODE

Those were the letters etched on the ledger in her secret drawer, he recalled. Sickened Preston asked her, "Amy, what does that mean?"

"Every. Body. Counts."

CHAPTER 19
CONNECTING THE DOTS...

HARTSFIELD JACKSON ATLANTA International Airport was the world's busiest airport. Today it showed. Of all the days for Preston to be stuck in traffic in front of the airport, he chose this one.

"What time is it? Are we going to miss our flight?" Tabby asked, hoping that he said yes.

"No. That's why I wanted to get here so early. I've learned to plan for Atlanta traffic no matter where you are."

"I still don't understand why you want us to leave. I can handle myself. Amy does not scare me. You know I'm from the West End."

"Yes, Tabitha I know where you are from, but I have to make sure that you are alright. If anything happened to you, I don't know what I'd do."

She saw the look of concern on his face and placed her hand on top of his, giving it a gentle squeeze.

"Baby, nothing will happen to me. Trust me."

"This isn't a trust issue, Tabby. This is a safety issue. Amy has changed. She's truly off her rocker and capable of anything."

He did not tell her that his wife had already killed one of his lovers and he did not want to chance history repeating itself. Especially not now.

"Come on, let's get going. I want you to eat a decent meal before you fly out."

Making quick work of getting the SUV unloaded, Preston and the skycap placed the luggage on the cart.

"It's only a four-hour flight. I doubt if I get hungry between now and the time we land."

"Tabby?"

She heard the agitation in his voice.

"Okay, okay. I will eat a good meal. I promise."

They walked across the busy cross walk into the airport straight to the Delta counter. The ticket agent checked the bags quickly and gave Tabby her boarding passes.

"All set. Enjoy your flight and thank you for flying Delta."

Knowing that she would have to leave him at the TSA checkpoint, Tabby began to walk slowly. She really did love Preston and did not want to go. Whatever he was dealing with, she wanted to stay and help him. But for some reason, he felt that she was in danger. He was so busy talking about the great sites she would be able to see that he did not realize she was lagging.

"Man, you're going to love it I tell ya'. The house is lovely. Everything you need is already in place. If you need something, you have plenty of cash and your credit cards. Okay?"

He stopped in his tracks and saw that she was a few feet behind him.

"Hey, what's this?" He wiped the tears from her eyes.

"I don't wanna go. Why can't I stay here with you?"

"We've been over this too many times already. It's for your safety."

"But why Canada? It's so far away."

"Not so. It is four and a half hours by plane. I am coming. I give you my word."

"You promise?" She whimpered.

"I promise. Come on, the line is moving."

"Where's Carter?"

Panicked, Tabby looked around for her son. He was nowhere in sight.

"Carter!" Both she and Preston called out.

A police officer saw them looking around frantically and assisted them.

"What's going on?"

"My little boy is missing. He was right here and now he's gone."

"What does he look like and how old is he?" The cop asked.

"He's three years old, fair skin, curly hair…"

"Blue eyes," Preston added.

The officer took the radio off his hip and was about to put out an alert for the missing little boy. Before he could, a young lady came over and asked Tabby what her son looked like.

"I think he's hiding behind that post, Ma'am. It looks like he's playing."

Tabby thanked her and rushed to a thick pillar near the checkpoint. There, Carter had his face against the pillar with his hands covering his eyes. He was playing hide and seek.

"Weddy or not, here I come."

Four small children ran from behind the other pillars and towards Carter.

"Oh my gosh, Carter, you scared me to death. Don't ever walk off from me," she said, picking him up and squeezing him tightly.

"I was playing a game, Mommy."

"Carter Preston Meadows don't ever do that again," Preston rebuked his son. "We could have lost you. Stay with your mommy. Do you hear me?"

"Yes, daddy," the doe-eyed little boy replied.

"I'm sorry Ma'am," a woman began. "He was playing with my kids and I was keeping an eye on them. I thought you saw him. He was safe."

"Thank you so much. I appreciate you watching him."

"No problem. Are you all going to Toronto?"

"Yes, we are."

"So are we. It will be good to get home. My name is Yvonne."

"Tabitha."

They shook hands.

"See, you've already made friends. Now I don't have to worry about you so much."

"Sure, you do. But get out of here and get to work. We will be fine. All of us," she finished, patting her baby bump.

"Take care of my son and my daughter," he said, covering her hand and kissing her.

"I will. I love you."

"I love you too, babe. Give daddy a hug, Carter. I will see ya' soon, okay Champ?"

It was going to be hard for Preston not to see his son every day, but it was for the best. He did not want anything to happen to him or his unborn child. Amy had been on a rampage. She was changing for the worst and he did not want his family caught in the crossfire. There were things that he needed to do. Some wrongs he needed to right. He had already waited five years too long. The time to act was now.

CRYING MEADOWS

Once he got back to his home he checked to see if Amy was around. She told him that she had a few errands to run and was going to be gone a while. None of the house staff were there this weekend either. He grabbed his gloves and put them on. After determining that he was home alone, Preston went to Amy's office and pulled out her old typewriter. Quickly he typed up a letter, folded the paper and stashed it in the bottom drawer of his wife's desk. He put the typewriter back in its place and closed her door. This was the beginning of the end.

❦

"Jasmine, you've lived in this apartment for months and you still haven't unpacked everything?"

"I said the same thing, Terry. It's a darned shame."

"Hush, Bianca. You and Terry can both help if you need something to do other than run your mouths," Jasmine laughed.

Today Jasmine decided to finish putting her house together. Bianca and Terry called at different times but both wanting to come over to just hang out. Angie called and said she was going to come over as well. The more the merrier in Jasmine's opinion.

She reveled in the fact that she had such good friends. This was the life she had always envisioned. By the time Angie arrived, everything was unpacked and put away. Terry had cooked a pot of spaghetti and Bianca was popping the cork off the wine.

"We have got to do this more often," Angie said, raising her glass for a toast. "To good friends and better gossip."

Glasses clinked, and each lady took a sip.

"Girl what is up with your boss?" Terry asked.

"Oh, she's just my boss now, huh?"

202

"Jasmine you know that's your friend," Angie stated.

"You are always singing her praises."

"Not you too, Bianca. Don't let them turn you into a hater."

"I'm not. She is weird though. You don't think so?"

"I've never really paid much attention to her. We hardly see one another."

"How does she act when you're working at her house?"

"She's cool, Ang. When I am in the garden, she's always right there with me, getting her hands dirty and asking questions. She really wants to learn."

"You been over there a few weeks, now huh?"

"Yep. It's cool. The extra money is good. I'm saving to buy a car."

"That's great. Have you seen, Preston? Mama said he moved into the guest bedroom last month and is still there."

"Hmph, I wonder what's up with that?"

"Me too, Angie." Bianca agreed, taking a bite of her food.

"Mama said Preston got a new woman, but she doesn't know who she is. Apparently, he is being discreet with this one. A first for him."

"Miss Ruthie knows a lot that goes on in that house, doesn't she?"

"Too much. She said the other housekeeper quit because Amy was crazy."

"Really? I wonder what Amy did?"

"It had to be something Jas, to make a person want to quit. Nothing comes between me and my money."

"Right, Terry. She could've found a better job though."

"Angie, a person would have to be nuts to quit. That job paid almost twenty dollars an hour and they did not do shit!

CRYING MEADOWS

Why you think Mama been there so long? The salary is ridiculous, and they pay for everything. Mama and Daddy went to Hawaii for three weeks. They did not have to come off one red cent. Amy and Preston paid for it all. First class flight, beach front room at this beautiful resort. Everything."

After dinner they all helped Jasmine clean up and shifted into the living room where the wine continued to flow as freely as the gossip. Bianca complimented the miniature cedar chest that jasmine had placed in the center of the coffee table.

"I can't believe all of the beautiful finds you've gotten from the thrift store. May I look inside?"

"Sure. It's nothing in there but interesting things I've found on the ground. Feather pennies, sticks. I even have a ring I found at the club."

"Ooh, what's this?" Bianca asked, examining the stick that Jasmine found before Christmas last year.

"This stick I found at the club. Neat, huh? I've never seen anything like it."

"Me either. My anthropology group would love to see this. May I take it with me to class tomorrow? I'll bring it back."

"Yeah, sure. I don't mind."

More wine sprinkled with more gossip and laughter was a recipe for a wonderful ladies' night out. Shortly before one in the morning, everyone went home. Sunday came and went in a blur and before she knew it, Jasmine was back at work. Her new life was almost too good to be true. She was happier than she had been in years. Even though she was just there Friday, Jasmine had missed the greenhouse. No sooner than the thought crossed her mind, her office phone rang. It was Bianca.

"Hey, Sis. The anthropology group went crazy over the stick. My professor wants to send it out, so she can trace its origins. Is it okay? They don't have to break it or anything."

"Be my guest. I'm excited myself to find out about it. Let me know what you guys discover."

"Will do. Later."

Jasmine placed an order for a few supplies, tidied her workspace and pruned some Bonsai trees. The little hairs on the back of her neck stood up and she turned around. It was Hannah. She smiled at the woman and waved before going outside to talk to her. A light fog set in.

"Hey beautiful. Where have you been? It's been a minute. How was your New Year?"

Hannah did not answer her question and turned her back. A soft cry began and then got louder. Jasmine recognized the sound. It was the cry in the wind that they used to hear.

"What's wrong?"

This time Hannah answered. "You are in danger my friend."

"Danger? What makes you think that?"

"Stay away from Amy Meadows. Get away from this place. You are not safe."

"Hannah, you're overreacting."

I AM NOT! TAKE HEED!"

"You're scaring me."

"You should be scared. Things are not what they seem. You will have to see. Come."

Reluctantly, Jasmine followed Hannah. The further out they walked, the denser the fog became.

"Five years ago, I was a resident at Impact House. Before that, I lived in Buford, Georgia. I came to Atlanta with a friend of mine for a concert and never went back home. After the concert was over, we went to a party where I was introduced to Crystal Meth. My first high ruined my life. From that day on all I wanted to do was get high."

CRYING MEADOWS

Hannah slowed down walking and lifted the sleeves of her gown. She turned her arms and hands over, palm side up. There were lots of track marks from needles and scabs on her arm that were caused by her picking at her skin. Jasmine stared at arms and then looked up.

She let out a blood curdling scream and turned to run away but when she did, Hannah appeared in front of her.

"Don't run away. I need your help."

"Wh-wha-what happened to your face?"

She was referring to the scars on Hannah's face that matched the ones on her arms.

"This is what the drugs did to me. I thought that something was crawling on me, so I picked my skin until I bled. One day I convinced my friend who gave me the meth to take me to my home in Buford. I still had the key. My husband had not changed the locks. I went inside, let the garage up so she could pull inside and together we took everything of value that would fit inside the car. Before we left the area, I drove by my son's school while he was on recess. He had really grown.

I missed him so much. We sold the stuff and got enough to stay high for a week. When I came down off my high, I wanted to kill myself. I met Nell at Impact House and decided to accept her offer of help to get me clean. I was doing so well. My husband and son came to see me. They wanted me as much as I wanted them. That is when I met Amy Meadows. She came to a meeting we had and told us all the benefits of coming to Meadows Mission."

"You were at Meadows Mission?" Jasmine barely recognized her own voice when she spoke.

"No. The place Amy took me, and a few others wasn't the shelter that you stayed at. She took us to a beautiful house, telling us that she was waiting on our apartments to get ready at the high rise. None of us made it out of that house alive."

Jasmine's head snapped. "What are you saying?" She heard wrong. Right?

"Amy convinced us to eat a meal she'd prepared. It contained Datura Stramonium."

"Angels Trumpet? The plant? But that is the plant used to make scopolamine. That's dangerous."

Hannah knew that Jasmine would make the correlation.

"It's more than that. It's deadly."

"The paramedics revived you when they arrived?"

"No."

"I don't understand. You survived. Did someone help you?"

"No one helped me. I died."

So that means you're a, a gh-?"

"Yes."

Again, Jasmine tried to bolt but Hannah was right in front of her.

"STOP! I told you I need your help."

Jasmine closed her eyes and began to pray.

"Lord please help me. I'm scared and want you to come save me."

"Follow me. NOW!"

A terrified Jasmine did as she was told. They were headed in the area where Hannah always disappeared. An opening appeared and for the first time, Jasmine saw the cluster of Angels Trumpets hanging from their stems.

She was not sure why she had never paid attention to it before. This beautiful flower was known as 'The Devil's Breath' and was the deadliest plant on Earth. She looked over at Hannah, whose face was once again pretty and smooth.

CRYING MEADOWS

"I think I'm going crazy. Did I do too many drugs? This can't be real."

Shaking her head, she willed her mind to get rid of the illusions in front of her. But every time she opened her eyes, Hannah was still there.

"My time is up. Amy must be stopped. Get the ledger. Help my family find me so I can be at peace." Hannah began to walk away.

"What ledger. Wait. You can't just walk away."

Jasmine followed Hannah around the bend and saw her stop by a large tree in the meadow. She turned around to face Jasmine, waving goodbye. The gardener watched in fascinated horror as Hannah sat on the ground and lay back on the Earth. Her body disappeared into the ground.

This time when Jasmine took off running, no one was there to stop her. Back at the greenhouse she hurriedly gathered her belongings, called Yuki to tell her she was ill and going home for the day and got out of there.

Once she got into her apartment, she locked the doors, closed the blinds, and went to her bedroom. Fear enveloped her. Not fear of a ghost but fear that she was going crazy and losing her mind. She would never be able to face Blayke again. The love that she thought she had found would now be lost to her because no one wanted to date a psycho.

Hot tears wet her pillow as she cried until she dozed off. She tossed and turned throughout the night, dreaming of Hannah. Waking up after a fitful sleep to a growling stomach. But no matter how hungry she was, Jasmine had to face a harsh reality. She was too scared to leave her room.

CHAPTER 20
FAMILY, FRIENDS, FOES...

DORA LEE MEADOWS HAD HAD a change of heart. As she sat basking in the sun of her Grecian villa, all she could think about was her baby boy, Preston. He had called her the other day and divulged some very interesting things. One of them being that he was no longer happy in his marriage.

"Mother, I know that I've screwed up in my marriage, but I am really trying to make things work with her. She's making it so hard."

"We women are emotional creatures dear, so you must understand that when we are hurt, we will try to make you feel as we do."

"Yes, I took psychology in school. Hurting people, hurt people."

"Indeed, dear. Unfortunately for you, not only did you step outside the confines of your marriage once, but you did multiple times. That can make a woman question her value to her husband and her self-worth. And to make matters worse, you produced a baby."

"I know I hurt her, but Mother you've met Carter. Is he not the most amazing little boy?"

"Oh, yes. Even with his coloring you can see the strong Meadow's genes in him. And those big locks of curls. How adorable. But think about how Amy would feel if she knew of your son with another woman. That would kill her."

CRYING MEADOWS

"That's just it Mother. I found a few empty packs of birth control in the bathroom trash at home. It appears that my lovely wife has been intentionally trying not to get pregnant, even though she knows that my inheritance is contingent upon us having a family. I'm at my wits end." The lie rolled off his tongue easily.

"Oh my. I can see how that can pose a problem. You are at an impasse."

"You can say that again. And Mother may I confide something else in you?"

"Of course, Son. Anything."

"I am deeply in love with Tabitha. It matters not that she is black. She has a warm heart and makes me feel one hundred feet tall. With her, I feel invincible."

"I've had the pleasure of speaking with her. She is a beautiful woman, and she has childbearing hips. Even though she is not on our level financially, she is extremely bright and socially adept. You could do a lot worse. I am quite fond of her and I love the way she interacts with your sister's children. The family likes her."

"That pleases me. Especially since she is with child again. I'm praying for a girl."

"Preston Scott Meadows, I'm going to need you to get a few of those rubber thingies I hear the young people talking about."

"Yes, Ma'am," he had agreed. "Mom, how did you deal with Dad's cheating?"

"I didn't, Dear. During the era that I was raised, women were told to turn a blind eye to that sort of thing. After all, it was in a man's nature to cheat. My father had several mistresses, and my mother knew about them all. But we were always taken care of and my father treated my mother like a queen when he was with us. Not once did he miss a recital or holiday. His family came first."

"Were you hurt that Father got Guadalupe pregnant?"

"At first I was angrier than anything. Then one day, I stopped caring about what and who your father did, and I began to enjoy my life."

"Are you saying you started having affairs also Mom?"

"I'm saying, I started enjoying my life, Son."

Preston chuckled. "I understand that. But why did you keep Guadalupe on, knowing she was sleeping with your husband?"

"Like I said, I stopped caring. I loved your father, but I began to love me a bit more. I retained her services because she was important to your father. If he was busy, then he wouldn't have time to bother me."

"Mom, I have underestimated you all these years. You're a sly foxy woman."

"And don't you ever forget it either. I love you, Son."

"Love you too, Mom."

For the past few days, that conversation replayed in her mind. She did not want Preston to marry Amy in the first place. The Blessingales, while they were an extremely wealthy family, were a strange lot. Cora Lee wanted all her children to marry for love.

Preston said that he loved his wife, but a mother knows her child. He only married his wife out of duty and obligation; to make his father proud. Abbott, Sr., had pushed the union so he could forge a business deal with Amy's father, George.

"Now look what you've done, Abbott. Made a mess that you're not here to clean up," Cora Lee thought inwardly.

Since Preston did such a fine job re-establishing the club and had indeed produced an heir, with or without his wife,

CRYING MEADOWS

Cora Lee decided she was going to give him his inheritance when she got back to Georgia. But since that was not for another week, she put that in the back of her mind and enjoyed her massage.

"My darling Bill, you do have a way with your hands…and tongue."

✦✦✦

Preston should have taken up drama in school. When he had called his mother the other day, he had given a stellar, Oscar winning performance. Hopefully, he was able to convince her that the reason he would not be able to have a child with Amy is because she was trying to prevent it without telling him. The whole 'woe-is-me' act used to work wonders when he was living at home. By the time she got back stateside, he would know if he still had the Midas touch.

There were a few things that he had done to ensure that his interests were protected should things not end well with him and Amy. He picked up his phone and called his father's attorney to see if all the paperwork was in order.

"Thank you for calling Corley, Penter and Draper. How may I direct your call?"

"Bill Corley's office."

"I do apologize but Mr. Corley is in New York at a conference. Is there anything his assistant can help you with? He left her in charge?"

"No. I'll call him on his cell. Thanks."

Before she had a chance to reply he hung up the phone. Bill could not have chosen the worst time to go out of town. Preston needed him. Now! Shaking his head, he leaned back in the desk chair at the hotel and enjoyed the blow job that the front desk agent was giving him. A few more things were on

212

his list that needed to be crossed off, but they would have to wait.

❧❧

The Dean of Students walked into the Anthropology class and whispered into the substitute teachers' ear and handed him a card before stepping back out into the hallway.

"Bianca, may I see you for a moment?"

"Sure, Professor Ames, what's up?"

"Um, you have some visitor's in the hallway," he said, handing her the card.

"A detective? For what?"

"Not sure."

There were four detectives in Navy blue suits, waiting in the hallway.

"Miss Ladd, we have some questions for you. Can you come with us?"

One reached out and grabbed her elbow to escort her. She pulled away.

"Wait. What's this about?" She queried.

"We just need to ask you a few questions down at the station."

"Uh-uh, let me call my brother first. He used to be a cop, too and I need him to meet me there."

"That's fine. We just need to ask you some questions. You are not in any trouble. I assure you."

Bianca gave him a skeptical look but followed peacefully. The drive only took fifteen minutes but by the time she got there, Blayke was already there.

CRYING MEADOWS

"What's going on, Dan?" Blayke said to his buddy Dan, who was one of the detectives escorting Bianca. We just have a few questions for her and the teacher."

"About what? My sister's never so much as gotten a parking ticket and you guys haul her into the station for questioning. Come on man. What gives?"

The detective opened a door and escorted, Bianca and Blayke inside.

"We asked you all to come down because we had questions about this."

He held up an evidence bag and Blayke gasped.

"Where in the hell did that come from?" Blayke asked standing up.

"Hey, that's my stick. How did you all get it? I gave it to Professor Lenox before she went out on maternity leave to trace its origins."

"Damn it. I see why you all called her down here."

"Yeah, Blayke. It was important to find out where it came from," Dan replied.

"What do you mean you see why they called me down here, Blayke and what's important?" She asked, her head twisting back and forth between the two men.

"What's the word?"

"That's what we're trying to figure out now."

"Will you two quit talking over me like I'm not here? You called me down here to question me about my stick and then don't question me. What kind of mess is that?"

"That's just it, B. This isn't a stick," Blayke answered pointing to the bag on the table.

"What is it then?" At this point she was beyond frustrated.

The detective cleared his throat. "According to our forensic anthropologist, Dr. Black, it is a proximal phalanx. She's never wrong."

Bianca gulped loudly. "A bone?"

"Yes," the detective nodded. "Where did you get this from?"

She looked hesitant because she did not want to incriminate Jasmine. Blayke saw the look on her face and went to sit next to her.

"It's okay, Sis. You can tell us where you got it."

"Um, I got it from Jasmine."

Blayke stood up so fast his chair tipped over.

"What!"

"Who is Jasmine?" The detective pumped.

She pointed to Blayke. "His girlfriend."

"Are you serious? What the-? How did-? Fuck!" Blayke sputtered.

"Calm down, Blayke and take a seat. What can you tell us about this Jasmine?"

"She is not a murderer. I can tell you that much."

"I'm not saying your girlfriend is. Just trying to make sense of things."

"I know she's not a murderer also, because when she showed it to me, she told me it was a stick, too. I've never seen a bone before in real life and this one doesn't look like any of the ones in class."

"That is because whoever killed this person, sawed him or her and the blade shaved the bone. Doctor Black ran tests and she concluded that the bones were human. Specimens were submitted to the crime lab and the FBI for identification. Unfortunately, they have more pressing cases to deal with in the lab, so it may take a couple of weeks to get our results back. In the meantime, we are trying to put what pieces of the puzzle together that we can."

"All you have to do is call Jasmine and she'll tell you the same thing that she told me. She found the stick; I mean the bone at work."

"When was the last time you spoke to her?" Questioned the detective.

"I don't know. A couple of day's maybe."

"You don't talk to your girlfriend every day?"

"No, Dan. We give one another space. But...we have never gone this long without talking. I've just been preoccupied at work." Blayke faltered.

"I called her Friday to see if she wanted to go out, but she never called me back. She hasn't responded to any of my texts either."

Things were beginning to look suspect for Jasmine.

"Well, I won't have her come down for questioning just yet. I'll wait until we get the identification back and then proceed from that point."

"Thanks, Dan. We'll be in touch." Blayke shook his hand and he and Bianca left the station.

"Has it really been five days since you've last spoken with Jas?"

"Yeah, Sis. It has."

"What did you do to her?"

"Nothing. I visited her Thursday night and things were fine when I left. Plus, I've got a lot going on at the shelter and she's working two jobs now."

"So, let me get this straight. You have not talked to her in almost a week and haven't been concerned enough to go by and check on her? Hmm, what's wrong with this picture?"

"I'll go check on her."

"Cool, let's go," his sister said.

"*After* I drop you off."

"Hmph," Bianca pouted, crossing her arms.

The siblings made small talk on the way to Bianca's home. Blayke dropped her off but before pulling out of the parking lot he tried calling Jasmine again. Her voice mail came on.

"Hey Babe, it's me. I have left you over a dozen messages since Friday. You have me and B worried. I'm on my way over. See ya' soon."

Driving as fast as he could without breaking any laws, Blayke headed to Jasmine's. From the parking lot, he could see her apartment and things looked fine. The sun was beginning to set, and it was getting cooler, so he grabbed his jacket out of the backseat before going up. When he pulled the jacket off the seat, he knocked some files into the floor.

"This is the reason I've been so preoccupied, Jas."

The files contained the names and information of each person Blayke or a member of Off the Street Shelter had referred to the Meadows Mission Transitional Housing and Employment Program. It was only ten files in the back seat but there was a box of over one hundred files in the trunk.

For the past few nights, he had spent time combing over the files, looking for anything that would help him locate the people he once served. He did not want to call their next of kin just yet to see if they had heard from their family member because he did not want to set off any alarms.

All the people who went into the program were supposedly offered jobs at the club or elsewhere in the community, but he could only account for half of them. Something nefarious was going on at Lush Meadows and he was determined to get to the bottom of things. The finger that Jasmine found was a great indication of such misdeeds.

CRYING MEADOWS

While he was sure she was not involved in any type of foul play, he needed to question her about the bone before the Atlanta police did. Even though some of them were his buddies, they would lay into Jasmine if they suspected she had anything to do with a murder.

He walked briskly up the stairs and knocked on her door once in front of it. She did not answer He knocked again, only harder this time. Inside, Jasmine was jarred awake by the loud banging. She was not going to get up. Whoever it was would get the point and go away. Burying her head under the cover, she grabbed the pillow to keep the noise out. The person at the door was persistent. And then suddenly, the knocking stopped.

"Thank God," she said out loud.

"What are you thanking God for?" Blayke asked.

"Blayke, what are you doing here?" She jumped up with a start.

"Checking on you. Why haven't you been answering your phone or returning any of my calls? Didn't you get any of my messages?"

"No. My phone is in the living room."

"Look at you. You look a mess."

"Thanks. You can leave now."

"Leave? What have I done?"

"Nothing. It's not you. It's me."

"Oh, it's like that? I've heard that before," he stood to leave.

"Stop! I did not mean it like that. But it is me. I am going crazy, Blayke. I need mental help or something."

He sat next to her on the bed. "You are one of the sanest people I know. What makes you think you need help?"

"Because I have been talking to a ghost."

Blayke let out a loud laugh and doubled over in amusement. "You're kidding me, right?"

"I'm not, but now you can leave. I already feel bad enough. No one needs you coming in here making them feel worse."

"Forgive me," he sobered. "Tell me what is going on."

Reluctantly, Jasmine started from the beginning, telling him about Hannah Whitlock. She did not leave anything out.

"She told you she was at Impact House? That's Nell Peterson's organization."

"I know. She told me. Do not look at me like that. I know this all seems farfetched but I'm telling the truth."

"I'm not looking at you like this because I think you're crazy. I'm looking at you like this because I believe you. You know that stick that you gave Bianca for class?"

"Yeah. She wanted to trace its origins or something. What about it?"

"It wasn't a stick. Turns out it is a bone."

"For real? Human?"

"Very much so."

Blayke pulled the phone out of his back pocket and scrolled through his contacts. When he found who he was looking for he hit select and called the number.

"Hey gorgeous, this is Blayke Ladd. How are you?"

"I'm well, Sir. How's it hanging?"

"Long and strong as usual."

Who in the hell was he talking to? Jasmine thought as she began to regain her wits. She stared curiously at Blayke and her neck shifted into a craned position. Blayke laughed when he saw the look.

CRYING MEADOWS

"Listen Nell, I'm sorry to bother you and your wife so late but I need a huge favor." He stressed the word wife to let Jasmine know that Nell had a domestic partner. She relaxed in understanding.

"Shoot," the woman on the phone replied.

"Is there any way that you can look at your records to see if you've had a client by the name of Hannah Whitlock at Impact House within the last few years? Maybe about five years ago?"

"No need. I remember Hannah well. She was a sweet lady. Came down from her suburban home in Buford, hooked up with the wrong crowd through a friend of hers, got hooked on drugs and never went back home."

Nell had basically just repeated everything that Jasmine told him less than ten minutes ago.

"Did you refer her to Meadow's Mission?"

"Yes. She was doing well for a while, too. Then one day, Amy Meadows contacted me, asking me if I had heard from her. Guess she fell off the wagon and left. No one's seen or heard from her since. Not even her husband. I got wind that he was out looking for her. Damned shame. Drugs are the devil man."

"You can say that again. Hey, thanks so much for the information. I may need to call you again if that's okay."

"Sure thing. Take care."

The screen on his phone went black after the call disconnected.

"What did she say?" Jasmine asked, scooting to the edge of the bed.

"She just confirmed everything you just told me. And I know you two didn't sit and plan this story together."

"So, what are we going to do?"

"*We* aren't going to do anything" he said pointing back and forth between them. "*I'm* going to see if a few of my old comrades are down to help me do a little hunting."

"But Hannah asked me to help her."

"And you have, Babe. The fact that you were courageous enough to tell me this story, not knowing how I was going to react, says a lot. You have done enough. Let me take it from here okay?"

He kissed her on top of her head and held her in his arms before placing another call.

"Dan, its Blayke. Is Detective Gunner still with the precinct? Great. I need your help. Can you pick him up and meet me at Off the Street in about an hour? Thanks. See ya' soon. Unbelievable," he breathed.

"What?"

"I think we are about to open Pandora's Box."

CHAPTER 21
BRAVE, STUPID, OR BOTH...

BEFORE BLAYKE LEFT HE REASSURED Jasmine that he was here for her. As hard as it was to tell him the truth about Hannah, she was glad she had. Now maybe, they would be able to figure out what was going on at Lush Meadows and with Meadows Mission. However, if he thought that she was going to sit idly by and do nothing, he had another thing coming. All fear set aside, Jasmine got up and showered. While talking to him, she formulated a plan.

"Hello, Amy. This is Jasmine. I'm feeling a lot better and was wondering if I can come by Meadows Manor and plant the azaleas?"

"Hey, Jasmine. That would be wonderful. I am very happy that you're feeling better. We were worried about you."

"Awe, how sweet of you all," she said, frowning at the phone. "I'll see you soon."

She hung up the phone. Hannah told her something about a ledger and she was determined to find it. Although she did not know Amy that well, she did know that most of Meadows Mission's records were kept at home in her office. Blayke told her that a few weeks ago after he met with Preston about the people who were supposed to be working at Lush Meadows. The time for being scared was over. Jasmine had work to do.

A half hour later, she walked up to the gate at Meadows Manor where she was met by the security guard in the booth.

"Good afternoon, Miss Jasmine. How are you today?"

"I'm doing well, Henry. Came to do a little work today."

Smiling, he said, "my wife wanted to thank you for the Ivy that you helped restore. She said it's the talk of the neighborhood now."

"Tell her it was my pleasure. I'll see you soon, okay?"

"Yes, Ma'am," he replied buzzing open the walk-in gate.

She walked up the long winding driveway towards the main house. It was breathtaking.

If I had a house half this big, I would be satisfied.

Butterflies fluttered around in her stomach. Her nerves were beginning to get the best of her. But she could not back down now. Too much was at stake. Before ringing the doorbell, she took a deep breath and exhaled. A moment later, Miss Ruthie opened the door.

"Well hello stranger," she said. "Long time no see."

"Hey, Miss Ruthie. I've been a bit under the weather but I'm better now."

"So glad to hear it, sweetie. I'll let Mrs. Meadows know you're here."

"Thank you."

The cook came back a few moments later holding her coat and purse.

"I'd love to stay and talk but this is our weekend off. Me and Hamilton got a date. I'm the last one to leave."

"Alrighty then. You guys have fun and don't do anything I wouldn't do."

"Honey chil' I plan on doing that plus a whole lot more."

They said their good-byes and Jasmine waited in the foyer for Amy to receive her.

CRYING MEADOWS

"Right on time," Amy observed. "Let's get started, shall we?"

Jasmine looked at the black and cream blouse, the off-white silk pants, and black Gucci flats that Amy wore. Definitely not gardening attire. Not that she ever got that dirty anyway. While there have been times that Amy got down in the trenches to dig, that was not often.

They had set aside a day for digging only and once all the holes were dug, all Jasmine had to do was plant the bulbs. Today, that's what she'd be doing. As usual, Amy stood watch over Jasmine as she tended her garden. Initially, she told Jasmine that she was there to watch and learn but after the exchange she had had with Hannah, Jasmine felt that it was something more to it than that.

I don't know how I'm supposed to look around the house with her watching me like a hawk.

"Did the doctor say what was wrong with you Jasmine?"

It sounded like there was genuine concern in her voice. For a moment, Jasmine felt bad for not believing in the woman who had given her a new lease on life. How could she take the word of an apparition over a live, fleshly person? If nothing else, she would just look around and see if this so-called ledger even existed. What harm could that do? If it did not exist, then she would just go about her business.

The worst that could happen is that Hannah would come back and haunt me.

The thought of that made her laugh nervously. But if it did exist, depending on what was in it, she'd take it to authorities and maybe they could help solve the murder of Hannah Whitlock, if in fact there was one.

"Did you hear me, Jasmine? I asked what the doctor said regarding your illness."

224

"I'm so sorry. I was in my own little world. He said it was just a small bug. He is not sure where it came from but a few of his patients had the same symptoms as I did. I took some medicine, drank plenty of fluids and got some rest just like he said. Now I'm as good as new."

"Very good. We really missed you at the club." Amy's cell phone rang. "Pardon me dear, I must take this call."

Her boss stepped away, but Jasmine was straining to hear the conversation. It was someone named Sturgis.

What kind of name is that?

Whoever it was put a huge smile on Amy's face. When the call ended Amy walked over to Jasmine and gave her some great news.

"I hate to leave you here alone, but I really must jet. I have a meeting to go to. I should return around six-ish. Will you be okay?"

"I'll be fine. If I finish before you get back what should I do?"

"Just tell Henry and he'll come secure the house."

"Thank you."

Excited, Jasmine stood up and pretended to stretch as she watched her boss get in the car and drive away. Only when she saw the car turn the corner did she make her way into the house. To ensure that she was home alone, she called out.

"Hello? Is anyone in here?" Silence.

Immediately, she went to Amy's office and began looking around.

"Damn, this office is almost bigger than my entire apartment. Where do I begin?"

The desk was the obvious choice. It was massive executive desk that had seven drawers on it. The bottom right drawer was slightly ajar, so she started in that one first. Taking her time, she went through each sheet of paper, scanning it to make sure it was not something that pertained to Meadows Mission or anything that Hannah told her about at the golf and country club. There was nothing in that drawer but bills for the house.

Contents in the middle drawer made her believe she was getting warmer. There were a few invoices for food and new linen for the shelter at Meadows Mission. Jasmine was happy that she was able to go directly into the transitional housing and job program. It did not make sense to her if she would have had to be in the shelter for any given time. Going from shelter to shelter was not an ideal situation.

Just as she was about review some papers, she heard the entrance alarm beep as the front door was opened. Hurriedly, she put the documents back where she found them and went to sit down on the opposite side of the room. Cell phone in hand, she pretended to talk to a supplier.

"No, Sir. We are planting azaleas right now. Yes. Okay." She ended the fake phone call.

"Don't mind me chil', I forgot to leave the receipts for Ms. Amy for the food bill. Glad that I was only a few blocks away 'because had I gotten any further; she'd be getting this Monday morning."

"I understand Miss Ruthie. I was on the phone with a nursery regarding the flowers."

"You sure are doing a great job on that garden. It hasn't looked that good in almost five years."

"Thank you. I love plants and flowers."

"You're welcome and it shows. Do not work too hard. Goodbye." And with that, Miss Ruthie was gone again.

"Phew," she exhaled in relief. "That was close."

She returned to the stack of papers, finding a few more receipts for purchases made for the shelter. Still there was nothing suspicious about any of them. If anything, it further proved that Amy and her team cared for the homeless people they helped. Searching the next few drawers yielded the same results, a few receipts, and blank copies of intake forms.

This was taking a lot longer than Jasmine anticipated. Time was ticking fast. She had already been searching for almost an hour and had not found anything of significant importance yet. The last and final drawer had more papers in it, and she began flipping through them. Her cell phone buzzed in her back pocket, startling her and she knocked a cup of pencils off the desk. Some fell inside the drawer.

Instead of the pencils lying in place, they began rolling downwards towards the back of the drawer.

"What's this about?" She asked, following the pencil's path until they stopped. There was a piece of material sticking out from the wood and she pulled it, revealing the hidden compartment. She reached inside.

"Well, I'll be a monkey's uncle. Look what we have here."

It was the ledger. Just like Hannah said. Hands trembling, she opened it up and started going through it. There were so many names in there that she recognized. People who had been residents at Off the Street when she first came. Other than names and dates though, there was no incriminating evidence.

"There has to be something more to this than meets the eye."

Engrossed in the book, Jasmine decided to find out what that was.

⊙⊙⊙⊙

"Sturgis. How great to see you. I trust that you have something for me?" She said, rubbing her palms today and licking her lips.

CRYING MEADOWS

"Indeed, I do. Albeit maybe not what you are expecting."

"What do you mean?"

"God spoke to me and told me that my work here is done. I'm needed elsewhere."

"Excuse me?"

"My journey to serve others and minister the good news of God's love must continue."

"You're leaving? And what about Restful Blessings?"

"Yes, I am leaving, and I've sold the business to Truitt for a fair price. Also, the chamber has been sealed and is no more."

"But you can't do that. I need you and I especially need the chamber."

"I am at liberty to do as I please and you don't need me. Seek God."

"Why are you doing this?"

"The Word says 'thou shalt not kill' yet you murdered Charlie Turner. I was going to send him home, alive, to be with his family. God had redeemed him."

"Whatever. He's more valuable as compost than he ever was as a worthless, good for nothing, drunkard."

"You have made idols of your money and your husband. God is not pleased with you. Woe to you, dear cousin. His wrath is sure to come."

"That's absurd. Complete and utter bullshit and you know it." Amy had not been this angry in a while. If Sturgis left, she would be forced to return to her old ways of doing things.

"Put away from thee a wayward mouth, and perverse lips put far from thee."

"Would you stop quoting Scripture to me already? I know what the Bible says better than anyone. Charlie was worthless, and I did what was necessary."

"Know ye not that the unrighteous shall not inherit the kingdom of God? You disobey God and refuse to repent. Your mind has become reprobate. It is time that I separate myself from you."

"Cousin, we are in this together. We're a team."

"What fellowship does light have with darkness?"

"I'm a good person and you know it."

"Be not deceived: evil communications doth corrupt good manners. Should I stay, it is highly likely that I will become as evil as you. May the Lord God of our fathers shine His light on you."

"Where are you going next, Sturgis?"

"Oklahoma."

Like a little child, Amy stomped around the room and threw a tantrum after he left. There was no changing his mind. He was done. Everything that she worked so hard for could be destroyed without the help of her cousin.

Sturgis was as vital to the growth and maintenance of Lush Meadows as the people were. Without the special fertilizer the putting green would be just like anyone else's; average. Feeling defeated, Amy got in the car and put the pedal to the metal on her way home. She needed to come up with another plan.

As she pulled up at the gated entrance of her house, Henry stopped her.

"Mrs. Amy, this gentleman here says that he was supposed pick up your car for servicing. Is that today?"

Amy looked at the technician from the Mercedes-Benz dealership.

"Yes. It totally slipped my mind."

"We can reschedule if now's not a good time," the technician said.

CRYING MEADOWS

"No, that's okay. Just let me grab my briefcase and you can take the car. Henry will you give me a ride in your golf cart please."

"Yes, Ma'am."

She put her belongings on the back seat and sat in the passenger seat. The cart's motor was quiet and allowed her to be alone with her thoughts. Henry was talking a mile a minute, but Amy had no clue what he said because she tuned him out. As they approached the main house, Amy saw the curtain in her office move ever so slightly. All the staff were gone for the weekend. There was only one person at her home.

"Henry, will you drive me around the house? I'm going to meet Jasmine in the kitchen," she lied.

"Yes, Ma'am."

On the way around back, they passed the garden. Sure enough, her gardener was nowhere to be found.

"Thanks, Henry. I really appreciate the ride."

"My pleasure, Mrs. Amy. Have a good evening," he finished, tipping his hat to her.

"Some colored folks are really sweet and kind", she said softly as he drove away.

"Now let's see what Nosey Nancy is doing in my office."

Gently, Amy opened the back-sliding door in the sunroom just enough to slither through it. If she did not open it too much it wouldn't beep and alert Jasmine that someone was in the house. Whatever she was doing in the office, Amy wanted to catch her in the act. Not sure what she was going to encounter once in her office, Amy stopped and opened the safe in the kitchen. There she retrieved her monogrammed, Tiffany Blue Titanium Pearl Glock Seventeen. It bore her initials A.J.B. for Amy Jo Blessingale.

The gun was a gift from her grandmother who was a true pistol packing mama. She taught all her grandchildren how to shoot, boy or girl, and now they were all exceptional marksmen. Inside, Amy prayed that Jasmine was nowhere near her office and it was the heat causing the curtain to move. The last thing she wanted to do was shoot the one person who was unknowingly helping her hide her deepest, darkest secrets.

CHAPTER 22
POINTING THE FINGER...

DETECTIVE DAN SANTIAGO SAT WITH his eyes protruding and mouth wide open. He was speechless. Blayke had filled him in on what he thought was going on at Meadows Mission in conjunction with Lush Meadows. It was mind boggling to say the least. Even though he had been off the force for a few years, Dan knew Blayke to be a solid cop. As crazy as it all sounded, the summation of all the small pieces of evidence made sense.

"Dan, you're the only one I know who wouldn't think that I was on drugs."

"Hey, this whole thing is bananas. At this point I'm probably high too 'because I believe ya' man."

"Now you see why I asked you to grab Gunner. We need him right about now."

"You got that right. Let's head that way. I'll call the assistant district attorney and see if she will get a warrant from Judge Bayless. That old coot is probably up cavorting with his young wife."

"How is she?"

"Who?" The detective snickered.

"Your wife, jackass. Assistant District Attorney Tracy Santiago."

"She's good. Did I tell you, I knocked her up?"

"Congratulations you lucky bastard!" Blayke said, slapping his friend on his back.

"Thanks. You ready?"

"Yeah. Why does this shit give me the willies though?"

"Same reason it does me. Grab Gunner and let's hit it."

Blayke, Dan and Detective Gunner headed over to Lush Meadows. En route to the country club, Dan called his wife and gave her the briefest summary of what was going on the reason he needed a search warrant.

"The Meadows carry a lot of weight in Georgia. Tread lightly," she warned.

Both men were deep in thought as they drove up Piedmont Road. The traffic was heavy for it to be a Saturday evening. As Dan drove, Blayke decided to call Jasmine. He wanted to give her an update on what was going on. The voice mail picked up when he called. He did not leave a message.

The club was crawling with high society guests when they arrived. Valet parking was backed up. People got out of their cars in their fancy attire and headed inside. Blayke and Dan pulled into the circular driveway and parked.

"Excuse me, Sir but you can't pa-", a valet attendant began but stopped when Dan flashed his badge.

"I'm here on official business. Is Preston or Amy Meadows available?"

"Mrs. Meadows already left for the day and I haven't seen Mr. Meadows in a few days. The manager on duty may be able to help you. You'll find her inside."

Walking inside, Dan said, "I wonder what's going on tonight."

"Casey and Beau are getting married."

"How do you know?" Dan turned his head towards Blayke.

CRYING MEADOWS

"It says so over there," he said pointing to the large banner near the ballroom.

The manager on duty was a short, round woman with wiry looking hair and horn-rimmed glasses. She reminded Dan of the gym teacher from the Porky's movie.

Flashing his badge, he said, "Are you the manager on duty?"

"Yes. I'm Mrs. Roundtree."

"Shut up, Blayke," Dan smiled, knowing his friend was going to say something facetious about the woman's name and how it correlates with her body shape.

"How may I help you?" She looked back and forth between two men.

"I'm here on some official business. Can you please point me towards your maze and rose gardens?"

She hesitated. Blayke stepped in. "Mrs. Roundtree, we'll be in and out of your hair without you knowing we were here," he attempted to assure her.

"Well, okay. We have a wedding about to start and I need this day to be perfect for the bride."

"Don't worry. This will be a day that she'll never forget."

Mrs. Roundtree had one of the kitchen staff members escort the gentlemen to the rose garden.

"So how do you like working at Crying Meadows," Blayke questioned.

"You know about this place, too? I thought it was an urban legend when I first started working here."

"My girlfriend did, too."

Jasmine. She was on his mind and he could not shake it. Since they arrived at the golf and country club, he had tried calling her again twice. Still no answer.

"She works here?"

"Yes, she does. She is the pretty little number who's the landscape designer. Her name is Jasmine," Dan volunteered.

"Oh, you mean Shorty with the fat ass?"

Blayke gave him a stern look.

"Sorry, man. I forgot," the young man repented.

"Obviously."

"Here you all go. The gardens are to the right of the gazebo."

"Thanks. We got it from here," Blayke told him.

As soon as they stepped out on the grass, Detective Gunner began to fidget.

"What's going on Gunner?"

"I think he's on to something, Blayke."

"Already?"

"Yeah."

The further out they walked, the antsier he got. Gunner was a well-trained cadaver dog who almost never got it wrong. His accuracy rate was well above ninety-five percent. Once he got near the first hedge, he alerted Blayke and Detective Dan.

"You think he found something?"

The dog started scratching at the ground.

"If he says he found something. Trust that he did."

Dan pulled the dog further into the maze and Gunner kept scratching at different spots.

"I think we're gonna need more dogs." Observed Blayke.

"And cops."

"Dammit. I broke my word."

"To whom?"

"Mrs. Roundtree. I told her that this would be a day that Casey would never forget."

CRYING MEADOWS

"You didn't lie."

An hour later, Preston's phone was ringing off the hook.

"Is that your line beeping, babe?" Tabby asked.

"Yes, but it can wait. It's just the club."

"What if it's important?"

"On a Saturday night? It's not. The Schumer-Lambert wedding is going on tonight. They can survive without me for one day. I'm face timing the most beautiful girl in the world and her cute son."

Skeptical, Tabby did not say anything. But when his other phone began to ring, she spoke up.

"Now look Dammit, are you going to talk to me and Carter or what? Turn that damned thing off," she demanded.

"It's the club again. Mrs. Roundtree. She just paged me nine-one-one."

"Call her, Babe. See what she wants so you can talk to your son before he has to go to bed."

"Hold on." Preston dialed the number to the club. Before he even got his 'hello' out, Mrs. Roundtree yelled into the phone.

"Mr. Meadows, please get to the club now! The place is crawling with cops. And dogs. Big dogs!"

"What! Why? Where's Mrs. Meadows?"

"I don't know, Sir. We cannot get reach her. But they have a warrant and everything. Sir, they shut down the Schumer-Lambert affair. Mr. and Mrs. Lambert are having the hardest time consoling their daughter. Please hurry, Sir," she pleaded.

"I'm on my way. Babe, I've got to go."

"What's going on?"

"Something at the club. Cops are there."

"Oh, Lord. Be careful, Preston."

"I will."

Twenty minutes later, Preston pulled up in front of Lush Meadows. Oddly, there were no valet drivers out front. He cut the ignition on his sports car and went inside. All the guests, including the bride and groom were seated in the formal dining room along with the staff. There were several cops keeping watch over them as detectives questioned them.

Embarrassed, Preston walked into the room with his chest stuck out. He was not going to let them see him sweat.

"Who's in charge here?" He demanded.

"That would be me. Detective Dan Santiago. Homicide."

"What's the meaning of this?"

"Our cadaver dog alerted us that there was a dead body buried near your maze. We're waiting on the bulldozers now."

"Bulldozers? You can't- "

"Before you proceed, read this warrant. It will tell you everything that I can do. Where is your wife, Mr. Meadows? We need to talk to the both of you."

"At home, I guess. I have not spoken to her in days. We had an argument."

Fuck, Amy. I knew this shit would backfire one day.

"About what?" His cell phone rang. "Santiago. It did? Yeah, I am already here," he said, looking at Preston who shifted uncomfortably. "Thanks. Mr. Meadow's, do you know Jeff Fitzgerald?"

"The name sounds vaguely familiar."

"He used to work here. Now does it ring a bell?"

"Yes," he snapped his fingers. "He used to work in the grounds department. Why?"

"We have reason to believe that he may be buried on this property."

237

"Come on with these preposterous allegations. He resigned a long time ago. No one has heard from him since."

"On the contrary, Atlanta police just heard from him. We found his finger in your maze and it's pointing directly at you and your wife."

Preston was not going to allow Amy's shenanigans to take him down and keep him away from his child.

"Detective, this is neither the time nor the place to discuss this. We can discuss this at the station later."

"Great idea. We'll head that way." Dan placed his hand on Preston's upper back and began directing him towards the door.

"This is ludicrous. There aren't any dead bodies on these grounds."

"I beg to differ. Do you have a good lawyer?"

"Of course, I do."

"Good. Call him because you are coming with me. Let's go, Blayke."

"Right behind you."

It did not take them long to get into the car since they were already by the door.

"We need to stop by Jasmine's. She is not answering her phone. I'm worried about her."

"Jasmine, the landscape designer?" Preston said.

"Yes,' Blayke turned around in the front seat to face him.

"She's at my home planting flowers. After Mrs. Roundtree called me to tell me you guys were here, I called my wife. She did not answer the phone, so I called the security guard at our gate. They're in the garden."

"He said she was there?"

"Yes. Has been since about four o'clock today."

Without being told, Dan did a U-turn in the middle of the street and headed in the opposite direction.

"Can't this thing go any faster," Blayke ridiculed the Ford Taurus.

"You can always walk," Dan retorted.

"Whatever, man. Preston, call the security dude and have him go to the main house and check on your wife."

"I'm on it." He pressed speed dial. "Henry, go up to the main house and check on Mrs. Meadows. No, nothing is wrong. I just cannot reach her on her cell phone. Thanks. I owe you. He's going right now."

Henry drove the golf cart up the driveway and got out. The front door was locked. Getting behind the wheel, he drove around back to check those doors. The patio door was standing ajar and he went inside. Everything seemed okay and then he heard sobbing coming from the front of the house. Quietly, he tiptoed closer to get a view of what was going down.

"Please, don't do this. I haven't done anything wrong."

"Meh, that's to be determined," Amy shrugged. "I don't like the fact that you were in my office. What were you looking for?"

"Nothing. I swear?"

Tears streamed down Jasmine's face. In hindsight, she should have minded her business.

"Tsk, tsk, Jasmine. Do not insult my intelligence by lying to me. I thought you and I were friends. I got you out of that deplorable shelter and gave you a good job. You were welcome in my home. Why would you betray my trust like that?"

Angry, Jasmine snapped back. "Why would you kill all of those people?"

CRYING MEADOWS

"Mrs. Meadows killed someone" Henry whispered, standing in the hallway near her office door.

"I was only obeying God. They got exactly what they deserved. And had you not gotten off the devil's candy when you did, you would have met a similar fate."

"Obeying God? He wouldn't co-sign this mess."

"Then you don't know His Word."

"His Word says 'though shalt not kill, Amy."

"It also says, "For the wages of sin is death; but the gift of God is eternal life through Christ Jesus our Lord."

"You're crazy just like Hannah Whitlock said."

Amy took a step back hearing that name. "Hannah? How do you know about her?"

"She told me everything. Even how you use your non-profit as a front to kill innocent people. And she told me about this." Jasmine moved the ledger that she had been hiding behind her back.

What! Henry panicked. He wanted to help Jasmine, but he was an unarmed guard and Mrs. Meadows was strapped. The lights from a car shined through the window briefly and then disappeared when the engine cut off. The familiar beep of the front door opening cued Amy, so she took a couple of steps back behind the door.

Feeling as if the cavalry arrived, Henry went into the office.

"Henry, watch out!" Jasmine yelled.

Startled, Amy fired the gun. A bullet struck the old man in his abdomen.

"Now look what you made me do. And Henry was one of the colored people who I liked. Hand me my ledger, this instance," Amy said.

Jasmine cocked her head to the side.

Did she just say, 'one of the colored people'?

The sound of heavy footsteps sounded in the hallway as Dan, Blayke and Preston ran towards the commotion.

"You want this book? Then here, catch!"

Jasmine threw the ledger towards Amy and charged her at the same time. The book hit Amy in the shoulder knocking her off balance. It was just enough distraction so that Jasmine could grab the gun. But Amy was strong and did not let go like Jasmine thought she would. Falling to the floor, both women rolled around, tussling for the gun.

Preston kneeled on the floor near Henry and pressed down on the man's stomach, attempting to ease the blood flow from his guards wound.

"Call the ambulance," Preston screamed. "Hang in there, old man. Help is on the way."

Things moved in slow motion as Blayke felt helpless, watching his girlfriend fight with the crazy woman.

"Jasmine," Blayke yelled going to her aid.

"Freeze!" Dan ordered, drawing his weapon.

Before anyone could intervene, a loud resounding blast filled the room. A thud followed the blast. The gun was on the floor. Detective Dan kicked the gun out of reach. Sirens sounded in the distance and drew closer. Hopefully, they would only need an ambulance and *not* the coroner.

CHAPTER 23
BURIED SECRETS...

ENRY WAS GOING TO LIVE. Thankfully, the bullet passed through the muscles surrounding the abdomen and never entered the abdominal cavity at all. By the time the ambulance pulled up to the house, blood was everywhere. It looked much worse than it was.

Dan leaned over Amy and turned her over to see if she was hurt. He was a bit startled at first because when he saw her face, she had a smile on it. He stood her up and placed her in handcuffs.

"Lady, I don't know what you're smiling about but it's over. You have the right to remain silent. Anything you say can and will be used against you in a court of law. You have the right to an attorney. If you cannot afford an attorney, one will be provided for you. Do you understand the rights I have just read to you? With these rights in mind, do you wish to speak to me?"

"God bless you, Sir," she stated simply.

The woman was off her rocker, Dan thought. What a day. He knew that it was a possibility that he would be dealing with some strange things when Blayke asked for his help, but he never imagined this. Apparitions, dead bodies, and a crazy, rich chick; it was all a bit much for him.

Blayke embraced Jasmine and looked her over to make sure she was not hurt. The paramedics wanted to check her out because she did have some blood on her forehead. Turns out it was splatter from Henry.

"Didn't I tell you to stay home?" He reprimanded.

"Yes, but I felt like I needed to do something. Sitting in my room being scared wasn't going to do me any good. Look," she said bending down and scooping up the ledger. "I found this. Not sure what the dates signify but there are a lot of names in here from Off the Street that I recognize. And Blayke?"

"Yeah, Babe?"

"Tina and Chris are listed in here as well."

"What? Let me see that?"

Blayke scanned the pages as Dan walked over. Sure enough, Christina Porter and Tina Brown were there. A uniformed officer escorted Amy and Preston to the squad cars that waited outside. Tears clouded Blayke's eyes.

"These dates on this side are the dates they entered the Meadows Mission program. I know because I remember this like it was yesterday. This column must be the date that they died. Fuck man! Chris wanted to get her life together. She wanted her kids back. I never should have sent my people to this program," he said angrily holding up the damning book.

"Don't be so hard on yourself man. You did not know. All you knew was that you were trying to help your folks get clean, stay that way, and get a good job. This isn't your fault."

"I should have known. The numbers she was reporting were not accurate. I always suspected something. I should have known." A distraught Blayke punched the bookshelf in Amy's office, causing books to topple. A folded letter fell out of one of the books.

"What's this?" Dan picked up the paper and read it.

CRYING MEADOWS

Preston,

I'm extremely disappointed at the last conversation we had. I don't see how you ending our relationship is going to improve things in your marriage. Your wife doesn't love you and she hates me. Since you've been gone, she's made my life miserable. I don't know how long I can continue to work here. She knows that we slept together and has threatened to kill me if I so much as look at you. I know that people say things like that all the time when they are mad, but the strange thing is, with Amy, I believe it. She's spooky and I'm terrified. I love you, but not enough to die for you.

Forever yours, Mari

"Meadow's was banging the housekeeper," the detective stated emphatically.

"Yeah, I know. A friend of mine named Terry who I work with told me. Her mom, Miss Ruthie is the cook here?"

"Hmm, interesting. I'm sure the D.A. will want to speak to the both of them. Officer, will you please bag this letter as evidence?" Dan ordered.

"That's probably why his name is in this book," Jasmine noted.

"No kidding?" The New York accent of Dan's was heavy when he said that. "Lemme see."

Dan flipped through the pages quickly, slowing down when he found Preston's name. A couple of pages over, he scanned down the list and then stopped.

"Did you go through this whole book, Jasmine?" Dan questioned. He had a concerned look on his face.

"Not all of it. I was trying to see if I could make sense of the dates and got sidetracked. Why?"

244

He held the book in front of her. "Your name is in here, too. Right under Victor Gonzalez."

"The fuck?!" Blayke said, snatching the book from Dan and the book was snatched from him.

"Bag this. Now! Is this the proper chain of custody for evidence, Santiago?"

"No, Lieutenant. I wasn't thinking."

"Get these people out of here," the lieutenant commanded.

"C'mon Blayke. I'll drop you all off at your place. I've got to head back to the country club. It's a madhouse over there."

"Thanks. You can take us to Jasmine's. It's on your way to the club." Blayke snapped his finger. "Jas, did you know Jeff Fitzgerald?"

"Who?"

"He worked at Lush Meadows. His was the finger that you found."

"No, I've never met him in person but one day, Zell and I were talking, and he said that Jeff told him that he saw Hannah and had spoken to her."

"Maybe she was asking him for help the way she did you," Blayke perceived.

"Possibly so. But why did she kill him?"

"Most people, when they have incriminating information, usually try to exchange it for some cash. Maybe he tried blackmailing her. Who knows?"

That is exactly what happened. When Hannah contacted Jeff, she told him the same thing that she had Jasmine. One day Jeff confronted Amy with the truth, and she took the hedge clippers and stabbed him in the stomach. While he was on the ground, she opened the large scissors and began stabbing him repeatedly. They were alone near what is now the rose garden. Just like she did with Marisol, Amy undressed Jeff, dug a hole, and rolled him in it. She didn't think about him anymore after that.

Having dropped Blayke and Jasmine off at her apartment, Dan made his way back to the club. He and the Atlanta police were in for a long night. All the guests and employees had been questioned and released long ago. The entire club was a crime scene until they determined otherwise. The detective was handed a pair of nylon shoe covers before he went outside. He was amazed at the way Detective Gunner and his team were able to pick up the scent of dead bodies even after all this time.

Volatile compounds made up human remains. A whole range of scents related to death, whether it came from dried bones or the recently dead, were detectable. Human decomposition, even when it was mixed, was traceable. There was no hiding anything that Amy had done over the last five years.

Skeletal remains were recovered near or under the maze that Amy had planted. It was installed as a cover for the dastardly deeds. Over fifty bodies unearthed so far, and the numbers were still rising. Lush Meadows was crawling with cops and members of the crime lab. The club was shut down. Yellow tape was at the gate and bordered the perimeter of the club.

Crime scene investigators and the uniformed officers all wore the protective gear like Dan's. From the looks of it, it seemed as if they were investigating a bio-chemical spill instead of homicides. Large, battery powered ultraviolet lights were positioned all over the lawn and golf course. Crime lab analyst, Nina Kidman came outside with several people, all holding large canisters with sprayers attached.

"Everyone get in place. It's time."

Those who had canisters began walking over the grass, spraying as they went along. Nina spoke into her radio.

"On my signal and I want you all to hit the lights. Go!"

All the U.V. lights came on, causing the grass to illuminate in a soft blue glow. The grass was luminescent as far as the eyes could see.

"Jesus," she said shaking her head.

"What is this Doc?" Dan asked.

"DNA. We sprayed luminol in the grass. The ultraviolet lights were to help us see where there were traces of blood. This whole place is a crime scene."

"Looks like we're going to need more bulldozers."

"Not necessarily, but we will need more dogs. What in the hell went on here? The media will have a field day with this. No pun intended."

As well they did. The Socialite Psychopath was what they called her. The local news broke the story immediately and it did not take long before it was broadcast nationally. No one could believe that someone so angelic looking could be such a devil.

But Preston knew.

His wife showed him her true self long ago. When word got back to Cora Lee what was going on at Lush Meadows, she cut her trip short. Bill Corley found Preston the toughest defense attorney that Meadows money could buy.

"Why in the hell is Meadow's walking?" Dan asked outraged.

"His attorney had inculpatory evidence. He did not have a part in any of this. The wife acted independently," the assistant D.A. said. "I didn't have a choice. We had to release him."

"I hope your office can hold on to the wife. That woman is bat shit crazy."

"Trust me. She's not going anywhere anytime soon."

CRYING MEADOWS

The following week, the coroner released the remains of Hannah Whitlock to her family who was able to lay her to rest. That morning, Jasmine dressed slowly, thinking of all the great conversations she had had with Hannah. Had she been alive, she was the type of woman that Jasmine would have loved to call friend. Shortly after eleven in the morning, Blayke came to escort her to the graveside memorial service.

There was a twenty-four by thirty-six-inch picture of Hannah standing on an easel. She was beautiful before the drugs. Long, silver blond hair against perfectly tanned skin with pouty lips. She could have been a model.

"This is so sad," Jasmine cried, watching Hannah's husband break down. Tiny hairs stood up on the back of her neck. She was being watched again. Looking towards the trees, Jasmine saw Hannah standing there in the same beautiful white dress. All she could do was stare. A smile formed at the corners of Jasmine's mouth as Hannah waved at her.

"Thank you," the apparition mouthed. Waving one last time, Hannah walked away until she disappeared like a fine mist.

"Let's go," Jasmine said, standing to leave.

"You don't wanna stay and speak with her husband?"

"No. I got the closure I needed, and he'll get his soon. I've said my final goodbyes."

"Hungry?" He asked rhetorically. Eating was something that he knew she could always do hungry or not.

"Where are we headed?"

"Bianca invited us to lunch. We don't have to go if you don't feel up to company."

"Listen, I'm good. I know it is going to be a minute before I get over all that's happened, but one thing I know is that Hannah would want me to live and enjoy life."

Jasmine relaxed in the seat feeling reassured about life. Once they got to the quaint bistro in Midtown and found a seat, the conversation turned to the findings at the golf and country club. As Jasmine listened to the commentary, she seriously considered writing a book about her life. It was so crazy that no one would believe it was factual.

Life imitates art far more than art imitates life. Oscar Wilde you knew what you were talking about.

"Who knew that a person could be that demented?" Bianca asked, sipping her tea.

"Rich people will do anything to stay that way. Maybe Amy did not see any other way," Miles added. He had popped the question a few weeks ago and Bianca said yes. They were not planning to marry until she graduated from university next year.

"I still feel bad for her," Jasmine sympathized. Everyone at the table looked at her like she was had horns.

"What?" They said in unison.

"Because, she did not simply do all of that to retain her riches. She was trying to save her marriage. You guys did not have a chance to see her the way I did. Amy really loved Preston and he dogged her out. Made her believe that he was going to have kids with her if they won the IGA bid and then when they didn't, she was assed out. How fair is that?"

"About as fair as creating a non-profit organization under the guise of helping the homeless, only to kill them. Then she used their decomp as fertilizer for the grass on her country club's putting green."

"Touché, Bianca."

"Atlanta has not seen anything this heinous since Wayne Williams and the Atlanta Children's Murders. Amy Meadow's name is going to be synonymous with the likes of John Wayne Gacy and Eileen Wuornos," Bianca added.

CRYING MEADOWS

Amy Meadows wanted Lush Meadows Golf and Country Club to make history. It did that and then some.

CHAPTER 24
ALL RISE...

ADVISED NOT TO TAKE THE stand to testify in her own defense, Amy decided that she would anyway. "Listen to reason. You could endanger our case," her attorney pleaded. "At this point, the prosecution has the burden of proof because they have no physical evidence tying you to any of those bodies. We can win this."

"I'm innocent, Stanley. I am not a murderer. God's Word is sure and true, and I will be exonerated. Once they hear me speak, they will see. Trust me."

"Preston, please talk some sense into your wife. Jurors do not believe that people are innocent most of the time. They do not listen to understand. Our natural nature is to rush to judgment."

"Stanley, when Amy has her mind made up you know there's no changing it," he said unconcerned.

The trial had been ongoing for the past two months, but it took Fulton County almost a year to bring Amy to trial. Testimony after testimony went forth and frankly, Preston was tired of the whole thing. All he wanted to do was divorce her and marry Tabby. His phone dinged. It was a text from Tabitha.

A smile crossed his face as he looked at the picture, she had just sent him via text, of Carter and their newborn daughter, Corlee Nicole Meadows, who was named after his mother Cora Lee. Regardless of how bad things were for Amy, things were exceptional him.

His lawyer worked so diligently on his behalf that the district attorney could not bring charges against him. Also, with Preston's name being in Amy's ledger, they figured that she was plotting to kill him as well. Thinking back to a year ago, Preston remembered finding the book in her desk. While he did not quite understand the dates in the book, he knew it was a record of all the people she had killed. What would it hurt if he added a few more names? It was he who had written his name, along with Victor's and Jasmine's in the book.

The plan was to make it look like she had an agenda to kill others. Of course, the plan worked. So, did the letter that he planted that was from "Marisol". Eventually, the police found her body. They were grateful for the anonymous tip they received. Another body to add to the count. Soon after she was discovered, Preston's sisters coordinated with movers for him to pack up the house at Meadows Manor.

"You need to make a fresh start," Bella Rose told him.

Although he and his siblings did not always see eye-to-eye, they were there for him during his time of need. His mother is the one that broke the news to them that their brother had two biracial children. No one seemed to care. This pleased Preston. They embraced Tabby without hesitation and both of his children melted their hearts.

And thankfully, his mother had released his one hundred twenty-million-dollar inheritance and set up the trusts for his children. Life was good. And in three days, after Amy took the stand, it would get even better. Hours melted into seconds and before he realized, the big day arrived.

The trial of the century was about to resume.

"All rise. This court is now in session. The Honorable Judge Richard Danner presiding."

"Defense you may call your next witness."

"The defense calls Amy Meadows to the stand, Your Honor."

Amy stood gracefully and turned to look at the jury, giving them a beauty pageant smile, before taking the stand.

"Please state your name for the court."

"Amy Jo Blessingale-Meadows."

"Please raise your right hand. Do you solemnly swear that the testimony you are about to give is the truth, the whole truth, and nothing but the truth?"

"I do."

No one was able to talk Amy out of testifying. Her attorney did his best to paint a picture of a woman who loved people and whose mission was to help others not hurt them. By the time he finished his questions, he was mentally exhausted.

"The defense rests, Your Honor."

Nervously, Stanley tapped his pencil on his knee under the table. Most of the questions that he wanted to ask her, he could not because they could have been considered leading questions. During his direct examination, the prosecution did not object once. That was a device tactic used by skilled attorneys when they were preparing to rip a witness to shreds. When he looked at the district attorney, she looked like a shark circling its prey before the attack. Amy Meadows was in trouble.

"Prosecution may begin its cross," the judge advised.

Assistant District Attorney Santiago began her cross examination. She began with a series of closed ended questions, but Amy's answers were ambiguous.

Exhaling the young D.A. said, "Your honor, the State requests permission to treat the witness as hostile. The witness is avoiding answering the questions and is giving different answers than she gave to the police when she was first interviewed."

Stanley jumped to his feet and said, "I object, Your Honor!"

The Judge overruled his objection. "Permission to treat the witness as hostile is granted."

Hanging his head, Stanley felt defeated. He had spoken to Amy at length and some of the answers that she had given him were outrageous. He could only imagine what she was about to say to the prosecutor.

"Mrs. Meadows isn't it true that you were a horrible gardener when you first joined the Distinct Ladies of Leisure Women's League?"

"Yes."

"Then how pray tell did you become so knowledgeable in that field in such a short while?"

Oh boy, here we go, Stanley thought, shaking his head.

"My Lord and Savior Jesus Christ answered my prayers."

"You mean to tell me that God spoke to you and told you how to grow a garden?"

"Yes. He did."

"And how often does God speak to you Mrs. Meadows?"

"Every time I pray."

"And He just gives you what you ask for? Just like that?" She snapped her fingers. "Is that it?"

"All things whatsoever ye shall ask in prayer, believing, ye shall receive."

"Is that a yes?" The judge asked.

"Yes, it is."

The prosecutor asked a series of questions and then went in for the kill.

"Amy, may I call you that?"

"Yes."

"Amy, tell the jury what the Chamber is that you speak of in your journal."

Stanley turned green around the gills.

"The Chamber is the room where I make my fertilizer."

"Isn't the Chamber a room that's kept at a hot ninety-eight degrees where you take all of your dead bodies? Aren't they laid out on metal embalming tables with holes in them? Isn't it a fact that you researched online how to speed up the decomposition process in humans, so you could create the fertilizer you used for your grounds at Lush Meadows Golf and Country Club?" Her questions were relentless.

"Objection, Your Honor. Badgering the witness."

"Over-ruled. You may answer."

"Yes."

"Why do you use tables with holes, Amy?"

"So that when the body decomposes and turns to liquid, it will drain into the rubber containers I have situated underneath each one. I then mix the decomp with the leaves I gather and make my special compound."

"Your sole purpose for starting the non-profit agency was to recruit homeless people so that you could kill them and exploit their remains for profit."

"Objection, Your Honor. Where's the question?"

"Sustained. Redirect."

"Didn't you create Meadows Mission as a front for your nefarious deeds? Your ledger clearly names hundreds of people who were supposed to be helped by you but instead were murdered, isn't that true? Why did you do it, Amy?"

"Objection, badgering the witness."

CRYING MEADOWS

Amy, still smiling started talking. "For the wages of sin is death; but the gift of God is eternal life through Jesus Christ our Lord. Those people who died were sinners. Repentance was far from them and they were separated from God. I helped them return to God and His love. They are restored to spiritual life—communion with Him. Now that they are dead to sin, they can live with God. They are given eternal life through the trees and flowers that they help grow. It's perfect."

"Once the people are dead, who helps you move them?"

"I do."

"Do you mean to tell us that a woman with your small stature can lift those big bodies that are completely dead weight?"

"I can do all things through Christ who strengthens me."

The examination continued along those lines for the next couple of days. The D.A. was astounded by the fact that Amy believed everything she said. Finally, Stanley had had enough.

"Your Honor, the defense would like a sidebar."

"Attorney's approach the bench."

Both the defense and prosecution walked to the bench where they spoke in hushed tones with the judge. The judge banged his gavel.

"Court is in recess. Meet me in my chambers," the judge demanded.

The judge stepped down off the bench and the jury returned to the jury room. Muffled conversations got louder in the gallery and some people stepped out to use their phones. Preston and his family were among those who left out.

"I can't believe Amy flew over the cuckoo's nest," Abbott, Jr. said.

"Me either," agreed Robert. "This whole thing is really sad."

"Who were you talking to?" Cora Lee asked her son.

"My insurance agent. I wanted to see if it's possible to collect on a life insurance policy for a person who died from the death penalty."

"Preston Scott Meadows. How awful of you."

"Face it, Mother. With the answers that she is giving these people, they will surely hang her out to dry."

The Meadows clan sadly nodded their heads. No one from Amy's immediate family was present in the courtroom that day because her mother had a heart attack because of the stress from the court proceedings. The woman who had worked so hard to build a family was seemingly without one in her time of need.

It did not escape Amy's notice that Tabby, her housekeeper, was in the gallery. While on the stand, she could not help but see that Cora Lee held a beautiful olive-skinned baby in her arms. A little girl who looked just like her husband.

Preston finally got what he wanted. A tainted baby.

Not a pure baby like the one she would have given him. He insisted on screwing around with those people.

When you lie down with dogs, you rise with fleas.

That was her final thought right before the bailiff escorted her back into the courtroom.

Someone let the people in the hallway know that court was almost back in session. Preston saw Amy and her attorney deep in discussion when he returned to his seat. Stanley whispered in Amy's ear and showed her some writing on a notepad in front of her. He was trying to save his client's life. Her testimony earlier made her a shoo-in for a death sentence. The bailiff announced the judge's arrival.

CRYING MEADOWS

"Court will come to order. The defense has changed its plea from not guilty to guilty by reason of insanity. Does the state offer any objections to this plea change?"

"Not at all Your Honor."

"So be it. Pending an extensive evaluation by a court approved psychiatrist, the plea is accepted. We will reconvene in three weeks following the report. Court is adjourned."

Everyone left out the courtroom.

"Guess she won't be getting the death penalty after all, huh bro?" Bella Rose quizzed.

"That's good," he nodded. "She should have to live to face what she's done."

Blayke and Jasmine went to speak with Preston and his family.

"I'm really sorry this happened to you, Mr. Meadows. My prayers are with Amy."

"Thank you, Jasmine. We appreciate it."

"What are your ideas about the club?" Blayke asked. "Any plans to rebuild since the fire last month?"

Preston was happy that the club was destroyed. He collected a hefty insurance check that he got to pocket. A disgruntled family member of someone Amy killed set the place on fire and it burned to a crisp. Good riddance.

"No plans to rebuild. I'm just going to concentrate on my other ventures right now."

"Good luck," Blayke offered, walking off. "So, tell me, Miss Aster, what are you doing for the rest of your life?"

"Spending it with you," she answered, kissing him on the cheek on the courthouse steps as they walked into their future.

Three weeks later Amy was found criminally insane; a month after that, she was sentenced.

AVERY GOODE

The gardener was being watched intently from the window above. Basket in hand, she strutted across the yard without a care in the world. She wore a straw hat, an oversized gardener's smock and a pair of gardening Crocs that turned up slightly at the toes. An award-winning beauty pageant smile spread across her face as she admired her handy work.

Flowers of assorted colors sprinkled the garden and bloomed beautifully. It was a glorious sight. One that Amy Meadows would enjoy watching every day, from her room, for the rest of her life as a permanent resident of the Georgia Psychiatric Institute for the Criminally Insane.

CRYING MEADOWS

Made in the USA
Middletown, DE
30 June 2023

34215690R00158